MAFIA GIRL

DEBORAH BLUMENTHAL

ALBERT WHITMAN & COMPANY
CHICAGO, ILLINOIS

For Annie, Sophie, and Ralph

Library of Congress Cataloging-in-Publication Data

Blumenthal, Deborah.
Mafia girl / Deborah Blumenthal.
pages cm
Summary: As the daughter of an infamous mob boss, seventeen-year-old
Gia struggles to come out of the shadow of her family's notorious reputation
and be her own person.
ISBN 978-0-8075-4911-7 (hardcover)
[1. Mafia—Fiction. 2. Families—Fiction. 3. Fathers and daughters—Fiction.
4. Identity—Fiction.] I. Title.
PZ7.B6267Maf 2014
[Fic]—dc23   2013028440

Printed in the United States
10 9 8 7 6 5 4 3 2 1 LB 18 17 16 15 14 13

Cover design by Jenna Stempel
Cover image © lambada/Vetta/Getty Images

For more information about Albert Whitman & Company,
visit our web site at www.albertwhitman.com.

ONE

The white plastic Jesus dangling by a string from the rearview mirror is rocking in time to the music as Ro barrels up the Henry Hudson Parkway singing "Stop in the Name of Love."

Without warning she lurches into the middle lane then floors the gas so Mr. Trailer Trash in the pickup with the *God, Guns, and Guts* bumper sticker riding our tail and doing disgusting things with his tongue is left behind like roadkill.

"Do not fuck with a Porsche 911," Ro says, extending her middle finger.

It can go 197 mph, I'm about to add, then think better of it because our little Jesus is shaking his head and doing figure eights. Or it's me because we've shared a six-pack and haven't eaten except for the Ritz Bits that Dante—whose car we have stolen—left behind in the glove compartment along with Trojan Extended Pleasures and half a joint.

"Where are we going again?" Ro asks.

"The outlets. Looking for Louboutins."

"Why didn't we program the GPS?" she says, punching her head. "I don't, uh, really know where I'm going." She blinks hard as if that will clear her brain fog.

I tap tap tap on the GPS, only "outlet mall" doesn't come up and neither does "Louboutins" and I can't remember the actual name of the mall and I'm starting to feel queasy and wondering if this was really such a hot idea since I have two quizzes tomorrow that I haven't studied for. But that doesn't matter because right then we hear a siren in the background that starts out low and grating, like the buzz of a bloodthirsty mosquito circling your ear, and then it grows louder and louder—and in case you're deaf there's a row of *red*.

Flashing. Lights. In. The. Mirror.

"Mofo," Ro says. "First time we cut school and we get…"

"PULL OVER TO THE SHOULDER," booms the loudspeaker.

"No way," I mutter.

Ro shoots me a look of disbelief. "Gia, remember whose car is this?"

I do remember. She slows down and makes her way to the shoulder while I study the font on the can of Bud between my knees deciding if I think it really works with the design.

Bodoni, that's the name of the font I like. Bodoni.

"Don't say anything," she says.

"What?"

"Don't say anything unless he asks you something."

"What do you think I'm going say, 'do you want a hand job?'"

Ro and I start to laugh because right then that becomes the most hilarious thing in the world. Then the cop struts up to the driver's window and we are *not* laughing any more. No. I stare straight ahead.

"You were doin' eighty."

"Oh," Ro says. Dead silence. One one-thousand. Two one-thousand. Three one-thousand.

"License and registration," he says, which will be a problem.

Ro hands him her license, which isn't a license. It's a goddamn learner's permit. She leans across me and fishes around in the glove compartment until she finds the registration or maybe it's the insurance and accidentally knocks the condoms to the floor. Ro hands him the registration. Dante's registration.

"So you don't have a license and it's not your car," the cop says. "And you were speeding and drinking."

Ro doesn't answer, but she's breathing like an asthmatic.

"You," he says. "ID."

I turn to look up at him and he looks back at me and something like the wattage they must use for the electric chair shoots through me from head to toe. Because the cop is about the hottest thing on the face of the universe, and I am ready to roll on my back—but I mean, a cop? So I uncurl my middle finger at him.

"Gia," Ro hisses.

"What exactly is your problem?" he asks.

"*You.*"

He stares at me for longer than he has to and I stare back at him, never mind the heat and the shock waves. I refuse to look away first.

"ID," he says again, pointing to my bag in case I don't understand English.

I scratch the side of my nose with my middle finger, then hand him my learner's permit. "Here, hottie."

Another intense look before he examines my permit, looks back at me in surprise when he recognizes the name, examines my permit again, and then hands it back to me.

"Shit," he mutters.

TWO

What's in a name? E-v-e-r-y-t-h-i-n-g—if you have my name. Everything if instead of working in a law office or a bank or maybe the IRS, your dad hangs out in a social club that's probably bugged by the feds.

Everything if he's been perp-walked in front of the TV cameras more times than I can remember.

Everything if he's the one whose last name they whisper when people disappear.

If you haven't caught on yet, I'll bring you up to speed. My dad doesn't have a boss, he is the boss. The *capo di tutti capi*. Translation: boss of all bosses.

There. Now leave it alone.

And me? His seventeen-year-old daughter who half the boys in school are afraid to walk near, and the other half swoon after for their own sick reasons, which gives me the dubious distinction of being the most hated/loved girl in school.

Not that I care.

They call me Gia. Just Gia. Even the teachers taking attendance. Never mind my last name with the operatic mouthful of syllables and vowels. Unless you need a dinner reservation in a place that's booked, then doors open and you get comped with antipasti and *fritto misto*, and after the main course when you're stuffed, Napoleons and cannoli appear when you didn't order dessert, and then we act impressed and my dad overtips.

Aside from the name buzz though, my dad and mom insist that, after all, we are just like everyone else. A normal, middle-class Italian family that goes to church, raises money for the nuns in Palermo who run the children's cancer hospital, helps the neighbors when they fall on tough times, but most of all, minds its own business.

Only how do I explain Frankie with the Glock who drives me to school every day in a Cadillac Escalade and then waits in front of the hydrant for me at three o'clock, and Vinnie—aka "the Nose"—who routinely sticks his into my life so he can snitch to my dad about who I'm hanging out with? Fortunately Vinnie is such a dick that he has no clue that the cop with the electric green eyes...

But I'm getting ahead of myself.

THREE

It's not that I mind being driven to central booking in the back of a grungy patrol car that reeks of vomit, it's just that I so have to pee and Officer Hottie is getting on my nerves because he is driving at an excruciatingly slow speed, every now and then glancing at us through the barrier between the front and back seat.

"What's your name?" I say, to make convo. Ro slides her foot over and kicks mine, but I ignore her.

"Cross," Officer Hottie says.

"Are you or is that actually your name?"

"Michael Cross," he says with a smirky smile.

"So are you like a good Catholic with a name like that?"

Our eyes met in the rearview mirror. He doesn't answer. "Well?"

"Where are we goin' with this?"

"I was just wondering if you pray," I say.

"You think I need to?"

"Not for my sake."

His eyes meet mine and he looks away.

"So do girls find you hard to talk to?"

Ro kicks me harder.

"What?" he asks in disbelief.

"Well you don't seem to actually talk."

He shakes his head, refusing to get into anything.

"I mean it's too bad," I say, unable to leave it alone.

"Gia," Ro says softly, treading carefully. "Can you stop?"

"What?" I say, holding my hands out helplessly. "I'm just trying to lighten things up here by making con-ver-sa-tion, or at least *trying* to. But Officer Hottie doesn't want to talk to me, which is too bad."

"You have quite a mouth," he says.

"Getting warmer."

The convo ends when he pulls up to the front of the station and opens the back door to let his juveniles out. We're walked up to the front desk where we wait while the cop behind it makes a point of looking up and then ignoring us.

"What ya got?" he says to Officer Hottie.

"Two under, DUI, speeding, no license, possibly stolen vehicle, resisting."

"We. Are. Fucked," Ro whispers.

"Yeah," I whisper back, staring at Officer Hottie. "But it was so worth it."

Don't get me wrong, it's not like we ditch school and go joyriding and get picked up by hot cops on a regular basis. This was singular. They were doing construction on the new library and the work filled the air with flying soot, which we were convinced was asbestos, and it was seventy-five degrees in October and what better weather to declare it a mental health day, never mind the chance to avoid some of the cockroaches perpetually dissing me. All other days, Ro and I do a fair job of acting like the A students we are at the Morgan School on Manhattan's Upper East Side.

And no one takes that lightly.

Only now? With a police record? How much hush money would my dad have to fork over to—

"GIA!" my mom shouts, making the walls vibrate as she bursts into the station with Ro's mom and my brother, Anthony. She runs up and hugs me. "You scared me to death. You know I hate trouble."

"Sorry, Ma," I say because I can't think of anything brilliant.

"Do you know what this is going to fucking cost us?" Anthony says under his breath.

That's Anthony. Not *I'm glad you didn't get your head split open in the Porsche while going eighty.* Not *how are we going to keep this out of the papers?* But I'm in the middle of a police station and what is the point of getting into an argument with my stupid guinea brother. I look at him and look away.

"Later, okay?"

"Rosemarie," Ro's mom says, shaking her head. "What were you thinking?"

"I didn't think, I—"

"*Right*," her mom snaps, her mouth in a tight line. "You didn't *think*."

We all stand around until my dad's lawyer, Mario Della Russo, aka Super Mario, strolls into the station in his million-dollar chocolate-brown Armani suit with a cream silk shirt and his trademark alligator loafers.

"Theresa, Maria," he says, kissing my mom and then Ro's mom. "Always something, eh?"

He moves on to me. "My beautiful, beautiful Gia," he says, leaning back and admiring me before kissing me on both cheeks. "Are the boys still killing themselves if you won't look at them?" he says with a laugh.

"I'm still holding out for you, Mario," which he loves me to say so I say it.

He throws back his head and laughs the way he always laughs because old guys love to hear things like that and anyway we need a lawyer who totally loves us to bail me and Ro out of this total fucking mess.

"I will take care of it," he says with a wave of his hand like he's about to talk to the first-class reservations desk at Alitalia for an upgrade instead of the low-life cops at the stinking ghetto precinct we are stuck in. He speaks to the desk sergeant. There is a discussion, paperwork, more discussion although I can't imagine what there is to keep talking about because we're so friggin' guilty even though it's a first offense for both of us. But then I see him uncover his gold pen and sign some papers. Finally he turns to us.

"Come," he says in his soothing tone. "It's getting late. We don't want to miss dinner."

Super Mario is cool. Perpetually cool, cool, cool, no matter how hot the water someone may be drowning in.

I wave good-bye with my fingertips at Officer Hottie who stands ramrod straight and stares but doesn't wave back, then follow Super Mario out of the station into his Panamera.

"What did my dad say?" I whisper.

Mario raises his eyebrows and turns his upright fist in a circle.

Translation: I. Am. Screwed.

I set the table for dinner the way I always set the table, using the perfectly polished silver forks and knives and the lacy place mats that are really plastic lacy place mats so that you can wipe away the stains and pretend they never happened.

We all sit down and eat the way we always do without drama, at least for the time it takes to eat the stuffed artichokes and drink the first glasses of Chianti. Anthony wolfs down his dinner and my mom always says, "Slow down and enjoy your food," and my dad never says anything. His mouth just tightens.

Then I jump up to carry the plates with the mounds of artichoke leaves into the kitchen while my mom puts on her elbow-length oven mitts and brings the manicotti to the table. I serve my mom first and then my dad. He holds up his hand because I'm about to give him a portion for three.

"Basta, basta," he says, looking at me pointedly, which—knowing my dad—means not only enough manicotti, but also enough of everything I've put the family through. I put some of it back and he continues to x-ray me with his eyes because my dad gets most of the information he needs by reading people's faces, leaving them no space to hide.

I look back at him and mouth, "I'm sorry."

"Sorry," he says mockingly, lifting his chin. His mouth hardens and he looks through me until I look away. He's not going to ruin dinner by punishing me now. He'll think about it. Then after I go to my room and try to concentrate on homework, which I won't be able to do because I'll be waiting for him to come up, he'll open my door without knocking.

"Starting tomorrow, no more..." he'll say and let me know my sentence. I'll listen and take it because when my father makes up his mind, if you want to live, you don't try to negotiate.

FOUR

"Gia?"

The next morning I'm sitting in my usual seat in English, but Mrs. Carter can't see me because she's nearsighted. I wave from the back and then come up to her desk and she hands me back my paper on *Julius Caesar.*

"Excellent," she says. "It breathes."

"It breathes" is Mrs. Carter's way of saying that you didn't just rip your ideas off Wikipedia or SparkNotes like a mindless asshole who'll end up in trade school or buy a paper off the website that Dante and others I know regularly frequent.

All of us at Morgan School are way above that. About the only things not required to get into Morgan are a DNA swab and an E.P.T. test. To seal the deal, they ask for a tuition deposit stiffer than a payoff to a Colombian drug cartel.

But bottom line, the green light depends on who your parents are or how much they make. In my case, it's a bit of both. When my acceptance letter came, inscribed in magenta with one of those calligraphy pens, we all knew that an affirmative meant that my life would change for better or worse.

So I work hard. And when Mrs. Carter says my paper "breathes," she means I put my soul into it and that it has depth, which might sound stupid except I know what she means, and anyway I like her and the transported look in her eyes when she reads Shakespeare. And it's fun to psyche out all the flawed personalities because IMO Shakespeare's characters are cool, especially Hamlet who's troubled and all, but brilliant and hot. And their motivations are no different from ours, because who doesn't feel strung out like a desperate loser?

I walk back to my seat making sure to hold my paper so Christy Collins sees it and dies because she's convinced the only reason I usually get As is that the teachers are afraid they'll get whacked if I don't, which is ridiculous. Christy has never gotten an A, probably not a B either, but if money could buy grades, she'd be in Mensa. But never mind that, she's stone-cold jealous of me.

"Typical," she spits out as I pass her and her eyes glom on to the A.

I glance over my shoulder feeling a rush of pleasure at her snarky face.

"Can I read it?" Clive asks.

Clive Laurent is this totally unique, asexual, standout person who looks, acts, dresses, and thinks differently from everyone else on the planet. I'm convinced he was born a thousand years ago and somehow time-traveled and ended up at Morgan because he took a wrong turn on his way home to Camelot.

Clive has long, wispy blond hair and pale skin. No one has ever seen him without the navy cashmere scarf he wears knotted around his neck no matter how cold or hot it is. I think he's hypothermic if that's a word or a medical condition or state of being or something when you walk around perpetually chilled.

In addition to the scarf, Clive lives in a vintage Burberry raincoat, which weirded me out the first time I saw him in school. But then I heard him answer a question in class and I realized that he's completely brilliant and doesn't have a mean bone in his emaciated body. He was so deserving of extreme niceness by someone who isn't put off by his strangeness that he became my closest friend, not counting Ro.

It's not like Clive is some poor soul who sleeps on a park bench and dump dives for food. His family is beyond rich and he lives in a ginormous ninety-million dollar duplex high up in the Time Warner Center, and when you're looking out the window it feels like you're in a plane hovering over a twinkling skyscraper fairyland.

Clive's parents are media moguls so they're always flying around in their own private Gulfstream. So Clive is mostly alone with maids, a butler, and a driver with only an aunt and uncle on speed dial. His only other company is the delivery guys from the Whole Foods downstairs because he's always calling up and ordering crap. And all he does is read, read, read all day from his Kindle.

So every day Ro and I pack manicotti or lasagna for him so he'll have a hot, homemade dinner because that's the least I can do for a friend—because I don't have too many of those.

Clive takes my paper and tucks it into his backpack. When he gets home he'll scrawl little notes to me proving that he's even smarter than Mrs. Carter. Then he'll invite me to hang out with him and I'll say yes because he's sweet and kind and fun and has a wall of vinyls, never mind the pictures of the city that I love to take from his floor to ceiling windows to see New York in changing lights.

Especially from the bathroom.

Clive is the only person in the universe who has a white marble Jacuzzi in front of an enormous wall of glass with no curtains, so it's fun to take bubble baths there and drink Dom and then stand up naked in front of the window and hope that someone in some other part of Manhattan in a crappy little apartment will see me through a telescope so I can give them a cheap thrill.

Anyway, the A on the paper is deserved. I worked for it because inside my head, my conscience is always telling me *prove yourself, prove yourself* so that one day I will have an actual life and become more than the self-sucking don's daughter—the nickname I've been branded with since birth.

There's a second voice too. That one keeps reminding me that if I don't get As I won't get into the right college and be able to follow my secret plan for the future.

Almost no one knows about my plan. Not Ro, my separated-at-birth best friend and next-door neighbor. Not Clive—at least not yet. Not my mom. And especially not Anthony. He wouldn't believe me anyway because in his head the only career for a woman is domestic servant.

The only one who knows about my secret plan for the future is the person who keeps secrets better than anyone in the world: my dad.

When I told him, his eyes got all misty, something that doesn't happen much, except when he watches sad movies where good people or animals die. Then he doesn't just cry, he sobs.

Shut up. I know what you're thinking.

I didn't plan to tell him. But after my grandma's funeral last year, he was sitting all alone in the living room in his favorite gold velvet armchair. My dad is almighty powerful all the time, only right then he wasn't. He looked defeated, like he had shrunk inside himself. He was staring out the window as the rain poured down because on a day like that it made sense that the sun wouldn't have the nerve to shine. The TV was off and he just sat there like the most alone person on earth, because I guess when you lose your mom you feel orphaned, even if you have a family of your own. `

Grandma Giulia was his conscience. She was the only one who could smack his head and tell him what to do and he would never contradict her.

"Mama," he might say, holding out a hand. But he'd never go further than that, which is something because my dad has a temper and, believe me, if he gets pushed, you do not want to be there.

So when I sat next to him and told him my secret plan he looked up and smiled, then kissed the palm of my hand like a blessing. I held hands with him for I don't know how long, hoping that from then on he'd think more about the future than the past and not look so small and sad anymore. When his cell rang, I got up, sure he'd want to take the call, but he didn't even look to see who it was.

Now that I've told him, I try to ace every paper and exam because no matter what anyone says about us and how stupid our lives can be, I'll tell you something you should never forget: our family has brains.

"Keep Saturday night open," Ro says when we talk on the phone after school. "We're having a birthday party for Dante."

Ever since Ro's older brother Dante and I made out in the upstairs bathroom when I was ten, he's had a major crush on me. It happened at one of their family's annual July Fourth barbecues where my dad and Ro's dad—who owns the best pastry shop in Little Italy—wear stupid aprons with sayings like "I'm the Grillfather" and take turns cooking. My parents love Dante, which doesn't help. He worships my dad and is a masterful suck-up who leaves gifts for me and for them for every occasion, from birthdays to Groundhog Day. Designer scarves, Tiffany rings, Vuitton bags, Prada wallets, cashmere hoodies, sports tickets, and anything else major-league expensive that "fell off a truck," but whatever. It's the thought that counts, right?

So when Saturday night rolls around after about eighteen courses of manicotti, lasagna, grilled salmon, filet mignon, roast chicken, calamari, clams oreganata, sautéed spinach, escarole, zabaglione, fifty kinds of cookies, and Ro's mom saying for the twentieth time, "why don't you kids ever eat anything?"—Ro and I and Dante and his friend Marco and some guy I never met before who they call Little Paulie, who's about six-five, and some skanky girl named Viv with pink hair who is getting on my nerves because of her gluten-free diet thing, go down to Ro's basement. After fighting for about an hour over which movie to watch and Dante finally grabbing his baseball bat and holding it over his head and threatening to smash the fifty-five-inch Sony TV he just got if "you all don't just *shut up* and *stop arguing*," we do finally and watch *The Fighter*, which is amazing. Dante sits close to me and I can tell he's wasted because he's whispering to me over and over again, "you're so beautiful, Gia," and "it gives me a hard-on just to look at you in that sweater."

"Please shut up," I tell him so I can watch the movie. But instead he starts to massage my neck, which is all it takes for me to fall into a sex trance, fantasizing that it's Officer Hottie instead of Dante. Then again, Officer Hottie isn't here and Dante is and what the hell because he does have good hands. And then like a slut I turn to him and we start making out even though I know that's the last thing I should be doing because tomorrow he'll probably steal a diamond ring and ask my dad if he can marry me.

But I can't worry about that right now so I don't. I pretend I'm into him and living for the moment, which is one way to justify being a slut. But it is his birthday and maybe he does deserve more than just a Loro

Piana cashmere turtleneck because of all the crap he gives me. So when he grabs my hand, I follow him into the laundry room.

Ten. Nine. Eight. Seven. Six. Five. Four. Three. Two. One.

The door to my room flings open and my dad x-rays me so hard I can practically feel the burn. I stare back. And crumble.

"I'm sorry," I whisper again in broken record mode.

He doesn't dignify that with an answer. "You don't go out for a month," he says. "No movies, no out for coffee, no nothing."

I wait. There's more.

"And you babysit every Friday and Saturday for the Andreottis. And every cent, it comes to me to pay for the bill from Mario. You understand?"

I nod.

"No more cutting school," he says. "No more drinking. No more trouble."

"Okay, okay," I whisper.

"Not okay," he says. "You get serious. *Serious.*"

FIVE

Serious.

My dad has guilt-tripped me like no one else can with his honor code and expectations. So after barely sleeping, I walk down the corridor at school and see the signs about the upcoming student council election and a light bulb goes off in my foggy brain. Even though the idea of running for president of this place is definitely something I should run from, I'm immediately jazzed by the thought of jumping in where I don't belong and stirring things up.

At the very least, I could have fun buying art supplies and making posters and calling it schoolwork. But more importantly, I could get over on skanky people at Morgan who hate me, because most of them are. Spoiled. Stuck-up. Bitches.

Who dress in paisley or what have you and wear things like Belgian Shoes and have moms with names like Muffy who carry those stupid Nantucket straw baskets with scrimshaw medallions and talk interminably about going riding in Connecticut on the weekends or watching horse jumping or entering their purebreds at Westminster or playing golf, while the non-Wasp world, not in Litchfield or Greenwich, Connecticut, who are stuck in places like the fucking Bronx and

Queens and lower Manhattan, except for Soho, are mostly out of work and panhandling, fencing crap on eBay, lining up for chump change from unemployment, and jumping turnstiles because they can't even afford stupid MetroCards. I would love to drop-kick most of them so that they would open their recessive-gene eyes and get over that rarefied bullshit way of existing.

You probably think I'm being paranoid, that no one really has it in for me.

Wrong.

I've just locked the bathroom stall door behind me when Christy Collins and Georgina Richards, the two-faced Brit twit, walk into the bathroom. They obviously know I'm there because I'm sure they toe peeped, and who else wears purple or green Louboutins with four-inch heels and nail heads, even when it snows? At first whiff I know it's Christy because she wears massive amounts of musk oil or something else that she must think smells hot but actually smells like pond scum.

"This school has really gone downhill since they let that Mafia bitch in," she says.

"Really," says Georgina.

"I mean look at who her dad is," Christy says. "How can they do that? She and that other one are total mafioso trash."

I sit coiled up like a rattlesnake poised to strike. The plural is mafiosi, I'm tempted to call out, but never mind that. How could they let Christy into the school when her dad works on Wall Street and who ever thought we should bail out *those* people?

Pins and needles make my legs tingle.

The door slams finally and it's quiet again. I go out and wash my hands, scrubbing too hard. I strut down the corridor almost passing the school election table, but I stop when the kid behind the desk smiles at me.

"Thinking of running, Gia?"

He's actually serious. I smile and shrug, stifling a laugh. *Me? Run for president?*

On the desk are applications and white pencils with *The Morgan School* in magenta. I reach for one and slip it between my teeth. Then I move on.

President. How would that go over? A total goof? Or not? Maybe I could actually wake this place up and bring it into this century.

I put the thought aside.

But when I'm in the library after school with Ro and Clive, I poll them. "What do you guys think about me running for class president—truthfully?"

"Gia, you would be the absolute best," Clive says. "Yes, yes, definitely, and I'll be your campaign manager and your front man or whatever."

"I'll be your assistant campaign manager," Ro says. "And we can put posters all over the school and you can make speeches about how the students need more power and—Gia, you have to do it, you have to."

I think about it for a total of about eleven seconds, then slap my hand on the desk. "I'm running."

Clive and Ro applaud and the librarian shoots us a dirty look. "SSSSSHHHHH," she says, putting her finger to her lips.

We give her a dirty look back because how stupid is that ssssshushing crap when you're in the library?

"Pizza anyone?" Clive says, looking back pointedly at the librarian.

We go out for thin crust whole wheat pizza and spinach calzones and talk more about what we'll do to get me elected. We only have one month to make me the best candidate.

When you're seriously running for office, you do it not only because if you win you can lord your power over everyone, but also because you supposedly believe you can help the school. So you have to come up with campaign pledges and convince people that you're the one to end some of the bullshit school rules like no flip-flops or ripped jeans or texting in the stairwell and maybe promise that if you're elected, the food in the dining hall will improve because Daniel Boulud will be hired as a catering consultant, and so on.

So Clive and Ro and I and a new girl named Candy who just moved to New York from LA decide to brainstorm to come up with my platform.

Unlike everyone else at Morgan, Candy didn't know my name when she first heard it. Or said she didn't. What she immediately glommed onto was my shoe and bag collection, which instantly put me on her A list. Not to mention that Morgan kids don't exactly open their arms to outsiders, so until she met me, she used to sit alone.

"OMIGOD!" she yelled one day and blocked my path as I walked down the corridor. "I'd kill for those shoes."

I looked back at her straight-faced, then cracked up.

So now we all sit around talking about my campaign platform and as usual Candy starts out by using her hometown as her default point.

"In LA my school had a screening night and we would show these incredible new movies before they opened, so maybe you could set up screenings here like that to bring people together."

"That would be totally cool," Clive says.

I look at Ro and she looks back at me, raising an eyebrow. Dante gets bootleg versions of new movies that we watch before he eBays them.

"Done," I say. "Next."

"You're running against Jordan Hassel, that jock a-hole," Ro says. "So you have to beat him at his own game. What if we set up a monthly fund-raiser for kids with cancer and give the highest bidder front row Knicks tickets that I'm sure we could get for free?"

"How do you get those?" Candy asks.

"Done. Next."

"I'm for raising money for more scholarships," I say. "That way this place can reflect the real world."

"Amen," Clive says.

By the end of the hour we have my platform. We are going to blow Jordan Hassel and Christy's best friend, Brandy Tewl—I swear that is her last name—out of the water. The only thing Brandy has going for her is that her dad runs a chain of restaurants so she has her pick of places for parties. Brandy's campaign slogan is "stop the bullying," which is fairly amusing since she and Christy and Georgina are the biggest bullies going.

"You need a one-sentence campaign slogan," Clive says. "It has to be catchy, like nine-nine-nine or whatever."

I look at Ro and Ro looks at me. Clive looks at me and I look at Clive. Clive looks at Candy and Candy looks at Clive. I look at Candy and Candy looks at me.

"I have no idea," I say. "But it will come to me."

"Well, think it up fast," Ro says, "because we have to get started on the posters."

I go home and check online. Most of the slogans are vacuous garbage: *A New Beginning, A New Voice, Hope for Tomorrow.*

I don't know how, but I know that by the time I come back to school in the morning, it will come to me.

SIX

Interspersed with thoughts about becoming president of Morgan are my obsessive musings about Officer Hottie, whose face now appears in my head 24/7.

Only how do you track down a cop? He's not on Facebook. No mentions on Google. He's not in the phone book because on a cop's salary he probably can't afford a landline. I don't have the nerve to call the precinct because they'd ask who I am and what it's about, and what am I supposed to say, I'm chasing the guy who hauled us in for DUI, resisting arrest, and whatever the hell else the charges were?

"Maybe we could go speeding up the Henry Hudson again," I say to Ro, only half kidding.

"Gia. Someone like you does not fall for a cop. He wants to fry your tail. He wants your whole family to fry. He's probably up nights fantasizing about locking up your dad, so wake the fuck up."

"You're right, Ro."

"And you are full of it, Gia."

I am sitting in the white canopied bed that I got for my ninth birthday when I was convinced that sleeping in a princess bed was all it took to turn me into one.

And now like a third grader I am on top of the world because I have a brand-new jumbo pack of sixty-four magic markers—orange, red, blue, green, purple, yellow, brown, black, maroon, and what have you—along with calligraphy pens and rulers and fifty sheets of oak tag for my campaign posters fanned out around me.

The marketing possibilities are empowering and I'm getting that amped-up first-day-of-school high before reality hits. I'm trying to dream up smart pledges and promises and ways to get people to vote for me because I would definitely enjoy winning, but more importantly, I would rejoice at seeing Christy and Georgina and their tool friend crash-land and burn in loserdom even though on some level I could care less whether or not people agree with me, especially the kind that go to Morgan.

That said, I still do not yet have a campaign slogan. And if I don't stop writing Michael Cross in thirteen different fonts in every color and size, I am going to blow my chances of competing in this so-called election, which would not help me on the road to my secret plan for the future.

The phone rings. Clive.

"How are you doing?" he asks in his sweet, innocent, almost musical voice. "Have you come up with anything?"

"Uh…not yet," I say, filling in the *a, e,* and *o* in Michael Cross's name with my hottest pink marker.

Clive doesn't know about Michael and what happened, so I tell him.

"Oh my God, Gia," he says. "Did they drop the charges?"

"Super Mario is on it. But my bigger problem is the cop."

"What do you mean?"

"He's my latest and greatest crush."

"Do you know what I think, Gia? I think you should forget him."

"You sound like Ro."

"Well, she's right. It won't end well. I mean a—"

"I'm not worrying about how it will end, Clive, I'm worrying about how and when it will begin because I can't even find him."

"What's his name?"

I hear keys clicking and he's spelling out M-i-c-h-a-e-l C-r-o-s-s. "I don't believe I'm doing this," he sighs, "but I'm doing it. I am. I'm hacking into my dad's system…terrific…so give me five minutes and we'll see."

I end the call and begin pacing my room. How can Clive find him? Does his dad have some spy network he plugs into? Connections with the police? All I know is if anyone can figure it out…

I jump when the phone rings.

"Gia," he says. "This is your lucky day. Your guy is a rookie cop who works out of a precinct in Washington Heights, and FYI his dad was a cop too. There's more stuff, only there's this security block and I have to find a way to get the password…and I will…eventually. But anyway, Michael Sean Cross lives two blocks from the precinct and I checked Google Earth and there's a bar called Uptown Lounge half a block away that's described as a hangout for off-duty cops. So it's not a stretch to imagine him hanging out there because—"

"How did you *do* that? "

"My dad has this resource."

"Resource?"

"Sometimes he needs information fast," he says, which doesn't explain anything.

"I owe you. *Any*thing. Tell me…a Fendi weekender?"

"Just the slogan," Clive says. "And it has to be good. We have to blow them out of the water. I can't face being on the losing ticket."

"It will be, I swear."

"Off to Clive's," I tell my mom. "School stuff."

"What? At this hour?"

"I'll be back soon. We can't do this on the phone."

"Why not?"

"Maaa, it's *math*. Do you want me to fail? It's complicated."

"Frankie will drive you," she says

"Clive's driver is on his way. Don't worry."

My dad is out and my mom buys it because even though I'm grounded, this is schoolwork. I hail a cab a block from my street. It's raining lightly and the pavement glistens under all the red and green traffic lights giving the world a fresh Christmassy glow. And yes, okay, this feels right and special and positive and maybe there is some kind of magic in the air and this will work out because it's preordained, if you believe things like that. And when I'm feeling out-there and directionless, which is most of the time although I try not to admit it, I do start to think there has to be a bigger plan that I can't exactly see, because how else can you explain the way things work?

Anyway, even if it's all a crapshoot, I guess I'll survive. I check my watch because I don't have much time for fairy-tale magic, especially on a school night when I could definitely get caught by my dad who sometimes has me tailed, and that makes me nervous and I don't want to be, and shit, if I at least had a beer.

And then there's the bar. A grunge bar? Who would be there? Old guys? Ex cops? Off-duty cops? Drug dealers? Junkies? Would the assholes hit on me? Would the bartender see my fake ID and toss my sorry ass onto the street or worse call the cops, which would be a laugh, then again, crap, Super Mario has enough on his plate and he does *not* need more from me. Washington Heights isn't exactly Park Avenue and, Gia, I remind myself, you are a candidate for school president and you don't need something *else* for them to throw at you because half the kids are already convinced that you're a lowlife.

Then for some reason the idea of once again being driven back to that derelict precinct—like hello, instant replay, rewind, do over—cracks me up, and if you are out by yourself laughing so hard you're in pain, you definitely look like a psycho.

"What's so funny?" asks the cab driver.

"Inside joke."

"Inside joke, what's 'inside joke?'" he says with an accent from someplace not on my got-to-go-to itinerary.

"Uh...well..." Then my phone rings.

"Where are you?" Ro asks.

"Going up to the bar to meet Officer Hottie," I say, laughing harder at that than the fact that I'm running for president.

"Gia, what are you on?"

I look out the window. "Dyckman Street."

"I didn't mean—"

"We're here, lady," the driver says.

"Gotta go, Ro."

"Be careful," she whispers.

"What do you think I'm going to do?" I hang up before she can answer and use the backseat as a dressing room, peeling off my flannel shirt, spraying it with cologne because it stinks, and stuffing it in my bag, and then changing into heels while the driver is repeating, "What's inside joke? What's inside joke?"

"Something funny...to only you and your friends...like my sorry life."

I slam the door, inhale, and stare at the sky. It's dark and hazy and I can't find even one teensy star to wish upon and this is all so...out of the box.

Then it hits me. I have my campaign slogan.

SEVEN

Mick Jagger is singing as I walk in. *I can't get no…no no no…no SAT-IS-FAC-TION*, which makes me think that maybe God has my direct line after all. I hold up my head and push past the crowd along the bar.

"Hey, hot mama!" A thick arm snakes out and grabs me around the waist. I slide out of it and keep going. The place is jammed. Heads turn as I walk, but I pretend not to notice as I search and search for *him*, but *he* is not *here*, at least not *yet*. I check my watch. Ten. Is he off work yet? Maybe cops hang out at bars when their shifts are over, but what the hell hours are the shifts and why didn't I think of that before?

I'm probably wasting my time. No, I am wasting my time. I make my way up to the bar and order a beer. "ID," the bartender says, all flirty-eyed. I smile and hand it to him.

"Looks good to me," he says. It should—it cost enough from that sleazo East Village forger from the Balkans. I find a back corner of the bar and stand there nursing the piss-awful beer as I glance at my watch for the tenth time like an obsessive compulsive. Not much time left because the stupid taxi got stuck in horrendous traffic because of construction and an accident that involved a pimp from New Jersey duded up in a white suit with a cowboy hat who planted himself on the hood of his white stretch Hummer so people passing by all slowed down and were like, *whoa, w-h-a-t?* Bottom line, it took almost an hour to get to this dump, never mind the fare. So, Officer Hottie, if you're coming, you better get here soon because my mom will start calling and I don't want to answer from a bar with blasting music because, hello, that does not exactly sound like I'm in Clive's apartment sweating over math. And if my parents find out, I'll be shackled and homeschooled.

"Refill?"

The guy is older than my dad, seriously. I shake my head and manage a weak smile, then glance at my watch. Officer Hottie now has five more minutes. If he doesn't show, I'm out of this pit.

Now that I rethink this, I realize what a stupid idea it was. What was I thinking? Then I start going over the trouble I went through to get here, based on nothing more than Clive's guess that he hangs out here because he lives nearby. As I take a sip of my beer, I feel a hand on my ass and turn quickly.

"Do you mind?" I slap away the arm but his BO smell lingers and he laughs and shrugs and I look at my watch for the twentieth time and start the final countdown. The place is a total dump and I am out of here because this was about the uncoolest thing I have ever done.

I walk toward the door saying, "excuse me, excuse me, excuse me, excuse me" a hundred million times but the music is loud and suddenly everyone seems drunk and deaf and pissed and oblivious. And then I'm thinking about how it probably won't be easy to find a cab going back and why didn't I think of that before and what if my dad finds out? And then because I'm so obsessed, not to mention making my last ditch effort to case the place for Officer Hottie, I don't watch where I'm going, so the tip of my shoe catches on the leg of a bar stool that's sticking way the hell out, and I lose my balance and careen to the side. And then—wham—crash into someone going by. An arm suddenly reaches out and braces me, or I would have been sprawled on the floor.

"God," I yell out, trying to balance myself. I spin around all spastic, and I am staring into a face that stares straight back at me and doesn't respond, at least at first. It dawns on both of us at the very same nanosecond, and my heart starts thrumming and drumming and omigod, he looks so, so, so, so help me FABULOUS.

"Gia," he says, the muscles in his jaw pulsing.

"Michael," I say, steadying myself by reaching out and grabbing his shoulder, pinning our bodies together.

He looks so different out of the blue cop uniform. More real, more present, more blood and guts sexual and alive and strong and gettable and electrifying—if that is possible. Jeans, black running shoes, a black fitted T-shirt that hugs his strong shoulders and tight chest, never mind the tattoo below the sleeve peeking out like a tease on the swell of his bicep, begging to be touched.

I am aware of the heat of his fingers and the pressure of his grip on my upper arm that remains for a few seconds more than it has to. I let go of his shoulder reluctantly and step back.

"What are you doing here?" I straighten up and pretend to breathe.

"I could ask you the same thing."

"Just slumming, you know."

"You're not old enough to be in a bar," he says, his jaw tensing.

"The Dairy Queen was closed."

"Get out of here or I'll take you in for underage drinking."

"Is that your idea of fun, Michael?"

He looks at me and doesn't answer.

"I forgot, you're the strong, silent type…anyway…I was just going. Want to walk me?"

"What are you doing up here?" he asks again. "Buying?"

"I'm not a goddamn junkie, if that's what you mean."

"Then what?"

"I came looking…for you."

He looks at me in disbelief. "What?"

"You heard me."

"Why?"

"Stop it, Michael."

"Go home," he says dismissively.

"Will you call me?"

He closes his eyes and shakes his head.

"Well at least walk me to the door." I go outside and he follows.

"So what," I say, glancing at him over my shoulder, "you don't like Italians?"

He looks at me with a steady stare and doesn't answer.

"Or maybe you don't like girls."

A half smile. "Right."

"At least you can kiss me good night then," and before he can answer my lips are on his, and for maybe one or two real seconds, he stands there immobile and doesn't kiss back but doesn't resist either. But not only that, his mouth starts to open like his body is willing even if his cop brain isn't, but a moment later he eases back and pushes me away.

"I can't do this," he says in a husky voice.

I step back, waiting, not knowing what to do. Score another point for Gia making a complete fool of herself. Not that this is the first time. *Run, stupid. GO!* my brain says. Only I can't.

So he makes the decision and turns his back on me and heads for the street with one arm up to hail a cab. I didn't have to worry because when you don't want one, the cabs drop from the sky. It stops with a gut-wrenching screech, which kind of kills the mood.

"Go home," he says, turning back to me.

I pull out a Chanel lipstick called Attitude then grab his arm.

"What the—" he says then falls silent watching me scrawl my cell in giant numbers from his wrist to his elbow.

He shakes his head in disbelief.

"Call me," I say, getting into the cab.

"You're crazy."

The cab speeds downtown and I stare out the window.

Crazy, the operative word in our family. My dad is crazy—pazzo—too, so it's in the genes.

Only his is a different crazy. It's a there's-so-much-shit-going-down crazy and I-have-to-keep-it-together-to-handle-it crazy, so he does things like turn on the water to make coffee and then walk off and leave it running. Or go to his closet and take out one tie after another because he's suddenly blind as to what goes with what, even though his ginormous closet is set up by his tailor every season with each suit next to the shirts and ties that go with it. Then he'll sit on the edge of the bed, lost, until my mom walks in.

"Gio," she'll say softly. Then she'll pick out the tie that matches the shirt and knot it around his neck and then kiss him on the forehead like his guardian angel. I've seen that happen.

I get nervous when he gets like that. It tells me that something is about to go down even though I don't know what it is because he never tells us anything. We find out more from the six o'clock news unless it's really bad. Then someone yells *pack*, and he sends Frankie to get us, and—boom—ten minutes later, we're in the car speeding to an out-of-the-way motel in Jersey for however long. We pass the time playing cards and watching TV while my mom crochets afghans or sketches dresses because before she was married she made clothes for Valentino. And everyone mutters prayers and we order out and then complain about the takeout and my mom goes on a rant about how "everybody cuts corners and nobody makes their own sauce anymore," which makes *her* crazy.

Only now that I'm at Morgan, I can't disappear and go into hiding no matter what because I'd miss everything and fail and never become president. And even if I could, I mean, how would it look to disappear for days without a sick note, which is a joke anyway because in my life, about everything is sick crazy and not normal because for us the only normal is abnormal.

EIGHT

As I'm coming in the door after school the next day, the home phone rings. It's usually for me or Anthony. Or it's Aunt Mary calling to go to the mall with my mom. But we always check caller ID before we answer. Now it's ringing and no one is home and I'm checking and it's New York 1, the all-day news channel calling, which scares me because we're not exactly listed in the phone book, so how the hell did they get our number?

"Romano funeral home," I say.

There's a pause. "Excuse me, I was trying to reach…" The voice drops off.

"Sorry, wrong number." I hang up and it rings again. I go through the same charade, but they're on to me.

Silence.

Are they putting a tracer on the call? A few minutes later there's another call. CNN now. I freak and call my dad.

"We've had two calls from the news."

"On the home number?"

"Yes. Daddy, are you okay?"

Ten-second pause.

"Don't worry, Gia," he says, his calm, blanket answer to everything, which makes me worry more

"It's nothing, nothing. You know how they chase me."

"But I don't want them to."

"Gia, I'll see you later, don't worry so much."

There's a knock on the door a few minutes later. My mom isn't home because she's at the church helping them get ready for the women's bingo lasagna luncheon. Do I answer it? If I don't, maybe they'll break in. I go upstairs and look out my bedroom window. A cop car. Now a finger is glued to the door bell.

I open the door. Two cops, one with his hand resting lightly on the top of his gun.

"What do you want?"

"We're looking for your dad."

"He's not home."

"Where is he?"

"You know more about where he is than I do."

Cop one turns and looks at cop two.

"Let's go," he says.

They give me one more lingering look and then get into their car and drive away.

I was ten when I found out about my dad. It was something my parents always worked hard to hide from me, to keep my innocent world intact and at arm's length from reality, at least their reality.

I remember everything about that day. It was snowing lightly in the late afternoon. I had been up in my room watching the snowflakes hit the windows and then slide down in slow moving, slushy drips. The room was cold and I remember putting a sweater on Beppo, my teddy bear, to keep him warm even though I was old enough to know that was silly. My mom was making minestrone and the whole house smelled good from the onions and garlic that she browned in olive oil in the giant soup kettle.

When important things happen in your life, your brain has a way of archiving them so later on when you want to go over them again the memories are preserved, like a prom corsage pressed between the pages of a diary.

When I was little, I thought my dad was in construction or in the restaurant business. We would be in the car and my mom or dad would point out office towers or apartment buildings.

"See, Gia," they'd say, "that's daddy's building."

I thought he built the buildings. I thought he made them himself, putting one brick on top of another, the way Anthony and I built our mansion houses with red, blue, and yellow Legos.

Later on I thought my dad was in the carting business even though I didn't even know what carting was. Then I found out and knew they used the word carting because it sounded fancier than garbage. Well, he was in the garbage business, but not the way I thought. He was in other businesses too, like restaurants, bars, dry cleaners, used car business, casinos, and places outside the city too that I didn't even know about.

It was something that Anthony said to a friend of his one day about my dad being a boss. I always thought well, yes, he was the boss, the boss of his company, because I didn't know what a boss was. But the day someone got shot down on the street in midtown and the papers reported it with my dad's picture on their front pages, it all fell into place.

That, plus the way I began to get treated.

For the first time I felt this divide: people were either keeping their distance or just the opposite, trying hard to be my friend, inviting me places where I didn't fit in. I wasn't just me anymore after that. I was a part of something bigger and I felt split down the middle. There was the Gia I was to myself, my family, and my friends, and the one that everyone else saw and either wanted to be close to or steer clear of, like I had a contagious disease.

When I finally understood about my dad, it hurt just to think of it.

"Does dad kill people?" I once asked Anthony. He looked at me, annoyed.

"No," he said, leaving it at that.

"Does he tell other people to kill people?"

"Do your damn homework, Gia," he said, turning back to the TV.

I had a hard time believing all that. I knew what my dad was really like so how could that be true? No one cared about us more than him. He was always there for me and Anthony, bringing us presents and taking us out for fancy dinners, the circus, and Broadway musicals. Actors came out to meet him when they knew he was in the audience.

Whenever we needed advice, he always had the answers. And if we got sick and stayed home from school, he'd sit by our beds and tell us stories.

His kind side went beyond just our family. He helped everybody in the neighborhood who needed help too. He even paid the vet bills for a neighbor when his three-month old golden lab puppy nearly died after eating something in the street. The neighbor renamed the puppy after my dad, and every time the man walked the dog past our house, he would stop and cross himself.

My dad gave to everybody, except when I was really small and we didn't have money. That was when he told us that the love we had in our family was more important than anything money could buy and that it didn't matter if we couldn't put presents under the Christmas tree as long as we woke up together on Christmas morning.

I remember coming home from school that snowy afternoon and turning on the TV. They were doing a report about a crime and the next thing I saw was the screen filled with my dad's face. I shut the TV off because I knew he would get mad if he saw me watching.

He was working at home in his office that day so I decided to go ask him because I had to know. I opened the door and walked in without knocking first. The office walls are paneled in dark wood, and both windows are covered with heavy wine colored velvet drapes, always drawn. I loved the way it looked from the moment he had it decorated. It reminded me of a cave. I felt safe there. Even now, my dad's office is my favorite part of our house, although I don't go there much since it's mostly off-limits. I remember staring at the vase of fresh roses on the table near the window.

He has a mahogany desk with a gold letter holder where he keeps bills. Next to it is a tall lamp with a wine colored base and gold handles that look like ears that stick out too far. On top of it is a shade with tiny pleats. I remember how the room smelled, like lemony furniture polish. I sat in the red velvet armchair with the lace doily over the footstool and stared at him, waiting. He was reading the newspaper and finally looked up.

"Gia, what's the matter?"

I didn't know how to answer. I wasn't sure what the matter was.

"Those things," I said, "that they say about you...on the TV...Are they right?"

"What things?" he asked, lifting his chin slightly.

"That you're the one behind it when people get killed," I said, so low I didn't think he could hear me. Our eyes met across the room. I don't think either of us blinked.

His eyes darkened. "Don't listen to the TV. They're trying to make headlines to be popular. Just remember the only important thing is that I love you. That's all that matters here."

"But is it true?" I said, refusing to look away.

"Sometimes things happen, Gia," he said, looking down at the gold rings on his fingers and at his nails, always perfectly covered with clear polish. "People don't always act the way they're supposed to. They cross you." He looked back up at me. "If you're running a business you have to trust the people around you, like we trust each other, right?"

I nodded.

"So we have to do the right thing when other people don't do the right thing. If you're the boss, you have to act like the boss."

I must have looked confused because he shook his head and smiled. "It's complicated," he said, "and I don't want you to worry about it. You're safe here, that's all you have to know."

I swallowed hard and got up to leave.

"Come, come here," he said, motioning to me. I walked over to him and he hugged me, kissing me on the top of the head again and again, as if he was trying to fill my head with his love instead of the thoughts I came in with.

"Who loves you more than anyone else in the whole world?"

That was our game, the game we had played since I was a two-year-old. He asked me that question again and again, each time as if he had never asked it before. Every time he did I was back to being two again, looking up at my dad as if he were this giant, the most perfect man in the whole world.

"You do," I said, and he broke into a smile the way he always did.

"That's right. Now go and see if you can help your mother with dinner. She's making chicken cacciatore," he said. "You love that, no?"

I nodded. He patted me on the back and I walked toward the door. I turned to look at him one last time, expecting to see him already looking down, reading his paper again, but he wasn't. His face was darker, his eyes hooded, and he was still watching me.

I never asked him again.

NINE

I get a reprieve from being grounded because we have to do campaign posters, so Ro and Clive and Candy and I hang out at Clive's, and at dinnertime we're starving so we speed-dial for hot and sour soup, egg rolls, moo shu pork, shrimp and Chinese vegetables, ten-ingredient fried rice, sweet-and-sour chicken, and shrimp lo mein.

After everyone pigs out and we read the fortunes in the cookies—*All your hard work will soon pay off* (mine), *Don't let the past and useless details choke your existence* (Candy), *The one you love is closer than you think* (Clive), and *Be direct, usually one can accomplish more that way* (Ro). I force them into the bathroom to wash their hands ten times to get rid of the grease before touching the oak tag for my posters.

When everyone's clean, we sit on the floor in Clive's room.

"Okay," I say, clapping my hands. "Here it is, the long awaited campaign slogan: *Gia. Fresh thinking. Fresh answers. Vote outside the box.*"

Silence.

"Earth to Clive?"

"I like it," he says finally, "but you know the people you're running against, Gia. Can you handle how they're going to twist it and throw it back at you?"

"I can deal."

"Just one thing, Gia," Ro says. "When they start snickering and sticking it to you about the word fresh and calling you a slut, how do you plan to answer that?"

"That this is the year of the slut."

"What?" Clive says, his eyes widening.

"I'm kidding. I don't know. Any ideas?"

"Say that they have filthy minds for thinking that," Candy says, "and for perverting the truth. Act totally indignant."

We all look at Candy with new respect.

"You go, girl. That's exactly what I'll say."

Then we get to work coloring, never mind the blisters on our fingers from all the work, three hours later we do actually finish all of them and they come out fabulous. Then Clive's driver takes Candy home to Park Avenue and drops Ro off at home in Little Italy. I stay behind to hang with Clive.

"You never told me about that night with Michael Cross," he says. "Excuse me, Officer Hottie."

"He's in total denial about his feelings for me. Plus he probably thinks I'm jailbait—even though I'm not—and the daughter of a don and he's my arresting officer and blah blah blah.

"Did he actually say all that?"

"He didn't have to."

"What did he actually say?"

"He didn't say anything. He's not a talker."

"So how do you know he's into you and can't handle it?"

"By the way he looks at me."

"That's all?"

"Clive," I say. "Chemistry. Does. Not. Lie."

He's quiet after that and we sit there looking at each other.

"Maybe I should just marry you," I say. "And we could live happily ever after."

"I would love that," Clive says.

"And you'd give me a giant diamond ring and everything?"

"Absolutely everything."

I smile back at Clive, not sure exactly what he means. He said he's not gay, but he's not like anyone straight that I know either. Not that it matters.

I climb into his bed and pat the place next to me and then Clive and I snuggle together while the rain comes down hard so that the view of Central Park outside looks all drippy and speckled like it was painted by Seurat, the French artist we learned about in art history who freaked everyone out at first with his weird way of painting called pointillism. He put like three million paint dots or something on his canvas, and if you stand away from it, you see that, whoa, it totally all works, because what happens is those separate color dots you see next to each other close-up magically morph into different patches of colors from a distance.

And that made me start to think about whether in real life you need to step back from things to see the real picture and the true colors, aka perspective, and that if you're too close and fixated on the individual dots, you can get it all wrong and maybe what you think you're seeing isn't reality or the true picture at all. It's something else entirely.

"What are you thinking, Gia?

"Of George Seurat."

"Because of our painting?"

"What painting?"

"You know, the one in the living room."

"You have a Seurat? A real Seurat?"

"Mmm, over the couch."

"Clive, do *not* tell anyone."

"Why?"

"Because they'd steal it and kidnap you for ransom."

"Like they could ever track down my parents to pay."

I look at Clive and he looks back at me and we start to snicker and then laugh and a minute later we're keeled over laughing so hard we're practically choking and holding our stomachs because they hurt so much.

I mean what's sadder, the fact that my dad's people would probably get behind stealing the art, or the fact that his dad is MIA and wouldn't be around to pay?

Without warning all this emotion that must have been barricaded behind the laughter rears up like a tsunami and I don't know why, but everything gets less funny and backslides and grows darker and tragic and suddenly we're sobbing and, God, how did that happen? And we're feeling sorry for everything that's wrong in our lives and not the way we want it to be, although we know we don't have the power to change any of that. So we sob harder and I can't breathe and Clive is gasping for air too with tears running down his cheeks. And how pathetic are we, lost and alone even though we're not now because we have each other. And I don't even remember how all this started now, but I wish I could figure out what it means because my insides are collapsing.

It's been one week, sixteen hours, and thirty-seven minutes or so since I've seen Michael. I check my phone every time I inhale to see if he might have broken down and called. Or left a message. Or a text. But no. He is playing hard to get or not playing at all and just being a dick because he's so into the good cop thing, trying to do right and be ethical and all, despite the fact that I'm sure he's up nights thinking about me and suffering too because even his tough impassive cop face is not good enough to hide what's behind his eyes.

If there's one thing I am sure of, it's that I have an unfailingly sharp radar when it comes to picking up vibes on how men feel about me. And even though, yes, I might be completely deranged, I am convinced that I just have to work on Michael Cross. And that is what I'm going to do if I can get near him.

What I need is a way to track his whereabouts, which makes me think of the electronic ankle bracelets that they clamp on felons' legs and that my dad walked around with one time so they always knew where he was so he couldn't flee to a safe house in Reggio Calabria or wherever to hide. But how ridiculous is that? So I have to come up with a real plan.

But then my phone rings. And of course it isn't Michael. It's *Vogue* magazine. W-H-A-T?

I'm not sure what I'm hearing at first. But then I realize that the assistant to the fashion editor named Clotilde Marie Saint-Just is asking me to pose for them for an upcoming issue called "Under Age and Over the Top," which would basically be about famous young girls in the news, even though I'm not exactly famous and not exactly in the news either—not unless you count the TV cameras they stick in our faces whenever our family goes out somewhere together because they love to stalk my dad. But, whatever, because if they do the story, I will be famous in a different and better kind of way, so the idea blows me away.

I mean *me*? In *Vogue* magazine? GET OUT. I call Ro.

"How do you know it's not some perv who wants you to take off your pants, Gia?"

"To start, the caller ID said Condé Nast, okay, and I don't think you can set that up on your own. So, no, it wasn't bogus. And then they gave me the name of the photographer who's shooting it and his name is John Plesaurus and he is *big* and does a lot of their covers and you can find his name in any issue. And anyway I called his studio to check and they said yes, yes, yes, the shooting is scheduled for four weeks from now and it's legit and yada, yada, yada."

"One other thing, Gia. Your dad will never go for it."

I don't answer.

"Gia?"

"I'm thinking."

My dad is nothing if not vain, and I am his daughter with his DNA and his looks. We both have honey-blond hair, tawny skin, and green eyes. Me in the magazine would be a compliment to him. So bottom line, I have my game plan.

"I can do it."

"Do what?" Ro asks.

"Convince him."

"How?"

"I'll call you back."

Whenever my mom makes pasta con sarde, no matter what, my dad comes home early. His grandparents grew up in a small town near Palermo and they fed him pasta con sarde before he had breast milk, I think, and they passed that love to him in their genes, so the fresh sardines with the sweet currants and the parsley and the thick bucatini pasta just about transport him back to his childhood.

Tonight is pasta con sarde night, which may work in my favor. I help my mom with the salad and put in extra arugula, because my dad loves arugula, and then I dress it with oil and balsamic vinegar. I bought a chocolate truffle cake at Ro's dad's bakery and after we finish dinner I cut him a big piece and bring him his espresso and then I'm silent and patient and all attentive, transformed into perfect daughter mode, waiting for just the right moment as he sits for a little while enjoying the pasta con sarde afterglow or whatever until I can't stand it anymore.

"So guess who called me today?"

He shrugs. "Tell me."

"*Vogue.*"

He narrows his eyes, not getting it.

"*Vogue. Vogue* magazine. They want to do a photo shoot of the best-looking daughters of celebrities."

I leave out the underage part and put a second wedge of truffle cake on his plate. My dad stirs his espresso with the small silver spoon and very slowly runs the sliver of lemon peel around the edge of the gold-rimmed cup. He shifts slightly in his chair, crossing one leg over the other, before cocking his head to the side.

"In what, in bikinis?" he asks, because he's afraid of saying thongs or panties and sounding pervy.

"No, Daddy, in *designer* clothes!" Not that I have a clue what they're thinking, but it's *Vogue* and what are they going to use, low-end polyester shit from Walmart?

"I don't think so," he says, blotting his lips with the linen napkin.

I look at him. "Do you know why they want *me*?"

"Eh," he purses his lips. "I know."

"Because I look like you, Daddy. They said I got my incredible looks from my dad." I give that a minute to sink in. My father lifts his chin.

"They said that?"

"Word for word."

He stares out the window and then turns back to me. "I'll think about it."

I look over at my mom who I can tell is already on board so I just need her to move him from thinking maybe to saying yes. I remember a line from a movie where the wife says that her husband may be the head of the family, but that she is the neck and "the neck turns the head."

"Mom?" I say, just short of pleading.

"Frankie would go with you," she says.

"Absolutely."

"And be there the whole time."

"Well, except the dressing room part," I say.

"Don't be fresh," she says.

I hold out my hands.

My dad turns to me. "Maybe," he says. "If it's *Vogue* magazine and you're on the cover."

The cover? Who said anything about...?

"You're the best," I say, jumping up and hugging him. Now all I have to do is make sure it's the cover.

TEN

No, I am not thinking about what I'll be wearing for the *Vogue* pictures or what I'll stand up and say to the assholes at Morgan to get them to vote for me, because my body is on orange alert and that makes me wired and dysfunctional and scared and excited and in need of a plan, and the only one I can come up with makes me semi-nauseous, but I don't care.

School goes by in agonizingly slow motion the next day as if the hands on the clock have been weighted down and time is playing a sadistic game of torturing me because it refuses to pass. When it's finally lunch, I turn to Clive.

"Can I borrow Thomas tonight?"

"What for?"

I dread telling him, but I do.

"Are you sure that's a smart move, Gia?"

Smart? It's a pathetic, desperate move. "I have no cards to play, and it's the only one I can come up with since he hasn't called." *And my hormones are like…*

"You can have Thomas, but be careful, Gia. And what about your parents? Are they really going to believe that you're coming over to my place again for the math?"

"They take Ambien."

After dinner I help my mom with the dishes, then go up to my room. I do homework, shower, wash my hair, and put on pj's. I make a show of kissing my parents good night before I climb into bed. I hear them come upstairs and I wait while they take turns in their bathroom, watching under my door until the hall is dark.

I wait to give them a chance to fall asleep, and then I get up and quietly dress in jeans with a red tank top, low enough to show serious cleavage. I toss sling backs into my bag and slip into ballet flats that will not ratt-a-tat-tat on the wooden floor. I creep down the stairs and go out through the basement so they won't hear the front door.

Thomas is parked down the block from my house in a dark cul-de-sac where the streetlight is broken. I'm now convinced that before he worked for Clive's family, he must have trained with Scotland Yard because he's good and blind when he needs to be. I walk down the street slinking away from the streetlamps.

I get in the car and Thomas winks at me. No rant about me leaving the house at eleven or the idiocy of going to uptown Manhattan alone. I can only imagine what a loser he'd think I am if he knew I'm headed for a bar filled with lowlifes because I'm blind with longing for the cop who busted me.

"Thank you, Thomas."

He looks at me through the rearview mirror. "My pleasure, Gia," he says, a small smile on his face that makes me wonder whether he did stuff like this when he was my age.

"Do you think I'm crazy?"

"In a good way," he says finally.

I cross my arms over my chest, a wordless hug.

To fill the silence, Thomas puts on Jefferson Airplane, which Clive says is Thomas's favorite oldies group.

Don't you want somebody to love?

Don't you need somebody to love?

Is this particular song at this particular moment a coincidence? Or are there no such things as coincidences?

When we get there, he parks at the end of the street.

"I'll wait here for you," he says, giving me a compassionate—or maybe a pitying—smile.

"Thank you, Thomas." I make my way to the front door and check my watch. Eleven thirty. Do you know where your arresting officer is?

The blasting music hits me like a slap. Some group I've never heard of. I immediately case the bar. The lineup this evening is even more depressing than last time. Half the place seems hung over and the other half would look better if they were. And there is no one who remotely resembles gorgeous Michael. I detour to the unisex bathroom with the gag-worthy urinal and apply more sparkly pink lip gloss before leaning over the sink and staring at myself in the mirror to use up an entire sixty seconds.

I unlatch the squeaky door and head for an empty spot. And then stop. Cardiac alert. He's leaning against the bar, a glass of something like scotch on the rocks in front of him. Panic wells up in me because it never occurred to me to come armed with a smart, edgy, übercool conversation opener. I brace myself against the wall and study him.

Perfect profile.

Straight nose.

Sharp jawline.

Strong mouth.

His body is cut under a charcoal T-shirt. No cutesy message on it. Michael Cross does not buy souvenir T-shirts or wear clothes to show the world where he's been. It's none of your goddamn business.

I keep staring. Does he know he's one of the most beautiful men on the planet? No. He's too troubled. I doubt that he spends much time admiring himself in the mirror. The only thing I can't envision is where I fit in. Maybe because I don't. He won't let me. I wonder about the kind of people he would open up to and draw a blank.

As if he hears me thinking he turns and our eyes lock. He tilts his head slightly, an almost unconscious show of surprise. I lick my lips and swallow, unable to hold back the slightest smile.

What do I do now? Crap. What was I thinking? Why am I here? My brain flatlines.

Out of nowhere, someone drunk and annoying comes up to me, cutting off my clear view of Michael.

"Can I buy you a drink?"

"No, thanks," I say, shaking my head. That must be all Michael needs because he walks over just as Mr. Inebriated is saying, "C'mon, just one drink."

"She doesn't drink," Michael says, staring icily at the guy before turning his back on him and stepping between us, a human barricade. The guy looks back at Michael and eventually shrugs and walks away.

Michael and I stare at each other hungrily and the air between us becomes charged and I am suddenly more pumped and alive and energized and over-oxygenated and in someplace above earth I've never been to. He does that to me.

Every. Time. He's. Near. Me.

Does he feel it too?

"Why are you back here?" he asks, a trace of annoyance in his voice.

"The beautiful people."

A smirky smile. It disappears as fast as it appeared.

"You never called," I say.

"Right."

"You didn't want to?"

His eyes meet mine and he looks away first. "I didn't want to," he says robotically, looking back at me with a steady stare.

"Liar."

It's like someone else is using my mouth to talk—only it's not someone else, it's me. Only it's me on steroids or truth serum or a talking drug, and I don't know how it happens but it does whenever I'm around him, because his refusal to say what's on his mind forces me to compensate, if that makes sense. But it probably doesn't because nothing happening between us makes sense or is logical or normal and I am clearly out of my safety zone.

"What is it with you?" he says, shaking his head, his face softening slightly.

Always the guarded cop talk with the subtext.

"I wake up at night thinking about you, Michael."

Shut up, Gia, just shut up, I tell myself. But my mouth refuses to listen.

He narrows his eyes, his guarded stare saying he's trying to figure out where to go with this, but I don't need cop talk to tell me I've struck a nerve. He can't hide the look in his eyes that tells me what I want to know.

"So you do too."

"This is fucked up, Gia," he hisses. "Can't you see that?"

I feel like when I'm at school watching a fencing match. All the swordplay, the maneuvers, the delicate dance of back and forth, advance, retreat, advance, retreat, until finally—zap—one player scores a direct hit and the air reverberates with the electric buzz of the scoreboard as it lights up.

I feel it inside when he says my name, everything shifting into overdrive. I'm not the "you" in the car anymore. I'm a flesh-and-blood girl with a name, a name that plays in his head like a song you keep singing over and over and can't get free of, at least that's what I'm thinking is happening unless I'm blind and all wrong.

"It's not, Michael. It's real."

He closes his eyes and shakes his head. "It's wrong."

Out of nowhere someone comes up behind Michael and gives him a friendly punch in the shoulder. "Hey, Cross. So this is where you're hiding out," he says, giving me the once over. I let out a breath I didn't know I was holding.

"Jim," Michael says.

"Did you get moved or what? I never see you anymore."

"Alternate nights, man," Michael says.

"Who did you piss off?"

Michael smiles and shakes his head.

"Intro?"

"She's just leaving," Michael says.

"Need a ride?"

"She has one," Michael answers, not missing a beat.

"Catch you later, Miguel." Jim smiles and moves on.

"Let's go," Michael says, his hand closing around my arm.

"How did you know I have a ride?"

"You want low profile, don't arrive in a Bentley."

Does he miss anything? I follow him to the door and out onto the street where it's so quiet it feels like we've landed on a desert landscape. I can't help sliding up the edge of his sleeve to look at the tattoo. *Semper Fi*. Always faithful. The marine corps motto.

"No wonder you're such a hard-ass."

A hint of a smile.

"Admit it," I say, tracing my finger along the outlines of the tattoo. "You think about me too."

He bites the corner of his bottom lip and shakes his head. I take a step closer to him. I can smell his shampoo, something woodsy and clean.

"Don't come back here, Gia," he whispers. "Please."

I lean forward so my lips touch lightly against his. I expect him to push away again, but, like before, for a fraction of a second he stands still, eyes closed. Then as if a different part of his brain trips an alarm, his warm hands close over my upper arms and he eases away, closing his eyes for a moment.

"Good-bye, Michael," I whisper then turn and bolt down the street. Thomas is waiting exactly where I left him. I climb into the backseat of the car, disappearing behind the tinted windows. I pull the door and it closes with a loud thud, like the lid on a coffin. Thomas and I look at each other through the rearview mirror. He starts the car and pulls into the street.

"I'm a good listener," he says, staring ahead.

Only I don't have words to explain how I feel. I stare out the window, trying to make sense of what just happened and the jumble of emotions inside as tears run down my cheeks because it feels like I have to fight so hard for everything in my life and nothing is easy and normal and straightforward. And I go around pretending and pretending and praying for what could be, but I can't escape who I am and it's so clear that Michael doesn't want to get involved with the radioactive Don's daughter. He can't see past that. Or won't. And it's so unfair.

"Shut up about fair," Anthony always says. "Life's not fair, Gia. Grow up."

Only I can't accept that. I won't.

Before I can make any sense of it, someone is gently shaking my shoulder. I open my eyes and look up.

"Gia," Thomas says softly. "You're home."

I stare back at him, unaware that I fell asleep. "Thanks, Thomas, for everything."

"You're welcome," he says gently. "Any time."

Half asleep I stumble down the street. I look both ways. All quiet. I stare up at the house. My parents' bedroom light is off. Very gently, I slide the key into the basement door lock. It opens with the softest creak. I walk in and close the door behind me, relieved to be inside. The door sticks a little because the frame is warped so I push it, gritting my teeth as it creaks into place. It takes me a few seconds to find the light. I flick it on, then think better of lighting up the whole basement and turn it off, feeling my way in the darkness.

Thump! A hand from out of nowhere comes down hard, slamming my shoulder.

"Ow!" I scream as I get dragged into the basement.

A beam of light from above suddenly illuminates my face.

"*Gia*," my dad says.

I stare at him in his pajamas. He's glaring at me, enraged, shaking, his hand wrapped tightly around the end of a baseball bat.

"I could have killed you," he yells, out of breath, squeezing my shoulder. He's shaking so hard that the first thought I have is that he's going to have a heart attack and drop to the ground dead. I stare back at him, his eyes wide and hard.

He throws the bat down hard behind him and it lands with a loud smack and bounces and rolls across the concrete floor and hits the side of a metal cabinet with a clank.

"What's wrong with you?" he says, catching his breath. His voice becomes so quiet and intense that it scares me more than when he was yelling. "I thought you were somebody breaking in. You were supposed to be asleep. Where were you? What the hell were you doing outside at this time of night?"

"I...I..."

Before I can come up with an answer, footsteps stomp down the staircase.

"What's going on?" Anthony shouts, a gun in his hand.

"Oh Jesus," I say, ducking.

"Go back upstairs!" my dad yells. "It's just Gia, and put that fuckin' gun away."

"What the fuck?" Anthony says.

I don't know who my dad is madder at.

"And you go up," he says to me. "*Now!*" he yells. I walk up the stairs to the living room. He points to a chair. "Sit. Sit there." A vein is throbbing at the side of his eye. "Where were you?

"Out with friends."

"Friends. What friends?"

"You don't know them. From school, okay?"

"No, not okay." He stares through me and then looks away. I've never been caught before, at least not until the car thing with Ro. "You don't listen anymore! You get into trouble!" he yells. He shakes his head. He doesn't know what to do now. He looks around the room, as if he's hoping to find answers.

"Your mother will handle this tomorrow," he says. "But now… you're staying home…you're staying in the house at night. You're not going out. Not for math. Not for pizza. Not for nothing. If you have so much time to run around, you work. You get a job at the bakery."

"What? The bakery?"

"To pay Mario, to pay for the bills—the bills from cutting school and drinking and—"

"Daddy, I— "

"Go to bed now. No more."

If it wasn't bad enough that Michael dissed me, now I have to sell cookies and probably earn less than Mario spent on ink for his pen.

Welcome to my charmed life.

My so-called job isn't starting for a week, so instead of boning up on baking and packing cookies, I decide to concentrate on being *serious*, and making myself school president although lately it's hard to focus.

"Prioritize," Clive says, morphing into my life coach. We're sitting at lunch together the next day and I'm telling him what happened. There's no way I'm going to go to his apartment after school, so I tell him everything, talking as fast as I can before the bell rings.

"Prioritize," I say, parroting his words. I try that and rather than dwelling on being grounded for life and forced into menial labor, I focus on my campaign because the election is only a month away. We have the posters, but we haven't put them up yet. What we want to do is get into the school at night, put them everywhere, and surprise everyone the next day when it's wall-to-wall Gia.

Only that plan doesn't cut it with Mr. Wright, the principal.

"I'm sorry, folks. We can't have students putting up posters in the school at night by themselves," he says.

So we're on to plan B.

"There are no classes on election day," Clive says. "Let see if they'll let us put them up then. At least there will be people in school."

"We're not talking about the election for president of the United States," I tell the office. It's just a local city election. "The turnout will be light and all we have to do is quickly tack up the posters. We won't be in anyone's way."

We get the okay and Ro, Clive, Candy, and I get together early in the morning and, like Santa's elves, we parade from room to room and along the hallways. If other candidates plan to put up their own posters, I don't know where they'll go because when we're done the only space left will be on the ceiling or the floor where their faces will be stepped on, which is fine with me.

By noon half the posters are up and we stand back and view our work. Most of them are white with the writing in one major color group to keep it clean looking. We did a lot of them in grass-green lettering because how fresh is that? And we did some in dark purple and a few in script to look artsy. The idea was to keep the look crisp like the message, no matter how people would tease us.

We take a break before we head to the gym where the voting is going on. I carry a stack of posters and a folding ladder over my arm as I walk around surveying the space. The gym has high ceilings and I'm not sure whether our ladder is tall enough. It probably wasn't the smartest move to arrive at school in a pencil skirt and heels, but at six that morning, I wasn't thinking clearly.

Clive climbs up the ladder for me and puts up the posters and I stand back and check his work, yelling out obnoxious orders like "a little higher on the right," and "no, a little lower. More. Keep going, Clive. No, Clive, no. Too much, too much. Up again on the right." And even Clive who has the patience of a saint is starting to get a trifle sick of it and me, I think, because I see him stop and take a deep breath and shoot me a look before he makes the adjustments and all the fine tuning so that everything looks perfect.

I step back to look at the posters from a distance and walk backward farther until—whack—I slam into someone and lose my balance, and all I remember as I'm on the ground is seeing a crowd of people around me.

"Gia, Gia, can you hear me?"

Their voices fade and get lower and lower and lower until everything goes still and an eerie silence fills my head, and in the last few seconds of consciousness I'm thinking that, you know, maybe I'm not going to live to be the class president after all.

ELEVEN

They called a stupid ambulance. I find out when I come to because I must have been down on the floor unconscious for a while, which is totally embarrassing. I guess I didn't wake up as fast as I should have. Then the stupid ambulance takes me to the stupid Lenox Hill Hospital emergency room like I might need life support, and anyway I totally hate being in those kind of places because who do they put you next to except people dying of cardiac arrest or paralyzed by strokes or burning up with fever from pneumonia or some other raging contagious Ebola-like infection or what have you? And is that what you need on top of what you already came in with?

When I open my eyes again, some EMT guy, who's blond and surferish and not half bad looking, is holding my wrist and taking my pulse and then shining an annoying flashlight pen thingie in my eyes and lifting my lids, and I really wish he would stop it for chrissake.

"I think she's probably fine," he says, "but we should just check her out anyway."

Another voice above his says, "Christ, do you know who she is? We damn well will check her out," and then he laughs.

I pretend not to hear that and ignore them because, hello, no surprise. So I turn my head away and rub my eyes, and on the other side of me there's someone else, and I look up at his face and—oh my god—nearly go into shock because he looks so much like Michael Cross. And then I'm convinced that I'm not okay and I'm hallucinating or delusional because it couldn't be; but anyway, I blurt out, "Michael?"

"Yeah."

I sort of can't breathe then and whisper, "What are you doing here?"

"Riding with you in the ambulance."

Yeah, that's, um, obvious—even to me in this condition. "How come?"

"You tripped…over me…over my foot."

I look at him like what? "Start over."

"I was assigned to security at the school for the election and you walked into me and I tripped you."

And I'm like, *what*? Because I think it was all my fault because I remember walking backward in four inch heels and the eyes behind my head were obviously not working.

But I don't say that. I don't say anything because all this time he's leaning over me, my blouse is pulled up out of my skirt, I realize. And there is a significant amount of naked skin below his full gorgeous lips. I can practically feel his warm breath on me as he exhales. I stare at him and he stares back, and very gently, he reaches up and slides my blouse down, covering my stomach. And something about him slowly pulling the swath of silk across my skin…

The EMT guy interrupts the most erotic moment of my life and starts babbling like a moron.

"Who's the president of the United States?" he asks, to see if I'm brain injured or what have you, which breaks the steamy staring thing and destroys the mood.

"Abe Lincoln," I say because I'm pissed.

So that's it and for like the next four hours I have x-rays and a brain MRI, which is like lying inside an open casket and listening to a sledgehammer on your iPhone. And then they take all these vials of blood and that nearly makes me faint because I hate needles, particularly when they're sliding into my skin. And hours later everything comes back normal, normal, normal, which I'm clearly not, so that surprises me. But normal or not, I wrenched something in my back when I went down so I move slower than a slug.

When my mom gets the call from the hospital, she goes crazy as usual. But then when I call her a minute later and say, "Ma, I'm fine, the school was just being extra careful because I tripped and fainted, and, anyway, they didn't want to be legally liable in any way if they didn't do what they were supposed to do," she calms down and stops her usual chant of "It's always something with you kids, it's always something. If it's not you, it's Anthony, and if it's not Anthony, it's you." Then she takes a breath.

"I'm leaving now," she says. "I'll pick you up."

"You don't have to, Ma, I'm fine."

"I have to," she says. "I have to."

So there goes my plan to have Michael take me home. Anyway, it's two in the afternoon and traffic on the Upper East Side will fortunately be brutal so that leaves me about half an hour to be alone with Officer Hottie unless he decides to abandon me.

"Will you call me now?"

He looks at me and doesn't say anything.

"I mean as a courtesy, just to see how I am because I did nearly die falling over your foot."

He smiles his half smile. "You're something."

I try to sit up but my back fights me, so I "ow, ow, ow" a little harder than I have to, and Michael comes over and puts an arm around me, and I lean against him for support and nearly die from excitement being so close. It's a good thing I'm not wearing a heart monitor because the needle would go off the chart and they'd bring out the paddles to reset my heart.

Michael goes back to his chair and runs a hand through his hair. I watch how his eyes flit back and forth between me and anyone who passes outside the door and I'm wishing, wishing, wishing I could peek inside his head.

Suddenly I think of that old movie I saw called *The Bodyguard* with Kevin Costner when he was young and seriously hot, and I pretend there's this bodyguard vibe going on here because Michael's hunky and protecting me and he could play the part because Costner was strong and silent too. Like Costner, Michael's presence fills the room and he seems to have laser vision capable of seeing my split ends from the opposite side of the room. I lean back in the bed watching him exist, loving that at least for this moment in time we're breathing the same air, even if we're in a depressing hospital room and instead of clothes I'm wearing a shapeless shit gown with the opening in the back that shows my entire ass—not to mention that people who have died here have probably worn this same rag to the morgue or down the runway to hell.

I stare at him and he looks back at me and then he glances down at my feet and notices the jade green polish and the toe ring and I wiggle my toes and he fights a smile. So we keep sitting there and, no surprise, he refuses to chitchat or maybe doesn't know how, which prompts Miss Motormouth to spice things up with annoying questions.

"Do you think your sergeant is going to wonder about this?"

"Wonder about what?"

"I mean, I assume you had to write up a report and it must look like an awfully strange coincidence that I'm the same girl you brought in two weeks ago."

He shrugs.

"So how did you end up at my school?"

"Morgan is your school?"

That's when I know for sure that he's bluffing. He must have seen the posters.

"Gia—fresh thinking, fresh answers?" I raise an eyebrow.

"I saw the posters," he says with a half smile. "You got the fresh part right."

His eyes hold mine and for those few seconds, it feels like the air is as thin as on top of Mt. Everest because it's hard for me to breathe and it has nothing whatsoever to do with the fall.

"How come you were working there…at my school?" I ask, my eyes not leaving his. "Instead of, say, cruising around and giving tickets or whatever…"

"Extra pay."

"That's all?"

"What else?"

Even though it hurts, I get to my feet and walk over to him, perching myself on the arm of his chair. "To see where I go to school," I whisper, my lips nearly grazing his ear.

He closes his eyes momentarily. "Why would I do that?"

"I don't know, Michael, you tell me."

He doesn't answer.

I lift his chin with one finger. "Maybe to see me?"

He opens his mouth to answer then stops, abruptly turning toward the door.

"*Gia*," my mom bursts in, hurling her purse to the floor before grabbing me in a hug, nearly smacking Michael in the head. "Oh my god, I nearly had a heart attack over you!"

TWELVE

After a week goes by I'm feeling better, so I go to the bakery with Ro after school and meet Teddy, the manager, and stand behind the counter pretending I know what I'm doing while Ro sits at a table and sips cappuccino and makes faces at me because she's enjoying this. Then I make them back at her, which makes Teddy mad because I'm not concentrating while he's showing me all the cakes and cookies and telling me what they cost and showing me how to wrap them, blah, blah, blah. Then he covers my hair with a net and hands me plastic gloves.

"Am I handling plutonium?"

"This is a bakery," he says, "you have to be clean."

"I'm clean," I say before sticking my tongue out at Ro. "I'll start next week."

"Fine," he says. "Don't worry. This a great place to work."

"Umm, If you want to carbo-load and grow your ass."

He shakes his head.

Back at school, the election is going to get ugly. In keeping with the tradition of Manhattan's elite private schools, the race has nothing whatever to do with issues or values or ethics or how the school is run and everything to do with popularity.

I work at being nicer than usual to everybody. At lunch while we eat the gross chicken meatloaf, we pick out people and try to figure out who they'll vote for so we can get some idea who is going to win and who they are going to wipe the floor with.

"The Tewl has changed her hair color," I whisper to Ro.

She sticks her finger down her throat. "Yesterday it was light brown and now it's bright red?"

That is off the charts weird in the middle of an election because you look like you don't trust who you are and that you need help because you're going through a serious identity crisis.

Jordan the jock is actually striding through the cafeteria working the room as if he's relying on political advice about networking dating back to President Clinton's campaign.

If all that's not weird enough, even Domingo, the guy who cleans the cafeteria, passes my table and says, "you going to be the president?" And, whoa, I didn't know even the kitchen staff is following this.

"I'm trying," I say with an embarrassed laugh.

He smiles and picks up the trash on the table that people leave behind because some kids at Morgan feel they are *so* above carrying a single empty Arizona bottle to the recycle bin ten feet away in order to save the planet.

"President," Domingo says again, like I'm in line for 1600 Pennsylvania Avenue.

I'd never admit it, but I'm feeling pretty good about my chances until someone comes up with the brilliant idea of holding a debate with the candidates to give the election more cosmic importance or something. I can't exactly get to the bottom of who came up with that idea—because the school never did that before—but whatever, I can take the heat. Anyway, as everyone knows, I am a motormouth and good at thinking on my feet. They schedule the debate for an assembly that is only forty-five minutes long and everyone is invited to submit questions, which a committee of teachers will then sort through to pick the best.

Our next move is to prepare me, and Clive salivates at the thought. That afternoon instead of going home I get permission from my dad to go home with Clive who transforms himself into one of the more obnoxious kids in school and fires questions at me, pretending he's holding a microphone:

"Gia, tell us in a sentence or two why you think you'd make a better president than anyone else in this school?

"What is the first thing you'd do if you became president?

"What do you see as the biggest shortcomings in our school and how would you address them?

"Our biggest strength?

"What qualifications do you bring to the job?

"Have you held office in other schools?

"What would you do to stop bullying in our school?

"How would you help make the school more diverse?"

If all that isn't exhaustive enough, he goes on YouTube and gets a video of the Kennedy-Nixon debates like I could definitely apply lessons from those to what I would say at Morgan.

"Clive, you're taking this pretty seriously."

He takes that as a compliment. "I'm just trying to think of everything I can to prepare you, Gia, because you know how those people can get."

"I don't know, not really."

Aside from Christy and her garbage mouth group, I don't know what to expect, and anyway, I really can't concentrate because my attention keeps flipping back and forth between reality and my fantasies of Michael Cross, who, of course, has not reached out and touched me and probably never will because Mr. Hot Cop is probably totally chickenshit.

But Clive isn't thinking about Michael. He's thinking about making me class president. So we drill and drill and drill until he thinks I'm ready.

"I'm surprised you haven't rented out a TV studio to stage a mock debate on camera," I mutter when it's nearly ten.

"I should have thought of that," he says.

I finally pack up and leave his building at ten thirty and while I'm going down in the elevator I'm not thinking about the election anymore or the stupid people or the questions they will throw at me, because on my phone I see something I've never seen before.

A text. From Michael.

THIRTEEN

I get a cab on Fifth and as it goes south I look again to make sure that I really saw it.

Off at 11. Meet?

Cardiac arrest. *Yes. Where?*

Simone Martini Bar. Know it?

Yes. Actually no, I don't. What was I thinking? I google it and find it in the East Village on First Avenue and St. Marks Place. Then the name Simone Martini sets off memory bells so I google that and realize why.

Simone Martini was an Italian painter from Siena (1280–1344) who they talked about in art history. We saw a painting of his from this online tour of the Uffizi in Florence, which was cool. And then I remember that he painted a portrait of a woman named Laura something who the poet Petrarch was crazed over and sort of stalked.

Instead of going home, I get out in the village and call my mom, mumbling something about meeting a friend to work on the campaign some more so I'll be home later, but not really late. Who knows if she believes me, but my mom doesn't have the strength to check out all the stories I dream up and my dad is out and I know she's in the middle of a rerun of *Golden Girls*, her favorite TV show, because can you possibly mistake the voice of Bea Arthur?

I get there way early, so I circle the block twelve times like a streetwalker and then stroll in finally at 11:15 like this is so no big deal. The place has soft lighting, zebra fabric on the seats, and a tin ceiling, and I love the vibe so I am in the zone.

I spot him and go into overdrive. He's sitting with a drink looking lost in thought, only he has this telepathic awareness of me because he looks up and the electrical currents begin pulsing. I head toward him, and he stands, and he has to be six-four because even in my heels he's high above me.

I kiss his cheek and breathe in his lemony scent. He must have cleaned up and doesn't that say something? I slide out of my jacket and sit in the banquette next to him and live in the moment.

"How you feeling?" he asks, pretending not to see the low-cut silk tank top.

I shrug.

"Your back, I mean."

"It's mostly better." I hold off on joking about Percocet because that would be playing into his law enforcement antidrug thing and I know that script. The waiter comes by and I order a Coke to avoid flashing my bogus ID.

I can't say it feels easy or natural or comfortable or any other emotion that I've ever felt to be near him in a bar, his thigh inches from mine. What it feels is otherworldly, as though the rest of humanity is closed off behind glass like the dioramas in the Museum of Natural History, and there's just the two of us.

"I didn't know if you'd call," I say.

"Neither did I."

I look in his eyes and stare at his lips and force myself to look away. I start toying with the black leather and gold bracelets on my arm, tightening them, loosening them, tightening them again and feeling twelve years old again and not me. And where did that come from? Because right now I need my Gia alter ego on steroids, the one who says what's on her mind and isn't gnawing at the inside of her cheek.

I'm convinced that in cop school they teach you never to say anything that advances the conversation so that the other person will feel forced to fill the silence. I snap to and start wondering if he's like this just with me or with other girls too which tightens my insides because for the first time I think of other girls.

Does he have a girlfriend? What a complete jerk I am. I mean, look at him, how could he not?

"Why didn't you know...if you'd call?"

"Gia..." he says, lifting his head and looking at me. I'm looking back at him and fixated on those lips again and how they're parted now. I expect flames to shoot up and burn us.

"This is totally off the wall."

"What is?"

"My seeing you, my sitting here."

"Because you're a cop?"

"Because of a lot of things."

"Does that scare you?" I say.

"What? Being with you?"

"Yeah."

"I don't know."

"You know what scares me, Michael?"

"What?"

"Not being with you." Then I swallow extra hard and close my fingers around his upper arm and just leave my hand there and try to pretend that I'm not breathing ragged because I'm touching his skin.

Did I really have the nerve to say that? Why didn't I just shut up? And how can my mouth come out and say what I'm thinking? But it does and I can't seem to control that, and here we go again with my head telling my mouth what it wants to say, not what it should.

Michael tries to pretend my hand isn't where it is, but he stirs and something inside him changes. We sit there without talking, surrounded by ghosts of things in his head, and he mostly looks down at the fake black marble table. And then he stares inside his glass at his drink before he lifts it and drains it, and I watch his throat as the liquid goes down.

I don't know where things are going to end up so I pull my hand away and lean against him and he feels warm and solid. I run the tip of my shoe up and down his calf and then wait, but he still doesn't do anything except open his clenched fist and press his opened hand against the tabletop. And I watch and wonder what that hand would feel like...if it were touching me.

He licks his lips. "You don't even know me," he says finally.

"What do I need to know?"

He squints and looks at me to see if I'm serious, and then his face softens and he smiles his smirky cop smile. "I never met anyone like you."

I give him back a smirky smile.

Out of nowhere, because I can't think of something to say, and even though this place looks more Chinese than Italian, I tell him about Simone Martini. And he looks at me and listens and smiles and says, "yeah, I read about him."

"Have you been to Italy?"

He shakes his head. "No."

"Do you want to go?"

"Yeah, maybe, who knows?"

Then I go on about Petrarch who he says he remembers from

school, even though I don't believe him. "He was infatuated with a girl named Laura from the first moment he saw her in church," I say. "But she was married and never got involved with him, but still he wrote poems to her and was obsessed with her."

He nods, smiling.

Then I'm thinking that he is probably thinking that I'm trying to send him a subliminal message about crushes and lust and unfulfilled hookups and maybe like he should make a move or else. So I just stop. Mid-sentence. And look him in the eyes, and I start to ache inside.

It feels like we are on top of Mt. Vesuvius with smoke and molten lava erupting around us. I slide my fingers around his forearm again, squeezing it slightly. The touch has this visceral effect on both of us. He swallows and, God, it's just his arm. All I can think of is that I want him to kiss me.

"Can we go?" I say softly.

"Yeah, I'll take you home."

"That's not what I meant, Michael."

"I know." His eyes don't leave mine.

I want you to kiss me. But he doesn't. He looks away abruptly then reaches for his wallet and pays the check.

We go outside and walk past small boutiques with handmade peasant dresses and clowny platform heels, a cigar store with a wooden Indian outside, and then a sexy underwear boutique with panties without crotches and I start to laugh and can't stop and he starts to laugh too, but not as much, and I bump against him and hook my arm through his, which feels like the most natural thing to do.

And then the only thing I'm feeling aside from bone-crushing lust is a growing sadness because the end of the night is getting closer and I look up at the sky and ask for help because I want to just stop time and make this night go on forever.

FOURTEEN

We're nowhere near where he lives, even though he doesn't know that I know where he lives, and no, he is not coming back to my house in Little Italy for a Limoncello. And no, he is not even setting foot on the street because the rows of brownstones have eyes and ears.

There is a limit to how many blocks you can walk, especially in my shoes. And anyway, Michael is probably horny and feeling guilty and conflicted in his cop role, but more than that, scared shitless because I'm seventeen, not to mention the don's daughter. So, as usual, is the deck stacked here? He wants to put me in a cab then head to a bar to get wasted I guess, not that he says any of that.

"It's late. You have to go home, Gia," he says. "You have school tomorrow, right?"

"Shut up, Michael," I whisper, staring at his beautiful face.

We pass the dark entrance to a low, seedy apartment building and no one is around, so I go over and try the door. It's stuck at first but then it opens, and he stands there watching me, not sure what I'm doing. I grab his arm and pull him in after me and then lean into him and press my lips against his and start kissing him. He tries to turn away at first, but not really. Then he can't not respond because he's so into me too. And for the first time, he kisses me back hard and then harder and rakes his hands through my hair and pulls me against him and everything around us dissolves and our tongues are deep in each other's mouths. And I don't even have words to say how that feels because suddenly every cell in my body is exploding with longing and I'm so overcome that I can barely stand. We're in each other's clothes and his skin is so hot, his shoulders and back so hard and strong and he smells like lemony soap. And he's inside my bra and touching me lightly and I can't bear it. We're maybe twenty seconds from the point of tearing each other apart and getting down on the floor, until, that is, an old guy with white whiskers and a cane comes tap, tap, tapping his way down the stairs to go out and sees us in heat and waves the cane around wildly in the air and yells in a loud, crazy voice like a psycho.

"If you don't get the fuck out of here right now, I'm going to call the cops!"

We catch our ragged breaths and start to laugh so hard I double over, a victim of pain and sexual wreckage. All Michael does is stop and close his eyes and mutter "shit" and wait and breathe heavy, and finally he looks at me and whispers, "let's go." He takes my hand and we push through the door and he slips an arm around my waist and we walk fast down the street like we're in a hurry to go someplace. Only we're not going anywhere. When we get a few blocks away he stops and holds me against him for a few seconds and then he shakes his head and kisses me again before he turns away and finds me a cab, and without a word everything that started is over.

And I'm not sure what happened. Or didn't.

What I do know is that I'm back in a taxi going to Little Italy. The night is over. It's past the time I promised my mom I'd get home.

But my head isn't with me. It's still with Michael, replaying the kiss and the feel of him against me. But more than that, everything I imagined to be true might even be, though no actual words confirmed that.

He didn't ask me out. Or say he'd call. Or give me his number.

Still.

FIFTEEN

When I wake up the next morning with only Michael on my mind, I know something is different. I get anxious because there *is* something to worry about. But for about fifteen seconds I can't remember exactly what, which reminds me of when my grandma had cancer and she said that in her sleep she forgot all about having cancer and she'd wake up feeling fine but then when she remembered again, she felt like she was slammed on the head with a brick as the misery flooded back.

I'm being a drama queen, I know, but that's a little bit how I feel with the debate just hours away. So I skip breakfast because I have no appetite, and after a shower, I stare into my closet, deciding my move with the clothes and the subliminal message and all. And it's either super slut to stick it to them or Miss Conservative to play their game, not that I have too many things in the second category.

I end up somewhere in between, a pencil skirt and flat suede boots and a white cashmere cardigan, which I'm sure no one will realize would cost $800 in the store, but not to Dante, which is fine, because— really—screw what Christy and Georgina and everyone else knows about me or not because I love to beat them at their designer games.

When we go into the auditorium first period, I'm a zombie staring into space. They make the announcements about upcoming events like the canned food drive for Thanksgiving when we're supposed to help the hungry by bringing in real food like chicken noodle soup that you can eat from the can hot or cold or say tuna or salmon or sardines. But instead a lot of people cop out and empty their pantries of the stuff they wonder why they ever bought in the first place, like enchilada sauce or meat gravy or what have you, and that is cheap and uncharitable.

Then Mr. Wright steps up to the stage. "As you know, the election is in less than two weeks, and today is our presidential debate, so now I'd like to have the candidates please take their seats onstage."

My heart tries to kick open my chest and escape. Never mind that Clive has prepped me to death, right now I can't remember a single question he asked me, not to mention the answers I'm supposed to give.

After a round of applause, everyone turns to look at us. I walk up the aisle toward the stage, then—whomp—out of nowhere, a backpack slides into the aisle, and my toe catches on a shoulder strap. I hear a laugh. I manage to steady myself and then stop and stare down the aisle briefly. Every pair of eyes is staring forward.

Without exhaling, I keep going, aware that my head is now starting to throb. I take a seat in front of one of the three microphones and immediately pull the bottle of Voss water closer, even though the shape annoys me because it looks like shampoo.

"A committee of three teachers has gone through the two hundred questions that students have submitted," Mr. Wright says, "and picked out the ten that best reflect the myriad issues facing our student body." He clears his throat. "They will be asking the candidates these questions, and the candidates will each have a maximum of two minutes for each response."

I look over at Jordan Hassel, who is wearing a navy blazer and a blue oxford shirt with a tie with little squiggly things on it like snakes or snails or something, and he looks so psyched that I think he's on uppers. Brandy Tewl is licking her thin lips again and again and sliding her ring back and forth over her knuckle like an idiot.

Mrs. Collins, one of the English teachers, steps up to the mike that they've set up to the side of the stage, and after tapping and tapping and tapping it to test whether it's working, which it obviously is, she says, "Can everyone hear me? Can everyone hear me?" And after just a few kids bother to lazily answer yeeees, Mrs. Collins puts on her reading glasses and says, "What will you bring to the job of president of the Morgan School?

We all look at each other waiting and then Mrs. Collins realizes she was supposed to say who was to go first and finally she says, "Brandy, why don't you start?"

"I would bring energy and vision and a strong interest in making our school even greater than it is," Brandy says.

Lame, but everyone applauds. Then Mrs. Collins points to Jordan.

"I've led the basketball team for two seasons and have a proven leadership record in tennis and ice hockey too," he says. "So I know about leadership qualities and hard work and bringing a winning spirit to getting an important job done."

Applause by his jock entourage for another meaningless answer. I look out at the audience, and Clive is sitting in the front row looking as if he is about to stand up and help me form the words when it's my turn to answer. His eyes are positively moist because he's hanging on every syllable of every answer. And we went over this question, we did, I now remember, but that doesn't mean I plan to answer it the way we rehearsed it, which I know will make him nuts, but I don't care.

"Gia?" Mrs. Collins says.

I sit there for a moment and then clear my throat and look out at the audience.

"I've never been the president of anything. I don't play on a team like Jordan or run track or whatever…" I stop and wait. I can feel the level of tension in the room rising because everyone is wondering if I am going to go on or fade away like a loser. I clear my throat again and pull the mike closer.

"But I don't think that should stop me because I think what you need most to lead a school like Morgan is toughness and a belief in yourself so that you can accomplish whatever you commit to. And if nothing else, people who know me know that when there's something I believe in, I am single-minded and don't get sidetracked and I don't give up—at least not without a fight. So if you elect me president and put your trust in me and hope to see real change in this school, I will be your voice and your advocate and I will help empower the student body."

Applause breaks out and Clive and Ro and Candy look ready to jump to their feet.

They move on to more questions about experience and goals and whatever, and if you ask me afterward what they were I don't think I could remember one of them. All I know is I hear applause after I speak and I manage to get through it, and as it all goes down, I'm aware of time slipping by because I become fixated on the black metal hands of the clock making tiny, skittish leaps as they edge closer and closer to 9:50 when it would all be over and I can resume breathing.

"Our time has run out," I hear Mrs. Collins say finally. "So I'd like to thank all the candidates for their answers and wish them good luck."

My heart slows as kids are getting out of their seats and talking and slinging backpacks over their shoulders. But then from the back of the auditorium, someone yells out a question.

"I'd really like to know how Gia can sit in front of us and run for president of our school when we all know that her dad is a crime boss and a murderer, which I think is disgusting. Who does she think she is running for president of this school or anything else?"

Silence spreads through the room and all motion abruptly stops as if an evil magician sprayed paralyzing gas into the auditorium. The teachers jump to their feet embarrassed, abruptly motioning to the kids to get going because first period is over, but Mr. Wright makes a megaphone with his hands:

"The debate is over," he shouts. "That was inappropriate and out of line." He turns to the boy in the back, pointing an accusatory finger. "You see me in my office right now, young man."

But everyone is dumbstruck, and no one moves.

I sit there as if I've been bludgeoned, waiting to see the blood that's now roiling in my veins start to flow out of me as every pair of eyes in the audience stares at me.

The voice. I know the voice, but I can't place it. Someone I know from a class or—? Whatever. How could I possibly think it wouldn't come up? How did I dare to run for school president? Did I really think I'd be safe just because the questions were screened ahead of time? The don's daughter. No one will ever let me forget where I come from or who I am or the stereotype I'm saddled with for life.

It might as well be tattooed on my forehead. That's my entire identity. I am toxic. A wave of nausea washes over me, followed by a pressure in my ears, which makes all the murmuring that follows mix into a widening hum of white sound that seems to grow louder and louder, filling my head so full it makes me insane.

And the entire school is still looking at me.

Staring.

Waiting.

Do I answer?

Get to my feet and storm out?

Curse them out?

Or announce that I changed my mind and am not running for president anymore and am withdrawing, effective immediately?

What I want to do is race out the door and never come back. I hate these people, I do. And they hate me and blame me, and why did I ever want to come to this stinking, horrible, pretentious school?

Then I think of my dad and his stoicism, especially when he's in front of a sea of TV cameras and reporters yelling out embarrassing questions at him. He raises his chin and stands tall and maintains his dignity, staying totally composed no matter what. He never caves. Never.

I. Can. Do. That. Too.

Get to your feet, Gia, a voice in my head screams. I look out and see Clive. He's about to cry. I give him the slightest nod.

I will not crumble.

They will not intimidate me.

My family does not do that.

No matter what.

"I don't know who asked the question," I say, drumming my fingers as I look around the auditorium and manage to get my quivering body on my feet, going for a cool, practiced calm.

"Because whoever asked the question obviously didn't have the balls to come forward and walk up to the microphone and identify himself first or follow the protocol and submit his question ahead of time. But never mind protocol right now, that's not what's important. There's something I'd like to say to that, something I'd like to tell every one of you.

"If you don't think I should be president, then don't vote for me. Vote for Jordan or vote for Brandy because you know who you'll be getting. If you're afraid of me and my family and who you think I am and what you imagine I represent and could bring to this school, then don't vote for me, steer clear of me, and vote for Jordan or Brandy.

"But if you think for yourself and give people the benefit of the doubt, then maybe you should consider voting for someone who might bring some fresh thinking and real change to this school. But what's more important is to follow your heart and do what you think is right because that's the way I live and that's exactly why I'm running for president."

Clive stands up and starts clapping loudly. A moment later Ro joins him, then so does Candy, and then other kids join in from different parts of the auditorium and there's almost a hard, deliberate rhythm going. I push back my chair, nearly knocking it over, and walk down the steps from the stage and stride up the aisle.

What I don't do is run, even though what I want more than anything else right then is to be free of this school and everyone in it and back in Dante's car. Only this time I'd be driving it, flooring the gas, and flying up the Henry Hudson as fast as a 911 Porsche could carry me.

SIXTEEN

Clive finds me after the assembly and throws his arms around me. "Oh my God, Gia, that was a grand slam, a fucking grand slam."

I don't remember ever hearing him curse before, so this is progress. "I wanted to wring his neck."

"Wentworth is a pig," he says. "I hope he gets expelled."

"Expelled? They'll probably add his name to the top of the slate."

I try to leave before lunch, but Clive heads me off at the door and won't let go of my hand.

"You can't leave, Gia, you can't," he says, "because then they win. You have to stand up to them and not cave. You know that. "

I shake my head, but he ignores me and grabs my hand and pulls me toward the dining hall.

"I have to get my math book from my locker," I say.

"I'll go with you," he says.

"Do you think I need an escort?"

"Yes."

We walk down the corridor and I reach for my lock and then stop. I see it before Clive does.

"What?" he says and then his eyes widen.

Mafia slut has been keyed onto my locker door.

Clive sits close to me like my bodyguard in the dining hall. So do Ro and Candy, like human shields. But there's no need because a dozen kids come over and say, "you were great, Gia" or "you rocked" or "you're your own person," yada yada, yada. And they say they'd vote for me any day over those loser candidates, which makes me feel a little better.

I stop in the bathroom on the way to English, and after I slam the stall door shut, I hear the outside door open, followed by the cloud of eau de pond scum that makes my eyes sting, putting me on alert again.

I wait while toilets flush and the water runs and hands are dried in a nanosecond in our state-of-the-art dryer. Then finally I hear Christy cackle.

"Wentworth totally has balls. I didn't think he would do it."

"It was totally proper," Georgina says so it sounds like *prop-pah* in that Brit way like her mouth is stuffed with mashed potatoes.

"I thought the mafia queen would freak," Christy says with a high-pitched squeal. "How could she hold her head up after that?"

"She is so going to lose," Georgina says.

"We're going to *make* her lose," Christy says.

The bell rings and the door squeaks open. I stand up and—wham—a roll of toilet paper flies over the top of the stall, smacking me on the head.

"Bull's-eye," Georgina says, laughing as the door closes. I adjust my skirt and yank the bathroom door open fast, but they're gone and I feel paralyzed.

Fuck.

Anger mutates into emptiness.

I go back inside and stare at myself in the mirror. Do I deserve this? Did I invite it? Maybe I am to blame for my dad. But I also know if I weren't at Morgan, the little hate cabal would target someone else. They need to. It empowers them.

Tell Anthony, a little voice in my head says. *You want me to follow them home?* he'd say. *I'll teach them a lesson.* But I know I won't. I can't. I can't tell anyone. Growing up is learning to fight your own battles, my dad used to say.

Compared to school, the bakery feels like a refuge, and it beats going home and thinking about Wentworth and Georgina and yada, yada, yada.

"You're late," Teddy snaps when I show up at sixty seconds past four.

Someone else on my case?

"Fire me so I can collect unemployment."

"You're waitressing today," he says, ignoring me. "Maureen called in sick."

I make a face because I'd rather stand behind the counter and count out cookies than ask people what they want and hear that the coffee isn't hot enough or the pastries are too sweet or too big or too small or too something. I put on an apron and pin back my hair and help an old man from the neighborhood who comes in every afternoon as if cookies and cappuccino are his only pleasures in life and listen to him whisper to me, "if only I were fifty years younger."

Then I wait while people take forever deciding and hurry back to refill sugar bowls and creamers, never mind that everyone seems to want one percent milk and I have to explain that it's either skim milk or heavy cream and then it becomes four thirty and then five.

At five thirty I take my break and check my phone, and of course Michael hasn't called and that pisses me off. I think about sending him a text, but what would I say? Can we pick up where we left off? So I forget that and go make six espressos and take a call from Ro who is still amused that I'm working in her dad's bakery. Then I turn to clean off a table and get clean plates and I hear arguing inside the office next to the kitchen.

I go back to look, and Ro's dad sees me.

"Go help outside, Gia," he says softly, motioning me away before he closes the door. Only I don't move. Something in my head puts me on alert. I hear yelling behind the door and then a loud thump like someone or something has fallen to the floor, then a groan of someone in pain. Another groan. I stand in place listening, unable to move.

Ro's dad's voice rises above another voice, but the sounds are muffled. I get a sick feeling inside, but there's no one to ask, no one who'd tell me anything. I'm used to that. All my life I've been hearing, "Don't worry about it, Gia" or "There's nothing going on, don't worry." Then the cops would come. So would the FBI. In the middle of the night people would get cuffed and arrested and Super Mario would be everywhere and then magically they'd be out on bail. The next day it would be all over the papers, because there was nothing going on and nothing to worry about.

Except incidentals. Like dead bodies.

I downshift into default mode, playing deaf to the sound of angry voices, grunts, pounds, the groans of someone begging for mercy, pleading, "I never cheated you, I swear."

I look out at the café. Someone's waving for the check. Someone else is holding out her hands like she can't fathom why idiot me isn't coming over to help her.

Only I can't move.

The hypocrisy of my life overwhelms me. I search for enough strength just to stand instead of crumbling to the floor.

"Miss, miss!"

The door to the private office opens. Teddy looks at me. "Gia," he hisses. "You alive?"

I rush off robotically to give the woman the check and bring menus to the other table. Then I go back to working behind the counter, my hands shaking as I put delicate cookies iced in rainbow hues on plates, while bodies are beaten steps behind me. I carry out cups of steaming coffee and glasses of chilled milk, pretending my hands aren't quivering and hoping I won't drop plates or spill the hot coffee that sloshes back and forth in the cup.

I walk back to the kitchen area and stop for a few seconds to listen. The door is still closed. The voices get louder. There's a thud, then another sickening thud, and then another. Someone is getting beaten up again. He's outnumbered.

"That's unfair, that's unfair," Anthony would yell when he got into a fight. *"You have to level the playing field,"* he'd say, parroting my dad.

Only the rules of the playground don't apply now. Not here. I stand there frozen. And then the beating seems to stop

"Teach him a fuckin' lesson," someone growls.

I go out the back door for air. A body lies scrunched up on the ground, thick streaks of blood pouring from his nose and ears, running down his face and neck, dark red pools forming on the ground around him. I open my mouth to scream then stifle the shriek that closes off my throat. I run to the side of the building, crouch down, and start to call 911 and stop. I can't.

It doesn't matter anyway. It's too late.

I turn and throw up my guts and break into a cold sweat, my whole body shaking.

I go back to being deaf and blind, pretending not to see or hear what I'm not supposed to because what good would it do to tell someone?

I work at the bakery one afternoon after another. Nothing else happens, at least nothing that I see, but I'm haunted by what I saw and there's no one I can tell, not even an eyewitness hotline for people who want to remain anonymous because that would boomerang and end up in our front yard.

"Just shut up," Anthony always says to me when I ask him questions he doesn't want to answer. Maybe he's right. That's all that I can do. Only lately, it's getting harder and harder to pretend.

I think of my secret plan for the future and then I don't and I shut that part of my life off and so-called normal life takes center stage again. One week. Just five days before the election, but front and center in my life aside from Michael is now the *Vogue* shoot.

The photographer's studio is down on Varick Street, and the shoot's on a Saturday because we're all in school, so I get there at nine a.m. on the dot, and the fashion editor whose face is famous from the documentary about *Vogue* is there along with the beauty editor who introduces herself. When I walk in they are already sorting through a dressing room hemorrhaging with designer clothes and deciding who will wear what, which will depend on what we look like in what they have, I guess, but how would I know since I've never done this before.

I promised my mom and dad that Frankie, my driver and part-time babysitter would come along, which is annoying and infantile, but he does. And when he walks in with me they fixate on him like, *what?*

Then they immediately assume oh cool, her personal *bodyguard*, instead of more like baby guard, but whatever, that seems to up my rank to superstar.

So someone named Taffy Jean Harkness who works for the photographer John Plesaurus comes out with a neon yellow clipboard in her hand with yellow, green, and purple sticky notes stuck in perfectly straight rows down the sides. She attaches herself to me and tells me my orchid Prada snakeskin bag is *so divine* and then she examines my black patent leather heels with the red soles and about everything else I have on and acts like I'm Kim Kardashian or something.

I follow her to the back of the studio where they have a buffet table with food like sashimi and California rolls and miso tofu or whatever.

"Help yourself," she says.

"Thanks, I'm good," I say, because (gag) I don't normally eat that at nine in the morning. I sit down to wait while the editors go back and forth, dressed in really drab shit like gray leggings and long blah work shirts and no visible makeup and they could definitely use some, and anyway since they get all those freebies, why don't they? And like where does it all end up anyway?

So they continue to look over all the clothes and shake their heads like they're trying to fathom some really deep mystery because the top editor has some obscure theme idea that they aren't too sure about. So while they're racking their brains, I check my cell over and over hoping that Michael texted or called because of the painful way we left things but of course he hasn't. And that totally depresses me but doesn't exactly surprise me because I know he is freakin' confused about me and thinks that not doing anything is the smartest move. But how does that help either one of us? Because now, let's face it, there is. No. Turning. Back.

After me the other girls waltz in, because to them being there at nine must mean nine forty-five or whatever works for you. Neary, just Neary, who has no last name, is the daughter of a big Hollywood filmmaker and she looks kind of natural, like she doesn't have to prove anything because her life is already so totally out there in Soho, Hollywood, Cannes, and elsewhere. She's wearing no-name jeans, which is like reverse chic, I guess, with Uggs and a sort of low-end type, bulky, cheap-looking, red cabled cardigan with a hood that maybe came from a Salvation Army thrift shop. And she's got a Starbucks venti in her hand which always kind of annoys me because it's like what, you'd die without your caffeine fix 24/7?

Anyway a minute after Neary, Bridget walks in and she's the daughter of Jade Just, a top clothing designer, and her look is definitely more like "hello, everything that I have on, you just saw on the runway— if you made it there, assuming you're important enough and all." She's in black cashmere that's all wrapped up with a skinny alligator belt and leggings and some extraordinary black alligator motorcycle boots with killer chains that blow me away.

The last one to come in is a girl whose name I think is Logan, which I always thought was a boy's name. Jade whispers she thinks Logan is heir to Exxon. Logan is smiley and friendly and totally no-attitude and proof that money doesn't necessarily turn you into a pretentious asshole—although, c'mon, it generally does.

"Does anyone know what we're doing here?" Bridget Just asks with a laugh.

"Uh, no," I say.

"Or like what we'll be wearing?" Logan asks.

"I hope whatever they pick they won't make us look stuck-up and stupid," Neary says, crossing and uncrossing her legs.

We all talk about how we hope, hope, hope they'll let us keep the clothes, and then finally they bring out the outfits for us to try, and okay, most of them aren't the kind of things we would want anyway, like gowns with feathers and then some off-the-wall plaid stuff with rips and inserts and diaper pins and what have you, and I'm like, *WTF?* Only I don't say that. I don't say anything. I just try to act like I'm cool with all this.

The first dress they give me to try is a strapless, floor length satin thing in purple that's huge. But that doesn't bother them and they start to pin it because I guess the pins won't show in the pictures. After about an hour of pinning, pinning, pinning every quarter inch of the seams on both sides with about a thousand tiny pins—occasionally drawing blood—and at the same time draping necklaces over my head, like one from Cartier with grape-size purple tourmalines that match the dress, they stand back and evaluate.

One one thousand. Two one thousand. Three one thousand. "No," says the fashion editor, shaking her head.

After everybody agrees that the dress and the whole look is dreck and doesn't work, they come back with a short, frilly thing, which is gross and so not me, even though no one asks.

"Try this, Gia," the assistant to the fashion editor's assistant says. So I do and I stand around in it and eventually they nix that too and it disappears like the gown that they had to remove four thousand pins from. The same thing happens for the other girls with their loser outfits and for four entire hours all that goes on is trying on more clothes and shoes and trying to put the clothes together with bracelets and necklaces. We have a break for lunch, but I still don't want to eat. Even when they say that now they've brought in deli because, I mean, luncheon meat? So I go with veggie chips and a lemon San Pell.

Everything starts up again until someone named Carlos who's emaciated and wearing a short, bulky, ribbed blue sweater that looks hand knit by someone's grandma—over pants that are tight and way short like something a Michael Jackson wannabe would be all over walks in with a skinny, long-sleeve, black knit dress that is high in front and virtually backless. It looks like something Jil Sander designed when she was obsessing about the photographer Helmut Newton, known for his weird nude shots.

And omigod. It is undoubtedly. The. Hottest. Dress. In. The. Universe.

And they give it to *me*. I put it on and almost jump up and down because it is so cool, and I turn around and see that it just about shows ass crack cleavage, which I guess is the whole point. And I am only sorry when I'm wearing it that I don't have a tramp stamp that says *Michael* but of course my dad would crucify me if I did, along with the tattoo guy who gave it to me and Michael, or rather especially Michael, and especially, especially Michael if my dad knew he's a cop. But anyway, everyone stops what they're doing and turns and eyes me and wows about how it looks, so that is it!

I take it off and they do my hair, which they sweep back in a dramatic way and then mousse up with all this exotic European crap you can't find here.

Then my makeup: primer, foundation, three kinds of highlighter, two kinds of cream blush, and then smudgy eyeliner in three shades of smoky gray and black, which they blend and blend and it's all way heavier than I usually wear and definitely high-end slutty, but I guess the camera takes it down a notch. They put on three coats of mascara and deep red lipstick and black nail polish and finally an unreal real diamond bracelet with about eighty karats that was brought over in a ratty backpack on the subway by two guys who are dressed like vagrants but are packing serious heat.

Overall the look is over-the-top total vamp, and I vow that no matter what happens I am not walking out of there. Without. That. Dress.

Then comes hours of posing and trying not to feel and look stupid, stiff, and uptight, which I do anyway. Music is blasting in the background, which helps a little because I do love Rihanna and I am standing, sitting, shifting, one leg up, sort of twisted so that you get a view of the back and yada, yada, yada, for about two hours. And John Plesaurus, the photographer, who's about forty-five, but old-guy sexy with longish curly hair, is standing over me, nearly breathing on my neck. Then he's on the floor in front of me with his camera practically up me and he's sliding along on his back calling out things like, "Gia, that's beautiful, that's beautiful" and "Gia, show me more shoulder" and "Gia, look at me, look at me with those sexy eyes, Gia" and "oh, that's hot" and on and on like he's trying to get me down on the floor with him, then finally he must have the pictures he needs because he suddenly stands.

"That's it," he says.

Boom. Lights out. Music off. It feels like when you're in a movie theater and suddenly the movie fails and you're in total darkness and you feel like someone woke you from a dream.

John talks on his cell and talks some more, but he's watching me from across the room. He finally ends the call and comes over and takes my hands in both of his and thanks me with a kind of warm, intense look in his eyes that tells me that if I am interested, he is definitely a player. But I pretend I'm not picking up those vibes and say "thanks, really, but no," when he says you must be hungry and asks if I'm up for going to Williamsburg for incredible Ecuadorian food, whatever that is, with him and Taffy. So I just smile and say, "my parents are expecting me."

Frankie is asleep because it's as hot as a sauna in the studio from all the lights, and anyway he had a massive meatball hero for lunch so he missed the whole John Plesaurus come-on thing, which is just as well. So I go back to the dressing room to put my own clothes on again and now I totally understand why models get thousands of dollars an hour to do this mindless, boring crap all day long.

"When will the pictures run?" I ask one of the editors.

"We're not sure," she says. "Maybe February or March."

That feels like years. "Thank you," I say. "For including me."

"A reporter may call you," the editor says. "Just a few questions for the lead in."

"No problem."

I put on my coat, then kick Frankie's chair to wake him.

"Start talking to them about buying the dress," I whisper, pointing to it hanging over a chair.

"No," I hear them say when he asks. "No, it's impossible, impossible. We have to FedEx it back to Paris."

But Frankie keeps pushing and takes out his fat roll and starts counting out the hundreds, then adjusts the Glock in his ankle holster, getting impatient, cursing them out, and within a split second, they are exchanging looks and then packing up the dress, which he got for just under a thousand dollars, I think. And we're out of there.

After that, all I can think of is wearing it to see Michael, which is insane because exactly where is Michael? And what am I supposed to do—go back to the grunge bar and wait for him again? As if I could with my dad now on my case and Frankie and Vinnie taking turns spying on me. Calling Michael wouldn't work either because he won't take the call. And anyway, it is so his move.

What does give me some peace of mind is thinking that he is probably suffering the way I am, up at night fantasizing about me— assuming he doesn't have a girlfriend, which he probably does, but whatever. I am not like her, I am sure, because if there's one thing that people say about me all the time, it's "Gia, you are one of a kind."

After I call Ro and tell her about the shoot and call Clive and then call Candy, I go home and sneak the dress up to my room so my mom and dad won't realize that the entire back is missing. Then I call Dante.

"Come over," I say like a command because I need male feedback.

He's there in a flash and I lock the door to my room and take off the robe I have on over it and turn around so he sees the dress or what's missing from it.

"What do you think?"

He goes ape shit and grabs me and yada, yada, yada in a heartbeat and he says, "I'll get you sports tickets for the school fund-raiser. I'll get you whatever you want."

So the dress is already paying for itself.

SEVENTEEN

The writer who's doing the intro to the pictures for *Vogue* calls a few days after the shoot.

"Do you have a few minutes?

Happy to take a break from bio, I close my notebook. We chat about the kind of clothes I like to wear.

"Designer mixed with H&M and other stuff."

Where I shop. "Everywhere," because off the truck won't cut it.

"Do you have a boyfriend? "

"No...I don't." To be safe.

Then I think the questions are over because she says she really enjoyed chatting with me and I thank her and say I enjoyed it too, then she says, "Oh, one last thing."

I hesitate. "Yes?"

"You live in a very high profile world."

High profile?

"Your dad is in the newspapers all the time...and on TV."

I hold my breath.

"How does that affect *you*?"

Never talk to reporters, Super Mario once told me. They're your best friends until they sit down at the computer. The seconds go by. My face gets hot. I want to hang up and not have this conversation. "If I wasn't his daughter, you wouldn't be interviewing me for *Vogue* magazine—"

"Yes, but I mean the…"

I know what you mean. "So I'm really honored to be part of the story, thank you." I press end and hold my middle finger up to the phone.

I forget about *Vogue* magazine and do homework. And then I'm having a four-way conference call with Ro and Clive and Candy and checking email and searching online for the perfect red silk thong because I'm thinking about New Year's Eve and imagining a romantic night with Michael with dinner and champagne and chocolates. Although that is out of the realm and anyway, he's probably more of a hamburger and beer guy. But then I stop fantasizing when I hear loud voices downstairs.

My mom is crying.

Frankie and Vinnie are shouting. A sick familiar feeling creeps up my spine.

"I have to go," I yell into the phone. I know the cops are after my dad for something because they probably bugged his phone or the social club and decided that whatever he said or didn't say fingered him even though by now he knows to be careful and talk in a code that only he and his friends can understand.

"Ma, what is it? What is it?" I say, running down the stairs.

"Find your brother, find Anthony!" she yells, shaking her head. I have no idea where Anthony is, but she always feels better when he's around. So I get on the phone and start texting his friends to call me *now*!

This has happened before and I shouldn't get scared, but I always do because deep in my gut I get this feeling that life is spiraling out of control and all of us are powerless to stop it and my dad is always the target, always. And I mean how many times can you dodge a bullet?

Last time there were about twenty feds along with NYC detectives and it looked like they were trying to stop a terrorist attack instead of just bringing my dad and a few of his associates in, as if that was so hard. Then to make it worse, they made sure to call the *Daily News* and the *Post* and TV too so they could embarrass us and make themselves look good.

Within five minutes the outside of our house is lit like a movie set even though my dad isn't even home and we're stuck inside peeking through slits on the side of closed drapes to see what's going on.

When they finally find my dad in a restaurant, they make a show of cuffing him while his manicotti sits there half eaten. Like what would he do, try to run with fifty cops surrounding him, guns drawn, ready to shoot? With his hands cuffed behind him, they perp walk him across the street with the TV cameras rolling and then book him downtown for RICO and murder or manslaughter even though my dad actually never personally killed anyone. I know that. I believe it.

Anthony comes home in five minutes and he has to parade past the TV cameras too, trying his best not to smack them out of his way, which he is dying to do. Not to mention cursing them out while they're yelling questions in his face about what he thinks about what my dad did or didn't do and then wanting to know, "are you taking over after your dad? Are you next in line?"

He comes in slamming the front door hard and talks to my mom and Vinnie and Frankie who is perpetually cleaning his Glock, and they have a conference call with Super Mario who is already in his car on his way to help my dad.

"It's time for dinner," my mom announces, going into her default setting. She heads for the freezer and takes out a pan of lasagna because God forbid in life you should miss a meal. She slips it into the oven and slams the door too hard and we sit and fold our hands and pretend everything will be just fine and that we should try to eat and relax and act normal, even though there's no normal in our family.

Anthony opens some Chianti and I dive for it and drink about five glasses because aside from everything with my dad, how will I face everyone tomorrow at school in the middle of this media circus?

EIGHTEEN

The only thing I want to do when my alarm wakes me is hurl it against the wall. But not showing up will send a clear message to everyone at school that the don's daughter can't deal, and screw that, so I get out the door. And even though I'd rather hide on the subway wearing sunglasses and a baseball cap, that's not happening.

Frankie and I don't talk on the way to school, but he keeps looking over at me to see how I'm doing. And then I get a text and it's just *xs* and *os* from Clive, who doesn't know what to say but just wants to send me love, which is why I love him. He's one of the few people who knows and accepts the real me even though sometimes I'm not sure there is a real me with a single identity anymore.

I decide to hide out at Clive's after school to get away from Little Italy and the reporters. And for the second time I call and cancel work and they'd probably like to fire me, but they can't because my dad and Ro's are best friends and associates and yada yada.

Nothing really special happens at school in the morning. I guess even Christy and Georgina are afraid to open their mouths because with all the attention on my dad and the arrest I might explode and blow them to bits. There are no metal detectors at Morgan, at least not yet, and there's a chance that Mafia Girl might be packing heat, which isn't so remote since I know where Anthony keeps his gun and I did go with him to a shooting range when we were out West and I took lessons and no one could believe how good a shot I was.

I remember what the instructor all duded up in camouflage gear said, "Shit, girl, you're a natural born killer." That was a compliment, I think. So after that I asked my dad for a gun like the little .38 pink lady revolver I saw online, and he smiled but didn't answer, which wasn't a yes, but wasn't a no either.

After lunch I need my math book, so I head to my locker. *Mafia Slut* has been sanded away, a fresh coat of paint covering the evidence.

Amped-up heartbeat…early warning system.

Only now there's a folded piece of paper wedged into the side of the locker door. Someone copied a newspaper picture of my dad with the headline: *Mob Boss*, and underneath it scrawled: *Like father, like daughter.*

When I look up I realize that I'm not the only one to get the flyer. They're sticking out the sides of every locker door.

I must be on Clive's radar screen, because a moment later he runs over to me waving the copy that he got.

"These people are pigs," he says, making his way along the row of lockers, removing the flyers, tucking them into his notebook. "Every one of these is going to the principal's office."

"Like that will help?"

My mom calls and tells me to come home after school, but I can't stand all the cameras so I have a fight with her and win and Clive and I walk across the park and go to his apartment.

"Are you okay, Gia?" He puts his arm around me and pulls me closer to him.

"Sort of," although this never gets easier. I look over at Clive. "I'd never admit it to anyone but you, but what I wish is that I could be anonymous like everyone else with a dad who has a normal, boring job like a teacher or an accountant or a salesman so everyone would think his work is so dull that they'd never bring it up."

"I know," Clive says, staring off.

"I wish I had other kids' problems, like how am I going to afford new Uggs or a down jacket from the Gap or a trip to Disney World or whatever, you know?"

He nods again, biting his nail.

And not be bullied on a regular basis or see full-page ads in the papers about upcoming documentaries about the mob or think about my dad being dragged off to prison and our family becoming the target of my dad's enemies who want to show their muscle by gunning us down.

"I just want all the crap with my family to go away."

Clive must read something in my eyes that he's never seen before because he does something he's never done before. He opens up to me about his parents and how everyone thinks he's the luckiest person in the world because his family is rich.

"All I ever wanted was to have a brother or a sister and parents who came home at the end of the day and cooked dinner and sat down with me around the kitchen table and asked me about school or my friends or whatever." He shakes his head. "People who cared, Gia," he says. "I never even had anyone to fight with. No one."

I can't think of what to say to that because, I mean, who is he telling, Miss Average American Girl? My family is dysfunctional too, just in a different kind of way.

"Maybe friends have become the new family."

He considers that but doesn't buy it. "It's not the same."

The truth is that even though my life is crazy, I've always had the family stuff, usually too much of it. When it comes to being loved that's one thing at least that my parents got right. Only our family is so tight and afraid of outsiders that we don't let anyone else in and other people see that and don't let us in.

So Clive and I are both lonely and strung out in our own different ways, but I mean maybe other people are strung out in their own ways too, because I don't really believe that people who I think look normal are really happy, happy, happy all the time either.

But instead of thinking too hard about deep stuff like that we veg out in front of the TV. And while we're surfing past the History Channel and prohibition stuff and *Sopranos* reruns, which remind me of me and my life, I yell stop when Clive starts to skip past the New York 1 story about my dad being busted.

It's not because I want to see him on the big screen. It's because while I'm watching, I'm looking at the people around my dad and all the back-up cops, and my eye catches something in the corner of the screen, and I sit up straight and focus and—Holy Christ!—one of the faces of one of the cops looks familiar. Is it Michael?

Only no, it's not. My brain is playing tricks on me and I have to stop this obsessing because Michael is on some other planet.

Or might as well be.

NINETEEN

"Sure you're okay?" Clive asks.

I walk away from the TV and toward the window and look down on the entire panorama of New York City and Central Park and the crowds of people swirling around below us in slow motion, each of them going off purposely in one direction or another, like they've captured by some filmmaker who's made a living map of the world.

Only I'm not on it.

And I am feeling more alone than I've ever felt and I don't know where to turn anymore because if the guy I am obsessed with actually was one of the massive NYPD patrol that backed up the feds assigned to put my dad behind bars for the rest of his life, where does that leave me? And even if he wasn't, he is on their side. Otherwise what is he doing working for the NYPD?

Ro is right. Someone like me cannot fall for a cop.

I start feeling this overwhelming rage at Michael and everything he stands for. Then again, what did I expect? It's not like he led me on. Everything that's happened was my doing.

So really, what's left? Go home and maybe call up Dante. Tell him that I've been thinking about him, and I know where that will go. But at this point I don't care anymore. At least I know who he is and which side he's on and all that truth means a lot, and anyway, he's not all complicated like Michael and I can just close my eyes.

Clive comes back into the living room holding two mugs of hot chocolate. He hands me one, which I don't feel like having, but there's an expression in his eyes like a little kid who hopes you'll like his surprise. I take the mug and smile at him because that is so Clive to think of something like hot chocolate at a time like this. I sit down next to him and sip it.

"It's the best hot chocolate I've ever had."

He smiles this megawatt Clive Laurent five-year-old happy-to-please grin, which does make me feel better. Not only that, something about sharing hot chocolate with him does help, which could be the chemical perk-up thing in chocolate.

But whatever, Clive knows my mood is changing because he picks stuff like that up on this visceral level. I finish the whole thing and get warm inside and say without really thinking, "it's so warm in here, don't you want to take off the scarf?"

He looks away and doesn't answer.

"Clive?"

He turns back to me and his face changes and grows distant, which gives me an uneasy feeling. He looks down for a few seconds as though he's deep in thought before he reaches up and slowly unties the scarf. I sit back and look at all the books on his shelves, half of them about history, and think about how he reads so much and how smart he is. And I look up at him again just as he pulls the scarf away, watching my face, waiting, with this expectant look.

My eyes get wide and I feel my mouth open. There's a thin white scar all along his neck.

"Now you know why I wear the scarf, Gia. I tried to kill myself."

TWENTY

I'm speechless for I don't know how long.

Something like that never, ever, entered my mind and I'm in free fall and feeling sick inside at the thought of my wonderful, decent, gentle, sweet, loving, brilliant Clive actually doing something like that, which seems so desperate and not like what he would do. Almost worse is the thought of him suffering so much that he'd get to that point.

"No one knows," he whispers. "Please don't tell."

I stare at him and swallow and finally hear myself whispering, "Never. Never…don't worry…when…when did it happen?"

"A little over two years ago."

"What happened?"

He bites the corner of his lip and he looks so sad suddenly, so alone and so young. "I was home alone one night and the maids had gone to bed." He stares off, a hurt look on his face, as if he's reliving it. "I wanted to call someone, to talk to someone, anyone, because I felt so lost. Do you know how that feels, Gia? To need to talk to someone and have no one in the whole world to call who will listen to you? No one to confide in or trust? No one who cares? I went over all the names of the people I knew and I realized I had no one—not one friend to call. No one I could talk to who would understand everything. I started thinking that I had nothing to live for anyway and that if I were dead it wouldn't matter to anyone." He shrugs. "My parents obviously didn't care enough about me because they were never home and their work was more important that I was…"

I stare at him and feel the tears welling up behind my eyes.

"It was so easy, Gia. Just me and the razor. It would be over fast. So I went into the toolbox and grabbed a new blade out of the pack and did it—one straight clean cut, then another."

"Who found you?"

"My dad. He came home for a day or two—I wasn't expecting him. "His timing was impeccable because I had just done it."

"Oh God, Clive…what happened then?"

"He called an ambulance…there was blood everywhere. I fell on the bathroom floor and nearly passed out…but he screwed it up for me like he ruins everything in my life." He looks off again, sadness spreading over his face.

"What happened after that?"

"Therapy. Lots of therapy. Talking, talking, talking about everything. Pills. I was sleeping, sleeping, sleeping. It was like I was lost in a dream for two months. And nurses here, all the time, like prison guards. And then I stayed with my aunt and uncle."

"And now?"

"Now what?"

"Tell me you'll never do it again, Clive, please, please."

"I will never do it again," he says, repeating the words like an obedient child.

"You mean it, Clive? I want you to mean it, you have to, because I don't want to lose you. I *can't* lose you," I say as hot tears pour from my eyes because it hits me how much he means to me and I don't have many people either. And it's selfish to be thinking about me and what I need when this is all about him, but that's what I'm feeling and my father is leaving me and Michael is afraid to call me and I have so little left, and he is one of only two true friends I have in the entire world.

And I love him so.

"I can't lose you, Clive Laurent," I whisper. "I can't. Do you hear me? I love you and need you and you are so much a part of my life and you have to be here for me because I am here for you no matter what, no matter when, no matter anything, ever, ever, ever. Do you understand?"

"I hear you, Gia, I do. And I mean it," he says. "I was different then. Younger, whatever. I don't want to lose you either, Gia, so promise me you'll be here for me."

"No matter what. You have my word. And my word is everything."

"Because you're the don's daughter," he says, super straight-faced, mocking me, making those stupid quote marks with his fingers.

"Yes, and just shut up," I answer, sticking my tongue out at him, which makes him laugh. Although what I want to do is cry because I think of my dad again and how I don't know when he'll be back, and how I hate good-byes.

I suddenly yank my gold earring out of my ear and prick my middle finger with the post, then grab his finger and prick it too. We press our fingers together and our blood mixes, and through my tears I smile at him.

"You're now a made man," I say. "Welcome to my family."

And Clive is crying and laughing too and he looks happier than I've ever seen him and we hug and hug, and just screw everything else in the world that isn't right because he's the world to me and it feels like all the black clouds have lifted and that we're floating together in this new universe of oneness and happiness and special friendship and closeness and love…

And then my cell rings.

TWENTY-ONE

More shit with my family, of course, because it never ever ends.

"Somebody whacked Carmine G.," Anthony says like he's in overdrive, "and the heat's on so Ma wants your ass home now."

I can't do this again. I can't. I don't want to be part of this.

"I don't care, Anthony. I'm with Clive and I'm better off staying here than running home and parading past the cameras and being on the six o'clock news."

"Talk to her," he says, handing my mom the phone.

"Gia," she says in crazed mode. "Frankie's in Jersey somewhere, and I can't think without the two of you around, and God knows what will happen now because you know how they love to come after us to get your father mad."

But for the first time I'm not giving in. I don't care what my mom needs. I don't care what Frankie says. I don't care what Vinnie says. I don't even care how it looks or doesn't look for my dad and what he thinks because why is everything in the whole world about him?

Why doesn't someone think about me for a change and what I need and what I want and how it affects who I am and what happens to me? I am so tired of everything I have to put up with in school every day because of them.

And right now the last thing I need is a gang of so-called reporters shoving microphones in my face and asking me if I think my dad had anything to do with it like I would know what *it* is. Like I would ever know anything or actually tell them if I did.

All I do know is that the world is a better place without that pig of a gangster because Carmine G. was known for putting coke up his nose and concrete shoes on people he didn't like and torturing gays because he probably was one and couldn't deal and setting up middle-of-the-night meetings with my dad so that our whole house went crazy because my dad walked around furious that he had to get dressed and go out at three a.m. And then he'd come home exhausted, in a rage because he had to come to agreements with someone he'd like to throw into a pit of alligators.

"No one knows I'm here, Mom, and there are a thousand locks on the door and the pope couldn't breach this security if he wanted to."

"Gia…" she says.

I don't answer. We both wait for what seems like an hour.

"Mom, I'm not…"

"Okay, okay," she says finally. "Stay there, stay there. But don't go out. Stay inside."

"Okay."

"You promise?"

"I promise."

We hang up and then I'm back in default mode and feeling guilty about not caring what she wants, but am I going to spend my entire life running home when there's trouble or running away until it dies down? And I feel even guiltier because I think about running away from this life and then I stop that because how can you run away from something that you are? And even if you could, it's not like the world has amnesia.

Then I have nightmarish thoughts again about my dad and not seeing him and not being with him ever again. It could happen, it could, I know. But I just can't deal with that and try to push the thought out of my mind the way I do whenever I start going down that road, because it's unthinkable not to have my dad around anymore and our family ripped apart.

I think of the families of men in prison and how they spend their weekends and holidays getting on buses to spend the day in depressing visiting areas with armed guards standing by. I tell my head to shut up because Super Mario always saves him and always will, no matter what. He'll get him out of trouble whatever they try to pin on him, otherwise why would they call him Super Mario or Superman?

I look over at Clive and think about what he said and the desperation he must have felt, and I feel sick inside to think of him here, feeling alone and desperate. Life doesn't get more unfair than that. No kid should ever be left alone with no one to talk to, feeling totally shut out with no options.

I think about my life and I know that no matter what, I will never, ever try to kill myself because death is not a solution. And no matter what happens, you can always find a way to deal. I believe that.

"What?" Clive asks. "What is it, Gia?"

I sit there for a few minutes before I tell him and he leans over and takes my hand.

"Gia, I'm so sorry you are always getting drawn into these messes."

"Messes?" I look at him in disbelief and then crack up laughing because *messes* isn't exactly the word for what perpetually happens to me and my family and it makes me think of something like spilled Cheerios. But really, it's so crazy and off the wall that, yes, it does fit.

"Messes," I say out loud, trying it out. Yes, messes does fit. Big fucking messes.

And Clive laughs. "Yes," he says. "We both live with messes."

At some time during the night I hear music, only I'm deep asleep and not sure where it's coming from. And then I realize it's my cell because Mick Jagger is singing "I Can't Get No Satisfaction," which was the song playing at the bar when I walked in the first time, and it just seemed so symbolic of my whole life that I made it my ring tone.

Only now at—what is it, two a.m.?—I am not thinking about satisfaction. I'm thinking about who is calling me and I look down at the phone and see *private*, which kind of jazzes my brain because I don't get too many of those. And what I want to do is just not answer and turn off the phone, but since there's so much going on with my family...

"Hello...Hello?"

I wait and hear breathing, but not pervy hard breathing, just soft, normal breathing like someone is there but not willing to break the strained silence and speak. And since Clive is here with me, only one other person comes to mind, but I don't know if he'd do that. Although the more I hold on, the surer I am that it's him and he's up thinking about me, and that's based on nothing but intuition. But I have this built-in radar so that when I know things, I'm rarely wrong.

"God," I say, almost pleading and then keep holding the phone.

I know he hears me breathing too and this is getting so hard for me because he is so there and it's like each of us is imprisoned in our separate painful worlds and there's a barrier between us, like in the visiting room of super max prisons. And what can I do to change that?

I wait a minute more.

Say something.

But he doesn't. He can't. Off in the distance I hear the growing whir of a fire engine or an ambulance like a cosmic cry of distress. Is it coming from here or his part of the city? I can't tell. I feel like I need a compass to show me where on the map I am right now, so I hug the phone to my heart for a few seconds before I press end and then wait.

Call back, please.

But he doesn't.

The connection is broken.

TWENTY-TWO

Back to the bakery. I'm behind the counter, hair pulled back, starched white apron, positioned behind pyramids of sugary cookies like chocolate chip, chocolate fudge, vanilla nut, café au lait, anise, Italian macaroons, chocolate biscotti, lemon drops, raspberry dainties, and butter cookies.

I wear white gloves and it feels like I'm in a church, only the religion here is sugar worship, and for three solid hours I fold cardboards into snow white cubes and line them with white translucent paper, filling each box just so and then tying them tightly with white string.

Teddy is forever snooping to make sure I'm being neat and careful, and after do overs and do overs and him muttering something, I'm finally left on my own and I think about people who have this job and do this every day, five days a week and Jesus...

When he has nothing better to do, Clive comes into the bakery and hangs out even though Ro's dad doesn't like kids sitting there like all day and taking up a table if they're just having a cappuccino and a few cookies. So I keep bringing him more cookies and more and his bill is like a hundred dollars for cookies that he doesn't eat, but he doesn't care. I sit with him on my break and drink so much espresso that I get bug-eyed. Finally when it's seven I can leave and Clive comes with me and we parade past all the reporters outside my house, ignoring them and what they shout. My mom makes rigatoni and sausages and salad and I reach into my pocket and give her the pathetic twenty-one dollars I earned.

"Eh, good," she says. "You learn the meaning of work."

I make a face behind her back but don't say anything because then she'd tell my dad and he'd make me work weekends too for being fresh. I go up to my room and Clive comes with me. My mom sits in the living room and makes sketches of fancy Cinderella dresses she'll never wear and crochets lace doilies as if we need more.

The phone rings the next night. "Gia," Clive sighs, "my parents are back, so would you please, please, please go to dinner with us?"

I hesitate for just a minute.

"They're dying to meet you. I told them so much about you. We have a reservation at Le Bernardin, so please say yes."

"Um, fine," I say, staring into my closet.

What the hell do I wear to meet his parents, who are these major media moguls and world-class sophisticates, and what will they think of the little guidette?

"What time?"

"Seven. Thomas will get you."

Thomas is now my partner in crime and he's totally cool, especially after I gave him a joint once and he gave me one back, which we vowed never to tell anyone because it definitely could get him fired.

I look through everything I have and can't decide and then just say screw it and go with the backless dress because where else am I going to wear it? I put on one gold cuff bracelet and cranberry heels and lipstick to match and I'm done. I wear a jacket over it though, so that when I leave the house it looks like lah-di-dah, Gia is just dressed in a nice, simple black outfit that's totally appropriate.

Thomas is waiting and I get into the car and he takes me to West 51st Street. I bolt out of the car before he has a chance to open the door for me, never mind nearly falling on my fucking head again because there's this massive pothole that Thomas obviously didn't know about. But still he apologizes fifty times over and I stop and take a few large gulps of air and then try to relax.

Le Bernardin is unbelievably friggin' cool and there's this giant ocean painting, which is the first thing you see. It looks like if you reach up you'll get soaked by ocean waves, it's that real. The maitre d' greets me and I tell him I'm meeting the Laurents and he acts like yes, yes, yes, how boring, because he already knows that. And after giving me the once over, he walks me back toward their table.

I had an image of Clive's parents in my mind and it's not at all like what I see.

His mom is pretty in a cool, elegant, chairwoman-of-the-board kind of way. She's wearing a camel-colored cashmere dress with no jewelry at all except a ring with a diamond that could double as a paperweight. She has beautiful skin and blue eyes and sleek chin-length golden brown hair with amazing highlights. And she glances at my dress and seems to approve, but I haven't taken the jacket off yet and when I do she'll freak and think I'm a slut and snub me.

Clive's dad looks like he goes with her because he's wearing a simple tan and brown wool jacket that looks casual perfect and designer expensive with a tan shirt and a slim silk knit tie. His dad's name, I know, is Claude and his mom's is Alice, although they pronounce it Aleeze, Clive told me, because her mom is French.

Just to be on the safe side, I say, "it's so nice to finally meet you Mr. and Mrs. Laurent and they immediately say please call them by their first names, which obviously makes more sense, so I do.

"Gia, we heard so much about you," Alice says, "and Clive was right, you're lovely. And you like clothes," she says, touching the sleeve of my jacket. At that moment I feel comfortable enough to slip out of my jacket, and her eyes open wide. Just as I'm thinking oh crap, I just blew it, it's over, she says, "Oh, Claude, that's the dress I ordered in Paris but couldn't get."

After all the chitchat about the dress and all, we look at the menu, but duh, I don't understand anything. I mean, geoduck? Tairagai? But Clive and his parents are familiar with every little morsel. Clive jumps in and saves me and says, "Gia, you'll love the crab cakes," so I order them.

At the end of the meal, Alice starts to talk about a new magazine that they're doing a prototype for, even though I don't really know what a prototype is. And she hints that they could use someone like me for an article they're including on personal style and finally says, "Gia, would that interest you?"

"I…I'm not sure." I'm almost stuttering because, whoa, I don't really know. "What would I have to do?"

"Just take a quick trip over Christmas to Paris, London, and maybe Milan and Rome to see what you'd buy to lend a European feel to the piece."

And I'm like, *are you kidding me!? That's work?*

"Well, only if my parents are okay with it and if Clive could come to keep me company."

"Yes, yes, of course," Alice says.

Clive nods, never mind the pained expression on his face.

TWENTY-THREE

I wake up the day of the school election knowing that it's going to be the longest day of school ever. We start the morning by voting and the results are usually tallied by the end of the day. Or if not, by the beginning of the next day.

"You own it," Ro says, high-fiving me.

"It's a slam dunk," Clive says.

"It's not over until the fat lady sings," I say, which is one of Anthony's dumb expressions that I really don't understand, but it seems to fit.

For the entire day I pretend this is no different from every other day, never mind that Ro already told me that they bought a keg and plan on getting pizza and having everybody over once we find out officially that I'm the new class president. At three o'clock I meet Ro and Clive and Candy in the hall near the principal's office and we go up to the wall where they post the results. Only no results are up.

"Crap," Ro says, "I wanted to celebrate."

"I can't imagine what's taking so long," Clive says. "I mean all they have to do is count the ballots. How hard is that?"

Even though in the real world ballots are counted electronically, at Morgan we do it the old-fashioned way, which they must think is quaint. But it is actually more like how corrupt third world countries do it, with everyone filling out a paper ballot that they slide into a cardboard box marked *voting machine.*

We leave school with an empty feeling, wondering if we should celebrate prematurely then decide that would be dumb. So for one more night I remain a candidate and nothing more is said.

Only the next morning when we get to school and go to the bulletin board the results are still not posted. After lunch we go back to check. And there it is, the new student president of the Morgan School is *Brandy Tewl.*

"What?" Clive says.

"It can't be," Ro says.

"No," Candy says.

A vocab word pops into my head, flummoxed. It means bewildered, confused. That's what I am because maybe it can't be, but it is, and I get this uneasy feeling. Clive has it too because his face is suddenly paler than usual.

Down the corridor come Brandy, Christy, and Georgina and they're holding hands and skipping and smiling like they won the lottery. They stop in front of the sign.

"Yes!" Brandy says. "We did it. We won."

"We *fixed* her," Georgina whispers as they walk away.

I stand there and stare, not sure what I just heard.

Someone comes up behind me and looks at the notice.

"Jesus, Brandy?"

Other kids look and a few of them make a point of applauding, even though I'm standing right there. Then Jordan walks up to the board.

"Brandy?"

That's all. "Brandy?" as though if he lost it would at least be to me and if Brandy won then he really hit rock bottom. Without another word, Clive and Ro and Candy and I leave school in total silence.

"Go home without me," I tell Frankie who's waiting outside because it's his shift. "And don't send Vinnie later because I'm going to Clive's."

"Be careful," he says.

We all storm across the park without a word. When we get into Clive's apartment we hit his fridge and take out all the beer that he bribes the maids to buy for him and we get drunk and then crush the cans one by one by one while we're thinking about Brandy and Christy and Georgina, because how else do you handle losing to such cockroaches?

"They screwed you over," Ro says, coming out with what we didn't want to say because it sounds like sour grapes. "Maybe they threw out some of your votes or just ignored them," she says. "I mean who was in charge of counting anyway?"

"I thought the teachers," Clive says.

"Me too," Candy says.

I don't say anything, but at that point I'm thinking, you know, maybe it's a blessing in disguise because really, why do I need to be president of that place? I mean volunteering my time to come up with ways to make it a better school when the best way would be to just expel some of the people who go there.

My mom looks up expectantly when I walk in.

"Did you win?"

"No."

"Someone else did?"

"I'm not sure."

She looks at me like, *what?* because she doesn't understand that and neither do I, but I'm getting the gut feeling I get when things aren't the way they're supposed to be. But I try to put that out of my head because it's time to go to work.

I sometimes wonder why people have pastries at dinnertime, but I guess they have different schedules or different needs and if your life is sweetness-starved, pastries might be the ticket.

I'm standing behind the counter dressed in white like a nun minus the cross but feeling like one anyway since I have no real social life beyond Ro and Clive and Candy. And I'm counting out the cookies, which in a strange way is therapeutic because when you've loaded up a whole box and tied it tight, you feel you've accomplished something, and I feel good about that. Until I hear voices. Familiar ones. So out of context though. It couldn't be. But my heart is pounding like tribal drums because it knows, yes it can.

Georgina and Brandy are waiting in line. They're whispering together and glancing at me and finally when it's their turn they look me in the eye and burst out laughing.

"Oh, hi, Gia," Georgina says. "We didn't know that you work behind the counter here as a *server*."

I look at her dead on. "What would you like?"

They pretend they're deciding and stand there forever, holding up everybody else in line.

"Those," Georgina says finally, pointing to the lace cookies. "Because we're celebrating," she says, staring at me pointedly.

I start to wrap some up.

"No, no, we're staying," she says.

I unwrap them. "There's table service." Isn't that obvious? If it's not bad enough that they came in, they sit at a table near the front and order tea and coffee and cookies. Only when their cookies arrive they taste them and Brandy shakes her head in disgust. "They're so sticky," she says. "Can we get some other kind?"

"Like what?" the waitress says.

Georgina runs to the case again and makes a show of deciding, finally pointing to the raspberry cookies and the chocolate chip, so the waitress brings those and they sit there untouched because maybe they're dieting but more likely just dissing everything and getting off on being guests while I'm the help.

Georgina and Brandy start whispering about something and laughing out loud and Georgina takes out her phone and snaps pictures of Brandy like she's a celebrity and something about what's going on is starting to make me crazed because I know what will be happening next.

"Gia, hold it," Georgina says, as she holds up her phone to snap my picture.

Without missing a beat, a strong arm appears behind her and reaches past her neck and pushes the phone away.

"My dear, Gia is working, so please, eh?" Ro's dad says, steely eyed.

Georgina freezes. "Oh, I'm sorry, I didn't mean to…" The laughter at her table dies, the cookies are devoured, and a minute later they pay and leave without a word.

Ro's dad looks at me and nods slightly.

Just desserts.

TWENTY-FOUR

Some sense of justice points my feet to walk in the direction of Mr. Wright's office after lunch the next day. I ask his secretary if I can see him and he comes out and ushers me in.

"Gia," he says, "What can I do for you?"

"It's about the election."

Mr. Wright immediately looks concerned. "What about it?"

"I don't think that Brandy really won."

He closes his eyes momentarily. "Gia, this isn't the first time we've had an election at Morgan."

"I know but—"

"And it's not the first time that a candidate lost and wasn't happy about it."

I shift in my seat. "I—"

"You what?"

"It's not that."

He cocks his head to the side. "Not what?"

"I'd just like a recount."

"On what basis?"

"Something I heard."

"What did you hear?"

"Something Georgina said, 'We *fixed* her.'"

"Implying?"

I sit up taller. "Mr. Wright…I think the election was fixed."

He stares at me for a long, uncomfortable minute then shifts his gaze and stares out the window as if he's looking for outside guidance. Abruptly he turns back to me.

"The Morgan School would not tolerate any discrepancies between the way the students voted and the way the election turned out, so I will consider what you've told me. In the meantime, I'd appreciate it if you'd keep this to yourself until I get back to you."

So natch I spill to Ro and Clive, who are sworn to secrecy, and we try to put it out of our minds and hang out in Central Park after school, playing on the swings and working out at Clive's gym and walking a gazillion miles on the treadmills before going downstairs to Whole Foods and looking at weird stuff like mung beans and sea beans and tikka masala sauce and having foodgasms after pigging out on bittersweet chocolate and pumpkin tofu cheesecake, which sounds healthier than real cheesy cheesecake and then just waiting, waiting, waiting until we get some final word.

TWENTY-FIVE

I come home from school and drop my backpack in the hall. I turn, about to go upstairs.

"Gia!"

"Daddy!" I start to say, but the word catches in my throat. He stands there in his cashmere bathrobe, the same color as his tanned face, his eyes lighting up. I run up to him, pressing my face against the lapel, trying to hide the tears in my eyes.

"I'm so glad you're home," I say, my voice cracking.

He steps back and looks into my eyes, shaking his head. He keeps hugging me like when I was little and couldn't stop crying after I scraped my knee in the playground.

"Gia, my Gia," he says over and over in a soothing rhythmic voice, smoothing my hair until finally I calm down, and he lets go and smiles like everything is all right again and I'm being silly to think it's any other way. I wish so hard that I have the iron will that he does to just pretend everything is totally all right when it's totally wrong, because half of how you see things in life and react to them depends on your attitude anyway, right?

Anthony comes home next and then it's his turn to hug my dad, but the hug he gives him is shorter and harder and stiff and uncomfortable because Anthony doesn't want to be held like a baby, at least not like I do. They look into each other's eyes for five intense seconds and then Anthony studies the floor hard and shakes his head and that's enough for them to say whatever has to be said in their silent, wordless male language of swallowed-up emotions and pretend toughness.

After that everyone tries to be on their best behavior because we don't know what's going to happen next and my mom who uses cooking as psychotherapy brings out twice as much food as we need for dinner.

Instead of just, say, pasta fagioli and salad and focaccia bread, we feast on veal marsala and roast chicken and manicotti and ravioli and escarole and salad and olives and peppers, which is over the top, even for us. But it's like in that one giant meal, my mom is trying to feed my dad for the rest of his life with all he will ever need and want because food is her secret weapon against whatever might threaten safety and happiness. But before we get to desserts and after-dinner drinks, I turn to my dad.

"Can I talk to you...alone...in private?"

He looks at me curiously and uncrosses his legs, reaching out a hand to me.

"Come, let's go into my office."

He takes his wine glass in his free hand and we walk to his office. He puts the glass down on the small marble side table and then closes the door.

"Come," he says again, patting the place next to him on the couch. "Sit here next to me."

I sit and turn to him, trying to remember the last time I was in his office, just the two of us. It couldn't be, I think, and then I realize yes, it was when I was little and I asked him about his work.

"What? Tell me what's wrong. What is it, Gia?"

I don't know what I'm going to say, I only know it's something I have to try to say to change things, even though it probably doesn't make sense and will sound really stupid.

"Daddy, do you think you could change your life now, now that you're finally home again?"

He narrows his eyes and looks at me questioningly. "What do you mean change it—change it how?"

"Just stop being a boss now and do something else so we could be together like other families and the police wouldn't come around and you wouldn't have to go to jail and get in trouble anymore. Can't you just stop now and let someone else be in charge? Just step down and walk away from everything?"

He studies the floor and shakes his head slightly. "I can't change who I am," he says finally, looking up at me. "It's too late. It's too late for that."

He stares off in the distance for forever, like he's going over his entire life, but then catches himself and looks back to me. His face turns sad as though it dawns on him that there's more life behind him now than ahead. He tells me about growing up poor and trying to survive on the streets.

"I had to quit high school to work to help my family get enough money to eat," he says. "There were gangs in the neighborhood and they beat me up. And if I didn't learn how to live in that world and make the right friends, my whole family would have starved and I would have been killed by the bullies. I learned to do what I had to, to survive, Gia, not because I loved the work. It's not the way I would have lived if I had a chance to choose…believe me."

I don't know what to say after that. And neither does he. We sit there together in awful silence with all the regret in the air and there's no way to make that go away or pretend anymore. And we're both thinking about the hard truths and what's ahead for him, and I feel like holding my stomach to make the pain inside go away.

"But your life…" he says, "your life will be better, so much better."

At least different.

"You'll have a wonderful education, you'll be happy and do important work, and I'll be proud of you."

"I hope so, Daddy."

"Not hope so, Gia, you will, you will. You'll go to the best schools and have all the opportunities I never had, because you know what?"

"What?"

"Education gives you power," he says, holding up his fist. "I want you to remember that. And something else."

"What?"

"You are going to succeed. You are smart and tough and you are going to succeed, no matter what."

I nod.

"Say it," he says.

"I will. I promise you," I say, my voice catching.

We go back and sit down for dessert and Anthony and my mom look at us like, *what was that about?* But neither of us tells, and I keep thinking about what he said and how he said it, as if he wanted me to make up for everything that fell short in his own life, as if he needed that to go on.

We all work hard pretending to enjoy the food and all the cookies that I always bring home for dessert, and we try not to think about the other talk, and after we sit around being too full to move, my mom says, "did everyone have enough?" which is insane. And eventually after we clean up, I say good night.

I keep looking at my dad and he keeps looking back at me as if we're the only ones in the room. And all I'm thinking is how much I wish everything going on now could just go away so the air could be clear and tomorrow we could start life over. And he'd be home for dinner like other dads and then the same thing for the night after that and the night after that, so that everything would end happy, like in a storybook.

Only none of that is going to happen.

You can't live your life pretending you'll always get second chances.

I go upstairs to do homework. I'm reading Romantic poetry for English, and even though most of it is hard to figure out at first, it hits me that these poets from the 1700s, who were sitting in their little rooms in their damp English cottages or out in their gardens writing by candlelight or moonlight, were suffering as much as we are over their painful feelings and all the things that weren't the way they wanted them to be. They had depressing love lives too, obsessed with people who were either not loving them back or were married or dead. And no matter when you were born, some things never change and we all suffer the same inside even though everyone feels it's just them and no one could possibly understand what they're going through and how it feels.

Which naturally brings me back to Michael.

For no reason I pick up my phone and stare at the one text he sent me and try to will him to reach out again so that the relationship, or whatever it is that we have going or don't, isn't dead and over. And I start living in my memories like a pathetic loser.

Eventually I put the phone down and take a shower and then put on an oatmeal mask that's drippy and disgusting. I don't know why I bother about shrinking my pores because it's not like it lasts. I wait and wait for it to harden and then wash it off and oatmeal chunks clog up the sink, which will piss off my mom. I put on Whitestrips next and go back to the stupid phone to check it again, but there's still no message from Michael, and, shit, I wish I could ask someone what to do, which would be pointless because all they'd say is, "Gia, just forget him, he's not for you."

But that's not true. Michael and I have some primal, chemical connection and when we're close the magnetic pull is so strong we cannot stay apart. And no matter what, I'm not letting that go.

I fall asleep before eleven, which is early for me but everything that has been going on in school and with my dad and with Michael and with Clive and the fashion magazine story is swirling in my head.

When some asshole goes riding down the street at a hundred miles an hour on his Harley at two in the morning because he can, I jerk awake and sit up in bed. My heart starts beating fast like I might die on the spot. Where the hell does my mom hide the Xanax? I need the entire bottle. I don't think she trusts Anthony, who would probably fence them, so she hides them and that leaves me with nothing but Percocet, which I won't take because they comatose me and I can't walk around school like a zombie. That would make everyone think I'm bummed out about the election, so I force myself to try this relaxing breathing thing.

Which. Does. Zero.

I press the phone against my chest like a security blanket and study Michael's text again as if it's in code and will reveal some vital, hidden message, which is asinine, and then say out loud, "I'm calling him." If his phone is off, then it's off. And if it's not, let's see what he does in the middle of the night.

As it rings my heart pounds faster and faster and it rings again and again and then…

He's there. But he doesn't talk. And crap, are we just going to go through the silent breathing thing again? And I decide no. We are not.

"Michael?" I whisper so softly I'm not sure the words come out.

Five-second pause.

"Yeah."

If I had a brain I would have planned what to say next, even scribbled it on my palm like a cheat sheet. But it's the middle of the night and I'm too tired to think of something smart and out-there like I'm cool about calling cops in the middle of the night, so my mouth takes over.

"Hi."

"Gia," he says in a way that sounds resigned and defeated but also maybe a little like "you finally called." Or maybe that's just what I'm hoping it means.

"Did I wake you?"

"I'm always half up."

"How come?"

"I don't know."

I wonder about that for a minute because after an entire day of being a cop you'd think it would knock you out since the job has to be draining. And half the time you're on your feet or chasing crazies who are pissed off about something or everything and at any moment someone might point a gun to your head. So why can't he sleep at night? But I don't say any of that.

"Did you call me the other night? Was that you, Michael?"

I hear him breathing. "Yeah."

"How come?"

"You know how come, Gia."

"What are we going to do, Michael?"

"I don't know, baby. I don't know."

And just that word. *Baby.*

It totally kills me and brings me to my knees and changes

everything between us for real so I know this all hasn't just been about me and my out-there fantasies.

For some stupid reason right then I start thinking about studying poetry and how each word matters so much and, as Mrs. Collins says like a crusader for a cause, "carries so much weight." And then I totally understand everything she's been trying to teach us for three solid months about writing poetry and just writing and how hard it is because you have to go through like the entire vocabulary to find the few right words that mean everything that you don't have the time or space or nerve to actually come right out and say.

"Are you glad I called?"

"You ask me things I can't answer," he says.

"Can't or won't?"

"Is there a difference?"

"Yes." There's a pause of like four hours. "Why don't you trust me, Michael?"

"I don't trust anyone."

"Fucking cop."

"Yeah," he says, a smile in his voice.

"I'll call you tomorrow."

He doesn't answer, which is what I expect.

"Do you want me to?"

He exhales. "I don't know."

Which isn't no.

"And Michael…"

"What?"

"Answer the phone, okay?"

He laughs softly and hangs up.

TWENTY-SIX

When we get back to school on Monday morning, Mr. Wright's secretary comes into first period English and hands me a note, written on heavy beige paper with *The Morgan School* in embossed purple letters at the top.

Please see me after class.

The adrenaline pours out so hard I feel like I could levitate. I pass the note down to Clive. He reads it and looks up, and we stare at each other in a deep, meaningful way for a total of ten seconds.

I look at the clock and there's another twenty minutes until the end of class, which seems like a century, so I start to doodle, nervously writing words like *retribution*, *pay back*, and *fraud* in the back of my notebook, pressing down so hard that I break the point and rip through the page, and in some small way, violating the paper helps.

When class ends, I walk to Mr. Wright's office, but he's on the phone with a parent who's ranting about something stupid because I hear him say, "I understand, I understand," about fifty times and, "yes, we take those things seriously," and then another dozen or so "I understands," and some other stuff about "social conscience," and I can only imagine how many of those calls he juggles every day.

Finally he comes out for me and I follow him into his office. It's kind of prep-school cozy, filled with dark brown wooden furniture and a green velvet couch and some comfortable looking green-and-blue plaid armchairs on navy carpet. Lots of bookshelves with boring kinds of academic books and the ginormous Oxford English Dictionary that no one ever looks at because it's so heavy and the writing is teensy, and really, TMI, right?

He points to the chairs and I sit down. He sits behind his desk and removes his round tortoise shell glasses and rubs his eyes, which are bloodshot, as if he didn't sleep much last night.

"Since impropriety is not tolerated in any form and I'm willing to go the distance to prove that, I've decided to have an outside agency recount the ballots."

I'm about to say thank you and then stop. I nod.

Mr. Wright stares at me, as if he's expecting to find some kind of higher truth on my face. I meet his gaze and wait.

"We'll get to the bottom of this," he says.

TWENTY-SEVEN

Thanksgiving in my house begins way before Thanksgiving when my mom starts to put about twelve leaves onto the antique mahogany dining table and sends out the white linen tablecloths to be starched and ironed and the silver candlesticks to be polished. She sets up all the folding chairs because she says she can't think straight unless she can visualize where everyone will sit and where every platter will go, which is ridiculous but I know by now that you can't argue with her. So when I have breakfast I sit at the end of the table and lift up the white cloth and put down a place mat and try not to make crumbs because if I do she'll smack my head and have a meltdown.

What we do for Thanksgiving is invite about half the neighborhood over, which includes Ro's entire family and their cousins and all of ours and Anthony's loser friends, and when we start to count up all the people it usually comes to about forty. Then the question is how many turkeys and Anthony always plays big shot.

"Ma, leave it to me, okay?"

A week before Thanksgiving, he comes home with his trunk filled with like five, thirty-five pound turkeys from I don't know where because he's afraid if he doesn't bring home enough he'll get killed, but my mom sees them and yells.

"Anthony, what were you thinking, eh? Look at this kitchen. How many ovens do I have?"

"Three, Ma."

"So how am I going to cook five turkeys?"

He brings two over to Ro's and her mom has to cook them and then Dante usually steals a red wagon from some kid in the neighborhood and drags them back home that way.

This Thanksgiving because my dad is home and we're not sure how long that will last, we go a little overboard and get two cases of Dom because if this is his last Thanksgiving here, we're going to make it memorable. And then we order huge flower arrangements for the table and desserts from Ro's dad because after all the cooking, my mom draws the line at baking.

Before vacation we get a ton of homework and after dinner I go upstairs and start doing it and then stop to think about the recount again and how screwed up the election was. And then out of the blue I start wondering what Michael does for Thanksgiving, if anything, and for no reason at all I start to imagine that he probably has a loser Thanksgiving and that thought doesn't leave my head.

Then I wonder whether he has parents and where they live if he does and about brothers and sisters and the house where he grew up and yada, yada, yada, so, you know what's coming. I decide that at night I'm going to call him and find out because he said I didn't know anything about him, and I want to, have to, know more.

It's easier for me to call him in the middle of the night. My head wakes me at some point after two and, almost instinctively, I pick up the phone. When it starts to ring my head gets totally crazed and I get filled with longing and think about starting out by telling him that I'm naked under the covers, but decide nuh-uh, I could never do that because he'd just hang up on slutty me.

On the third ring, he answers and waits. Didn't he ever learn the word hello?

"Michael?

"Yeah."

"Hi."

"Hi, Gia."

"You in bed?"

"No."

"Where are you?"

"On the Henry Hudson."

"What for?"

"Waiting."

"For?"

"Speeders."

This is not what I expected. "You're still on nights?"

"For a while, yeah."

"Shit."

"Yeah."

"Can you talk?"

"Nothing else going on."

"I miss you."

Silence.

"You miss me?"

"Gia…"

"I know you do, you bastard. I hope you hurt."

He half laughs.

"So what are you doing for Thanksgiving?"

He snorts.

"What? Going home?"

"Yeah."

"Where's that?"

"Baltimore."

"To see your mom?"

"Yeah."

"Does she cook—the whole Thanksgiving thing?"

"I cook," he says.

"Really?"

"Yeah."

"She doesn't like to?"

Silence.

"It's hard for her."

"How come?"

"Long story."

"What about your dad?"

Silence.

"No dad," he says finally.

"Did he…die?"

"Yeah, he's dead."

I wait, expecting him to go on, but he doesn't.

"Is it cold out?"

He laughs. "Yeah."

"So what, you just sit in the car with the heat on?"

"Right."

"I wish I was there. To keep you warm."

"You're doing that."

I laugh.

"Shit," he says suddenly. "Gotta go."

He hangs up and I stare at the phone.

Progress.

TWENTY-EIGHT

Someone from John Plesaurus's office calls to say that John would like to messenger me some of the shots from the photo shoot, which is totally cool because I didn't expect to see them until they ran in the magazine.

"Tell him thank you, I really appreciate it."

Only it occurs to me that I probably do not want the envelope arriving at my house because then my mom or dad might open it along with the AmEx bill and *People* or Blue Cross garbage and solicitations from the church, and if the pictures look pornographic, forget the bakery, they'll chain me to a pipe in the basement for the rest of my life. So instead I give them Clive's name and address and tell them that would be a preferable move.

When Clive gets home from school he calls. "It's here, Gia, I have the envelope."

"Open it, open it," I shout, my foot tapping on the floor. There's a pause and I hear paper being torn and then paper rustling, then more rustling.

"Oh my God, Gia!" he yells. "You won't believe these pictures… *Oh my god!*"

"What? What?" I scream, jumping up and running down the stairs and getting into a cab barefoot and telling the driver to "go faster, go faster, go faster," and he probably thinks I'm having a coronary, which I am. Finally we get to Clive's and I'm so nervous I drop the phone and have to go searching for it on the filthy floor of the cab and then I sprint past the doorman who already knows me and waves me in, and I get into the elevator and the doors open on Clive's floor.

He's pasted the pictures up on a wall and I am totally out of my mind and hysterical because they are positively *incendiary*.

"I may just have to sleep with John Plesaurus to thank him," I say, only half kidding. "I mean just look at these pictures."

"Gia, you are a born model," Clive says. "The camera loves you."

Except for iPhone shots and pathetic family photos from when I was little, the only pictures, I've really seen of myself have been awful graduation pictures, where your face looks pasty because they white out your zits, or those photobooth candids, which only show a mini version of your face and neck and you have an idiotic grin on your face or your eyes are closed, but not any kind of close-ups of my face and body.

So the first thing I do is take the best two shots—that show my entire naked back with me turning my face around over my shoulder and doing this hot vamp thing with my eyes—and put them in an envelope. Clive and I go to the post office and I overnight them to Michael, who, of course, has no idea that I even know where he lives and will probably be pissed to find out that I did all this detective work on him, but whatever. So then Clive and I celebrate by going out to Per Se, this over-the-top restaurant in the Time Warner Center. We have gnocchi Parisienne with tarragon custard and cauliflower mushrooms and carrots with fines herbes and beurre rouge and some other entrees just to taste them. We try to order wine but they just smile and shake their heads because even though we show our IDs, they know they're laughably fake. So we go with San Pell and even though I don't know what I'm eating, it all tastes so fabulous that it feels like I've died and gone to heaven and Clive charges the seven hundred dollar bill to his dad.

I call John Plesaurus when I get home. "You are such a genius."

Of course he loves being told what he already thinks about himself.

"Gia, you were a perfect model, really, and you're so incredibly beautiful, and you know what?" He takes a deep breath and then there's like this thirty-second pause. "More than anything, I'd like to take pictures of your extraordinary body."

What follows is this embarrassing three-hour silence on the phone because hello, John is, what, like forty-five, and that is so not what I expected to hear from him and how do I answer that?

"Naked pictures?" I finally blurt out.

"Mmm, really beautiful nudes, but just for me," he says. "No one else would see them."

I swallow hard. "John...do you know who I am?"

Another pause.

"Yes, so?" he says in this supercool innocent way.

"So?" I laugh. "So? So John, my dad would chop you up into little pieces and leave you at a Dumpster if he knew you said that to me."

He doesn't take that entirely seriously, which he should, and sort of laughs it off.

"Gia, it's just a thought or maybe just my fantasy, okay, so why don't we leave it at that?"

Then I crack up and it breaks the mood and I thank him again and hang up and then stare at the phone and go *holy crap* and pray the feds haven't bugged it and that this doesn't come out on the front page of the *New York Post* or a supermarket tab tomorrow.

TWENTY-NINE

When my cell vibrates exactly two days later in the middle of the night, I wake up with a start and try to clear my head.

It's him an excited little voice in my head sings, and I'm trying to guess in those few seconds how he's going to react to seeing the pictures. Pissed because they're too hot and he thinks I'm too young and maybe a total slut? Or blown away and turned on because he gets to stare at half of my naked body in the privacy of his own home?

Based on what I know about Michael, I decide that nothing is simple and that he'll probably be feeling a freakin' combo of the two and he won't know what to say or feel or do, but just the fact that he's calling...

I answer then wait for him to talk because for once in his life maybe he'll say hello and start a conversation the way nine-tenths of the people on the planet do.

But he doesn't know hello. Or even hi.

"Gia?"

"Mmm."

"Who took these pictures?"

"Why?"

"Tell me."

"*Vogue*. A photographer for *Vogue*."

"You're going to be in the magazine?"

"Yeah."

"Jesus."

"Do you like them?"

He exhales. "Yeah."

"Just yeah?"

"No, not just yeah."

The wattage rises without him even being in the same room. I smile. "I'm glad. I wanted them to blow you away."

His half laugh.

"God, Michael, you're so impossible."

"Why?"

"Because you hold back, you're so afraid or whatever."

"Yeah, or whatever."

I yawn. I can't help it. Only it's not exhaustion—it's not enough oxygen to the brain from speed breathing because he called.

"Go back to sleep, baby," he says, maybe because he can't think of anything else after that, otherwise he's afraid of where the conversation will go with the pictures and all, but then again, I don't imagine phone sex is exactly his thing. "You have school tomorrow."

"So now you're playing like my dad?"

"No, like your law enforcement officer."

"Then fuck you...Officer Hottie."

"Hang up," he says, a smile in his voice.

"You hang up."

"Resisting," he says, getting into the game.

"Take me in," I say back.

"Is that your idea of fun?"

"Definitely," I answer. Then I press end and leave him hanging.

THIRTY

It's been almost a week and we don't have a school president, or we do and it's Brandy, but not really because they're still recounting. Only why is it taking so long? The day before Thanksgiving, Clive and I and Ro and Candy meet in front of the school because somebody said that there might be more information about the election.

"Let's look at the bulletin board," Clive says.

"One for all and all for one, united we stand, divided we fall," Ro chants, and we chime in along with her. But we stop when we get to the sign.

Based on irregularities in the tabulations, the school will be recounting the ballots.

Now it's officially out there.

"This is huge," Clive says. "Because if you win, it means we've caught them at their dirty game."

"I love that," says Ro.

"*Moi aussi*," says Candy, raising her fists in the air.

Maybe justice will prevail and I had a hand in it. So I am now in an extra good mood because of the recount and Thanksgiving coming and the trip to Europe that no one knows about.

I haven't asked my parents yet, but I'm sure they'll let me go because it's with Clive's parents and it's totally chaperoned and I'll be away and safe and everything will be five star.

"Come for Thanksgiving," I say to Clive.

"I would love that."

His parents are away of course, this time with friends in the south of France and he doesn't want to go there because the French don't celebrate Thanksgiving, duh, so he brings pumpkin pies and cookies from Daniel Boulud and crusty baguettes, and my mom and dad really like Clive because he's totally respectful and worships me and he's always telling them about how the teachers love my work, which they want to hear because of what they pay for my school. I think that at some level they think of Clive as one of their own and I tell everybody I've adopted him and that he's my new brother. Even Anthony laughs about that because he wouldn't mind having another brother so there is someone else around the house to deal with all the garbage he doesn't want to.

My dad motions to Clive to come talk to him. I casually walk toward them, pretending to be fixing the flowers on a side table. From the corner of my eye I see my dad put his hand on Clive's shoulder.

"You're a good friend to Gia."

"She's very special to me," Clive says.

My dad nods. "You are always welcome in my home, and I am here for you, whatever you need."

"Thank you," Clive says and then falls silent. I don't have to see his face to know how touched he is.

We both head for the kitchen to help my mom baste all three turkeys and Clive gives her a pottery cup with a hand-printed label that says *Herbes de Provence* that has fennel and basil and lavender and stuff so we sprinkle it on the turkeys and it makes the house smell like a kitchen in the south of France, or that's what Clive says, because how would I know. Everyone who walks in says, "Omigod, what *is* that?" and presses their hands to their hearts.

That of course makes Clive feel very special and then we also help my mom mash the forty-five hundred potatoes, a job that Anthony hates to do, but Clive doesn't mind. So Anthony goes upstairs to look at pornography on his computer or whatever, and then finally, everything is ready.

All forty of us descend on the table like locusts and everyone looks at my dad who says grace and makes a speech about thanks, and of course my mom and I get teary-eyed even though we hate that.

But I am thankful.

For having my dad with us. For my crazy family. For Clive. For the recount. For what hasn't happened yet, but will, like my secret plan for the future.

When all the emotional stuff is finally over, we dab our eyes and take a breath, then pass around big platters of white meat turkey and then dark and of course we start with my dad. After the meat, we move on to gravy and then the mashed yams and mashed Yukon Gold potatoes and string beans and brussels sprouts and carrots and parsnips, cranberry sauce with walnuts and oranges, sausage corn bread stuffing with sage, and then the bread and then the pumpkin and chocolate pecan pies and the sugar cookies and espresso and tea and then after-dinner drinks, and then Frankie drops to the floor because he has a massive heart attack.

The ambulance screeches up and the EMT guys give Frankie oxygen and it takes three of them to carry him out on a stretcher. By then everyone has switched over to speaking Italian because that way they feel closer to God and then they're praying and throwing their hands up and everybody heads for their cars to follow the ambulance.

But my dad holds up his hands. "Please, I will go with Anthony," and "we'll call you when we get there."

We all stay home and pray for Frankie and wait and wait and after that there's a total pall over what's left of the day. Clive and I help my mom clean up and then we go upstairs and watch a movie.

"Do you want to stay over?" I ask Clive.

"Would your parents mind?"

"Definitely not."

But I put him in the guest room, not my room, anyway. At three in the morning the house phone rings and I know it's my dad calling so I tiptoe into the hallway.

"Thank God, thank God," my mom says, which means Frankie pulled through and we have something else to be thankful for. I start wondering how the hell we're going to get him to lose weight because when you're ninety pounds overweight, you're basically a walking time bomb.

THIRTY-ONE

I am coming out of school with Ro and Clive and now that Frankie is home recovering and Vinnie's helping Frankie, my dad has actually agreed to let me cab it home or go with Thomas. And for once in my life I can breathe without a babysitter/spy waiting outside for me like I'm still in kindergarten.

There's an ice cream truck that always parks by the school and I decide to get a chocolate ice cream sandwich. I get in line and then look across the street while I'm waiting and I see something I've never seen before.

At least not outside my school.

He's wearing sunglasses and a worn leather bomber jacket over jeans and he's leaning up against a car with his arms crossed over his chest. He looks so breath-stopping hot that I feel faint. Am I hallucinating? It takes a minute for reality to set in and then I start to wonder how long he's been there watching and whether his plan was to just keep observing from a distance or to actually cross the street and come closer.

Instead of racing over, which my heart is telling me to do, I wait in line until it's my turn. I buy two ice cream sandwiches and slowly cross the street.

"Hope you're not allergic to chocolate."

He half smiles as I hand him the sandwich, taking off his sunglasses and hanging them from the neck of his sweater. He looks at me hard, his eyes burning green like they're lit from within, and he seems to forget the ice cream, but I start to rip the paper off mine with my teeth and point my chin at his to remind him. So he slowly and neatly peels away the paper and then holds my gaze.

"How are you, Gia?"

I manage to lick the ice cream first. "Hmm, better now."

The sandwiches are already melting from body heat. I watch his mouth move and the slow, hypnotic way he slides his tongue along the long side of the dark chocolate wafers, catching every drip while he watches me mimic his moves because this is definitely a game.

Only my hyperactive brain is already firing questions: What's next? What now? What exactly is his plan here, assuming he has one? But I'm not going to ask so I stand next to him and lean on the same black BMW and continue eating fast while he takes his time, which a shrink would definitely conclude means something major.

Ro is watching from across the street and probably going, *not that cop*, but I smile at her anyway. And Clive is watching too because I know he's curious about Michael after all I've told him. I look back at Michael working on the sandwich, and then, because I can't think of anything else to say and the silence is killing me and screw my resolve to not say anything, I say, "now what?"

"Work," he says, checking his watch.

"So you just came by to see me or what?"

"Something like that."

That sketchy bullshit answer infuriates me because if this stupid cop doesn't make a serious move soon…

"So you saw me." I turn to leave, but his arm reaches out and eases me back.

"Gia…"

"What, Michael?"

"Watch your back," he whispers, his face dead serious.

I cock my head to the side. "What do you mean?"

"There are rumblings…retaliation. That's all I know."

I look at him curiously then cross the street. Did he come because he wanted to see me? Or just to pass on the vague warning because he felt it was his duty? Or both?

Ro and Clive both look at me like, *what was that all about?*

I shrug my shoulders because I have no idea.

Later at night when I'm in bed, the ambiguity eats away at me and the scene keeps replaying in my head. The warning. The truth behind it, if there is. More than that my brain fixates on the video in my head of Michael eating the ice cream sandwich. His mouth moving. His eyes. The way the air seemed charged.

I sleep fitfully, turning and twisting, obsessed with trying to get to know someone who seems intent on being unknowable.

THIRTY-TWO

BOOM, BOOM, BOOM, BOOM!

Gunfire!

Then another barrage of gunfire. BOOM, BOOM BOOM!

I jerk awake, trying to figure out what's happening. BOOM, BOOM, BOOM, BOOM, my stomach seizing, recognizing the sounds but panicking because I have no sense of where they're coming from.

"Gia, Anthony, get down, get down on the floor under the bed!" my dad yells as my mom screams in panic.

Like a terrified kid who wakes up with nightmares, I dive under the bed for cover, pressing my hands over my ears to muffle the deafening sounds and trying to stop my body from shaking like I'm having a seizure.

BOOM, BOOM, BOOM, the shots continue, hitting the windows and sending chunks of glass raining down, crashing everywhere, splintering and cracking, our home being shot up and destroyed, like we're in the middle of a war zone—only we're letting it happen, powerless, unable to fight back and we're all cowering on the floor like scared sheep. I want to run down the hall into my parents' room but it would be stupid to stand so I stay scrunched up under the bed, my heart pounding so hard I'm sure my parents can hear it.

"Gia, stay where you are, but answer me!" my dad yells. "Are you okay?"

I try to answer but can't at first. "I'm okay," I manage to say, my words coming out haltingly, ragged, through my tears.

"Gia, are you okay?" he yells again.

"Yes, Daddy, I'm okay!" I manage to shout.

"Thank God!" my mom yells.

We all wait one minute, two minutes, three...and then hear sirens and know that help is coming and whoever did it is probably far away already. I crawl out from under the bed and make my way to the door. The floor is splintered with shattered glass and my feet start to bleed from the cuts, but I don't care and keep going.

My parents are crouched on the floor of their room, huddled together and it's like I'm seeing them for the first time because they look old and scared and helpless. My mom is lying there with her legs pulled up and I see red veins crisscrossing her milk-white skin and she's crying and screaming, "God help us, God help us, what's wrong with this world?"

Anthony comes in and his arm is bleeding because a bullet must have grazed it, and my mom yells, "Oh my God, what happened? What happened?"

"It's nothing, Ma," Anthony says, but the blood is dripping down his arm in a steady stream, leaving a red trail on the pale blue carpeting. My mom jumps up and goes to the bathroom to get peroxide and gauze and I grab a towel to press against his arm to stop the bleeding. And my dad is calling 911 for an ambulance and Anthony's yelling, "they'll pay for this," and everybody is searching for their clothes and I run back to my room to find jeans and shoes and when I come back my dad is buttoning his shirt and standing by the side of the window. He presses numbers into his phone and stares into the night.

"You know what to do," he whispers. "Now."

And just the command of his voice makes me feel sick inside. When will this war ever end?

When someone tries to wipe out an entire family—or at least scare an entire family—that's big news.

"If it bleeds, it leads," TV reporters say, so pictures of our house with the windows blown out are all over the papers along with pictures of Anthony being driven to the hospital in the ambulance even though the bleeding slowed down and the bullet didn't lodge in his arm.

The phone is ringing constantly and flowers start arriving, which is dumb, but people like to show they're sympathetic. And I am walking around thinking about Michael's warning and how he knew something and then in spite of everything around me spiraling out of control, it happens to be a school day, so I bandage all my cuts and stuff my feet into boots and get dressed and go.

Everyone is either looking at me like I'm radioactive or coming over and saying, "Gia, Gia, I'm so glad you're okay."

"I'm fine, thanks," I say about a thousand times, only I'm not because I'm totally freaked by the thought of going home and sleeping in my bed again. If that isn't enough, my mind keeps replaying the warning from Michael, but I don't have to think anymore about him because my phone rings at lunch and it is him.

"Gia, are you okay?"

"I'm fine, we're all fine, except a bullet grazed Anthony's arm and he had to have stitches."

He exhales. "I was worried. I'm glad you're okay."

But that doesn't exactly do it for me and I have to go to class so I hang up and this time I try not to think about what could have been.

We move into Ro's house for a few days while our windows are being replaced with bulletproof glass. It feels weird to move next door, but Ro's family is like mine, and her mom is like my mom's separated-at-birth twin, and our dads work together, so there's constant food and noise and I feel safer there. Then I start to think about Christmas in Europe with Clive, which could not come at a better time, so I ask my parents.

"Go, go," my dad says, relieved that he has a place to send me. "Yes, you can go, if the parents are with you."

I begin to count the days, the hours, and the minutes, because I need to escape.

From New York.

My family.

My school.

And my life.

THIRTY-THREE

Clive and I are actually at the airport, waiting to go to Paris. His parents, all upset by the news, called my parents and told them about the trip and promised that it would be good for me and that they'd be with us 24/7 yada, yada, yada, and that they'd watch out all the time and more than that, they'd treat me like their own daughter. Anyway, we have more than three weeks off and if I were home, all I could do is get in trouble.

The truth is my parents didn't need convincing. They wanted me out of the way because my dad is going on trial. It's going to be a media circus and they see Europe as a safer universe. So they thanked Clive's parents and my dad told them he was grateful.

"I'll remember it," he said.

I try to forget about the trial and my worries about him and what will happen because Super Mario always gets him out, and I live in the moment and the time in Paris and Rome and Milan and London seems to rush together in a joyous nonstop blur of extraordinary old hotels with suites with gilded antiques and door-size windows and marble baths and feather beds and long-stemmed roses and chocolate croissants and room service forever there to satisfy your every wish, at your door in minutes with endless wine and coq au vin and all kinds of pâté and stuff. And everything comes hidden under enormous silver domes and Clive doesn't think anything about all of that because for him this is just his normal abnormal life.

But I am constantly like, "I can't believe this, I can't believe this," which he thinks is funny, but finally one day he stops laughing and looks at me seriously and shakes his head.

"Yes, but, Gia, all this isn't what makes you happy, you know?"

"Maybe not, but it doesn't make you unhappy either, you know?"

"You'll see" is all he says, looking back at me.

In between going to boutiques and perfume stores and looking at shoes and dresses and hats and T-shirts and underwear and taking pictures of everything that I love because the article will be mostly a collage of cool pictures of out-there fashion that I love, we go low end and visit cheapie department stores, which are Europe's answer to Target and Forever 21, then to flea markets like Les Puces de Saint-Ouen in Paris and Porta Portese in Rome and the Portobello Market in London. And I buy things off tables, like beaded necklaces and lacy thongs for less than five dollars and we bargain because you're supposed to and take care with our wallets because of pickpockets.

Clive is watching all this and we're goofing on people and his parents. We stop for onion soup in a little café and it arrives all steamy and smells like heaven and has a thick glob of Swiss or whatever cheese melted all crisp over the top. I just about faint because it's so delicious and then I have to go to the bathroom only there really isn't one, it's just a hole in the ground that I have to squat over and I tell Clive and he laughs.

"I forgot to tell you about the ancient bathrooms."

It's a trip to see plumbing from the seventeenth century, especially when you're in completely new surroundings with someone who's your best friend, not counting Ro.

At night after walking our feet off all day long we usually go out to dinner by ourselves or with Claude and Alice and then sometimes they go upstairs to bed and we sneak out and go walking by the Seine.

"That's where you see all of humanity," Clive says.

We watch lovers and homeless people and pickpockets and mangy stray cats and homeless dogs and take pictures without letting anyone know we're taking their pictures, but then we get totally exhausted too and go to sleep at two a.m. and wake up when the sun shines inside the room through the enormous windows that look out on what seems like a panoramic painting in the Metropolitan Museum of Art.

Only it's not.

It's a living canvas. It's a sweeping view of slanty Paris rooftops and the church of Sacré-Coeur high, high up in the distance as if it's tucked away where it's safe and close to heaven and it's all so fairy tale enchanting that I can't stop taking pictures and want to cry because when things are so perfect it almost hurts to look at them and you want to inhale everything and hold it inside you.

My phone doesn't work here, which is just as well because I needed a break from my Michael obsessiveness, and anyway, maybe it will help both of us to be an ocean apart.

For our last few days we go to Milan and after visiting the Duomo and walking on the roof and gasping at the view, we go to a department store called La Rinascente.

"Go up to the bathroom," Clive says.

"Do you think I'm three and don't know if I have to go?"

He grins. "No, Gia, that's not what I meant. Go up to the bathroom and look out the window."

"What for?"

"Just go."

I take the escalator up and find the bathroom and go in and look out the window. And freeze. I'm staring at a painting in a museum, I think at first. Only it's not. It's the real world and it's the Duomo right there, framed by the window like a painting and lit by the golden afternoon sun, and it's the most beautiful, spiritual sight I've ever seen, so I tear up again, which is crazy.

Then I start thinking about other beautiful things like my dad and our family and how I'm missing them and what I feel for Michael and about this whole extraordinary trip, so I go outside and find Clive and look at him with my misty eyes.

"It was…overwhelming."

"I knew you'd feel that way, Gia," Clive says, hugging me. "That's why I love you."

Because everything is so perfect, I can't leave it alone and I have to make it unperfect. Enter Michael again and I start to wonder how this whole trip would be if I were with him, but not just the sex thing, which we would obviously be doing like ten times a day, but everything else—like getting blown away by the risotto and the veal cotoletta and walking on the narrow, winding cobblestone streets and cursing at the insane drivers and finding perfect little boutiques with shoes in colors you didn't know existed and freaking out about the palazzos with their glossy painted doors and the paintings in the museums and the people and what everyone is wearing.

I wonder if he'd get into it as much as I do and think about changing his life and staying here forever and escaping from crime and everything ugly from back home. But how can I answer those questions because I don't know Michael, at least not yet. And who knows if that is ever going to change because he's so impossible to get close to because of his emotional body armor. And maybe he can't escape either because it's been a part of him for so long.

For no reason I think of the mystery about Michael's dad who was a cop too and the stuff that Clive couldn't find out and wonder about how that could affect who he is and what he thinks. And when we get back and have our computers again, I'll ask Clive and see if he can hack into his dad's network again and get behind the firewall.

We leave behind the magical thinking and the fantasy world we explored when we land back in New York and head for the limo waiting for us at the airport. The driver takes our bags, including the twelve new ones with all the stuff we bought, and fits them all into the trunk. While we're waiting for Clive's dad, the driver lifts his newspaper and I glance up and in a nanosecond my world implodes.

On the cover of the *Post*, there's a picture of Frankie with a one-word headline: *Squealer.*

THIRTY-FOUR

"ANTHONY," I scream as I walk through our front door, before I even drop my suitcase. "Anthony!"

Then even louder, "Anthony!!"

He runs out of his room and looks at me.

"What's going on?" I say, waving the paper in the air. Very slowly he comes down the stairs and looks at me with the darkest, angriest expression I have ever seen on his face.

"Frankie turned."

"I found that out on the front page, Anthony. Why didn't anyone call me? Did you forget you have a sister?"

He doesn't answer.

"Anthony!"

"It just happened. We didn't want you to freak."

Frankie has worked for my dad for as long as I can remember. The feds were after him, everyone knew that, but we thought of him as family. He'd been taking me to school for years and he was at every family dinner on every holiday. Now, after he nearly died at our dinner table and he's back on his feet after we paid for thousands of dollars for nursing care, he turns?

"Why?"

"Why? To save his ass. They were close to putting him away for life on ten different charges, that's why. And the feds had tapes where dad was mad and said shit about him and what a dick he was. And they played those for him and it must have convinced him."

I watch him clenching his jaw. "What are we going to do now?"

"Who the fuck knows."

"But Super Mario is on it, right?"

"What do you think, Gia?"

I drag my bags up to my room and instead of a homecoming, it feels like a wake. My mom is at the church, probably afraid to leave, and my dad is out somewhere hunched down with his associates, and stupid me actually thought it might be possible to escape for an entire three weeks without family stuff flying in my face.

I now know for sure that my head is screwed on wrong and that I live in a dream world.

THIRTY-FIVE

I'm still on European time and jet lagged, and I'm walking down the corridor passing the bulletin board. I casually turn my head and—whoa—see my name, and for a few seconds I can't figure out why because there's this disconnect.

I'm *president.*

What? Me? The little guidette? Do they really want me?

"*Gia,*" Clive says, running up to me, putting his arms around me. "You did it."

Then other kids are congratulating me, and I'm saying thank you and thank you and thank you and getting the thumbs up, but my head is now thinking of my dad and how this is really for him because of how proud it will make him to know that I won. And how this is what he wants for me, because in his eyes it means achievement and respectability and success. And right now he needs any good news because it is in desperately short supply in our world.

But this is a new direction for my head. Am I up for this now? Can I do the job? Do I really have something to offer the Morgan School?

During the vacation they finally recounted the votes and the sign is up and I have really friggin' *won.* Clive and Ro and Candy are applauding and going crazy while I'm trying to process this, and all I know for sure is that from now on, I'm going to be looked at differently. For better or worse.

Even Jordan comes up to me and says in a really serious, decent, TV announcer kind of voice:

"Congratulations, Gia, and I mean that. I think you'll be a great president."

That kind of throws me, but I smile back at him. "I hope you'll be willing to help me," which is the kind of bullshit things that presidents say, I imagine, and he nods gravely.

"Anytime, Gia," he says with a warm smile. "Anything you need."

This is all too warm and fuzzy and I should shut up because—hold it—does Jordan actually like me? I don't dwell on that thought for long because then Georgina comes by and looks at the sign, her eyes widening in horror, and right behind her is Brandy Tewl.

"I don't believe this," Brandy says. "I don't, not after *I* won, not *her*."

They give me a dirty look and storm off.

Clive is leaning against the wall taking this all in and shooting me these amused looks, but best of all is when Wentworth comes by and looks up at the sign and then glances back at me with this suckworthy, patronizing smile.

"I guess I better watch my back now, right, Mafia Girl?" he says, "because, I mean, I know you must be watching yours all the time."

As I'm fantasizing about the joy I'd get smacking Wentworth's head, Clive must be having similar revenge fantasies because he sneaks up behind Wentworth and shoves the sharp corner of his math book between his shoulders

"Hands up, fucker!" he yells. Wentworth nearly jumps a foot off the ground and we all start laughing at him until he slinks away. Even though I feel like a suck up, I go to the newspaper office and ask them if I can write a few paragraphs about how I'm going to keep my campaign promises about the fund-raising, the tickets, and especially the scholarships. I'll also ask for volunteers to help me even though in truth I feel like barfing when I think of working with some of the people in this school. But when I tell Clive that, he just laughs.

"Gia, you really don't have to worry about that because it's not like people here are going to be lining up to volunteer unless they think it will help their applications to Harvard."

And as usual Clive is right.

I get the note from Mr. Wright when I'm in bio.

Please see me at three.

When the bell rings, I head for the office. There's no one at the secretary's desk, so I walk in and knock on Mr. Wright's door. He looks up and waves me in. Sitting in the office is Domingo, the cafeteria worker. What?

"I thought I owed you an explanation, Gia," Mr. Wright says. "Mr. Caruso found the evidence."

"What evidence?"

"The votes," Domingo says.

He opens the shopping bag that's next to him and takes out a stack of folded pieces of paper. Only they're not just pieces of paper, they're ballots.

"Where did you find those?" I ask.

"In the garbage," he says.

I feel a lump in my throat. "Thank you, Domingo. Thank you very much.

"But why did you take them? How did you know?"

"Someone was trying to hurt you, right, Miss Gia?"

I nod.

"We appreciate it, Mr. Caruso. Thank you," Mr. Wright says. "You can go home now."

But Domingo doesn't move. He looks at me dead on. "You're different, Miss Gia. You always throw away the garbage, even if it's not your garbage."

And then I realize that he may be one of the smartest people in the school.

After school the next day, Clive and Ro and Candy and I head to Central Park. It's one of those extraordinary days when you're convinced it's due to global warming because on January 5, how can it be sixty? We all take off our down jackets and walk around in sweaters, and like a six-year-old, I'm excited about going to the park and fooling around and then getting hot chocolate and hanging out at Clive's to do homework. We walk toward Fifth Avenue, but when I look up, I see someone I don't expect to see. He's standing in front of his red Jag. I stop for just a minute and stare.

"Gia," he calls, even though he knows I see him.

Anthony.

In all the years I've been in school, my brother has never waited outside for me. Not only that, he's wearing a suit and a white shirt and tie, which he doesn't do unless there's a wedding or a funeral, so I freak and think, uh-oh, has Frankie died? Did my mom send my brother to drive me straight to the funeral home? Then I think no, I'm in jeans today and my mom saw me and there's no way I could go in this so I'd have to go home first, and no, that's not why Anthony is here, which brings me to think about other things.

"Anthony."

"Wanna get some lunch?"

"I had lunch three hours ago."

"So dinner, whatever," he says. "Get in, c'mon."

I say good-bye to Clive and Ro and Candy and kinda shrug when they look at me like, *what's going on?* because I have no idea. So I get in the car and he pulls out.

Anthony's car has white leather upholstery and even though his room is always a pigsty, his car is immaculate, which I can't exactly figure. He keeps it parked outside the house and every few days he washes and waxes it himself. Even the white wall tires never have a speck of dirt on them. Once I actually saw him scrubbing a little dirt spot off the white leather seat with saddle soap and a toothbrush. I kind of stopped in my tracks because where did that come from?

The only annoying thing in the car is the cheapo cardboard deodorant tree hanging from the rearview mirror that reeks of artificial pine.

"Why do you have that shitty thing hanging there?"

"For the good smell."

"Like a good cheap taxi smell?" It must be the word cheap because he rips it off the mirror, opens the window and throws it out.

"Okay?"

I look at him weird. "Yeah, but I didn't mean you had to throw it out immediately."

He shrugs and keeps driving. We approach a red light and Anthony starts honking at the guy in front of us who slows down because he thinks the guy could have easily made it through the yellow.

"A-hole," he says.

"A woman started crossing with a stroller. What do you want him to do, mow her down?"

He looks at me and doesn't say anything. "What are you in the mood for?"

Actually nothing since I'm not hungry and it was his idea to eat, not mine. "Whatever."

"Want to go to Rao's?"

"Are they serving now?"

"For me they are."

"Okay, whatever."

He heads uptown and I just sit there because I really don't have a huge number of topics I feel like discussing with my brother. I notice that he's wearing the cuff links I bought him in Rome. I point to his cuff. "You like them?"

"Fuckin' A," he says. "They're gorgeous."

"Does Dad like his?"

He glances over at me. "He's wearing them today. He loves 'em."

The cuff links are gold, almost like the beans Elsa Peretti makes for Tiffany, only these have a few tiny rubies on the side, which upgrades the whole look, I thought. The pair for my dad has a few more rubies and some tiny diamonds too. And for my mom I bought an eighteen-karat gold cross with tiny emeralds because she loves crosses and owns more of them than the Vatican. And every day, no matter where she's going, she wears every single one, a total of about twenty, in different sizes and shapes, in case someone may not realize she's a serious Catholic.

When we get to Rao's, Anthony manages to find a spot close to the restaurant windows so he can keep an eye on the car. We go in and it's pretty empty at that hour and they give him a huge greeting like he's made their day. I've totally lost my appetite, but I'm not going to sit at Rao's and not eat, so I order a seafood salad and so does Anthony, but he also wants meatballs and ziti. We eat and Anthony looks like he's in heaven, which always happens when he eats, which is why he's about twenty-five pounds overweight. But I don't go there because when you're chowing down at Rao's, you don't exactly want to hear a lecture about how fat you are.

"Where's Mom?"

He looks at me. "Home."

"Oh." I pick up another forkful.

As usual, Anthony manages to drop some seafood salad on his shirt and he goes "shit," and the waiter runs over with a cloth napkin and a bottle of club soda, and Anthony says thanks and does a lousy job of trying to get it out, and what he's left with is an oil stain with an enormous wet spot around it like a bull's-eye. But based on his skills with his car, I'm sure he'll rise to the challenge when he gets home.

"How's school?"

"Okay." I kind of look at him strangely because Anthony always hated school and never ever talked about it. After high school that was it for him and he never mentioned it again.

"You're like the president?"

"Not 'like,' I am the president."

"Cool. So what do you do, make the rules?"

"Yeah, I decide totally everything." I shake my head because my brother is obviously a bigger moron than I thought. "It's not exactly a job that comes with total power," I say to disabuse him because he must be thinking that I'm like Castro was over Cuba or something. "It basically means I get to do the stupid volunteer stuff that no one else really wants to do anyway."

He nods and that kind of ends the conversation about the school and being president and I look up and—whoa—see one of the girls who was at the photo shoot with me at *Vogue*. It's Bridget, the daughter of Jade Just, the designer. This time she's wearing this over-the-top black cashmere sweater dress that looks like someone took a knife and arbitrarily made some significant slits in it so that it's clear she's got on a royal blue satin bra and a matching thong, plus these extraordinary over-the-knee suede boots in a dark eggplant color. We make small talk for a minute or two as she stands at the table.

"Are you alone?" I say finally. "Do you want to sit with us?"

"No thanks, it's fine," she says. A second later John Plesaurus walks in.

I guess Bridget Just has an extraordinary body too and maybe she's fine with having a *Vogue* photographer take porno pictures of her just for his personal viewing pleasure or whatever, because John Plesaurus is obviously not only a great fashion photographer but also a deviant child molester. So I smile at him and then turn back to Anthony, who, a second later, asks too loud, "who the fuck is that?"

I roll my eyes. "The guy who shoots for *Vogue*.

Anthony looks at me confused.

"He's their favorite photographer."

"Oh, from those pictures?"

"Yes, from those pictures."

After that I make a point of not looking up and watching them and I'm getting antsy about sitting there because all I'm wondering is whether this meal is before or after for them. And my mind is going places it has no business going because what do I care what she does? I'm wishing that Anthony would just hurry up and finish the stupid meatballs or take them home or whatever. Finally he cleans his plate and signals for the waiter to come over because I know he wants dessert.

"I have a ton of homework, can we just go?"

"Never mind," he says to the waiter, "just the check." He pays and we go outside and get into the car and I'm watching him and waiting and he starts the car and finally I can't stand it anymore.

"Anthony, what the fuck is going on?"

He looks at me and bites his lip, staring off into the distance. An eternity later, he turns back to me. "The jury came in," he says, so low I can barely hear him.

Neither of us says anything and I stop breathing.

"Dad's not coming home anymore, Gia," he blurts out finally. "This is it."

Then I see something I rarely see. My brother is crying.

I sit there looking at him, getting more worked up than I would have if I just went home and found out or read it in the papers, because someone put him up to this lunch and I know it wasn't my mom or my dad.

"What does Super Mario say?" The words come out in a rush. "He's on it, right?"

Anthony doesn't answer.

"Anthony…what does he say?"

"He says we're fucked."

"What? What do you mean?"

"Gia…you don't know how much they have against him this time."

"Like what?"

"Like wire taps and all the Frankie shit."

"But Dad's gotten off before. He always does, no matter what."

"That was before," he says, staring off like he's lost.

I wait for him to go on but he looks back at me, his eyes scared and empty and he shakes his head as he starts to sob.

THIRTY-SIX

Clive must have been watching the TV. "Come over, Gia," he says. "Stay here with me."

"I can't leave my mom. She's a wreck."

There's silence on the phone. What can he say? "I'll be here if you need anything. Anything, Gia."

"I love you, Clive."

"I love you more, Gia."

Ro and her parents come over, and then Anthony's friends, sending my mom into desperate, total despair cook mode, working too fast and preparing everything in her entire Italian repertory and it's like a wake where you try to act like you're there to pay your respects, only my dad is alive, even though, despite appeals and appeals and appeals, I don't know if I'll ever see him again without a partition between us.

And that morbid scenario makes me feel needy and crazy and abandoned and weepy and loveless, and I start to obsess about being alone and lost and think of Michael, who I haven't seen since I got back, and all my crazy, screwed-up feelings make me cry because— oh God—my dad just got put away, so why the hell am I thinking about being with someone in law enforcement, you know?

I'm not sure if it's the headlines on the five and six and ten and eleven o'clock news that night or the fact that I disappeared in Europe for three weeks and have not spoken to him in, what, a month? Something telepathic must be going on between us because at two in the morning my phone rings.

"Hey," I say.

"Gia."

"How are you, Michael?"

"How are you?" he says, like with everything going on.

"Crappy."

"I know."

Silence, the painful silence that's always there and feels like he's on one side of the continent and I'm on the other.

"You were away," he says, more like a statement than a question.

"Yeah."

"Where?"

"Rome, Milan, Paris, London."

"Right."

"I'm not kidding."

"How come?"

I tell him about Clive and his parents and the magazine and he listens and listens.

"You have some life."

"Yeah."

"I want to see you," I blurt out. *Yeah, I want to see you too*, I wait to hear. But no, not Michael.

"Tomorrow," he says. "I'll wait for you after school."

"And then go to work after five minutes."

Exhale. "Not five minutes, I need to see you too."

I'm on my way into the kitchen when I hear my brother talking to my mom in a tone that puts me on alert. I stop outside the door and listen.

"All our assets," he says, "they're seizing all our assets."

"Everything?"

"We'll have to sell the house and maybe move into Grandma's apartment, and we'll keep some money to live on…but they get everything else…everything."

It feels suddenly like the whole world is crashing down around us. Not only have they taken my dad away, they are punishing all of us for being in the same family.

"Everything," she says over and over. "Everything we have after a lifetime."

Suddenly I'm filled with anger and I burst in. "Mom, my God, didn't you know? Didn't you know that one day this would happen?"

She holds out her hands. "You don't think about that. You can't," she says, "or you can't go on."

"But why didn't you ever try to stop him? Why did you accept everything? All the shit he was into." I'm feeling a rage at my mom that I never knew I had inside me.

"You have to accept everything with a man like your father," she says. "There's no other way. I talked to him, I did what I could, but he lived the way he lived." She shakes her head. "So I committed a crime. I loved him," she says. "I loved him no matter what. And now this is what I get, this is how they punish us."

"But you didn't—"

"Stop, Gia!" Anthony yells. "Don't blame her. Leave her alone. It's not her fault."

"I can't stop. Look at what's going to happen to us now."

"Fuck the feds," Anthony says. "They're not going to stop us."

"Dad said that too, Anthony, and look what happened to him. Do you want to end up in the next cell?"

"Don't talk like that, stop it," my mom yells. "Stop the fighting. I don't want this. We're a family."

"We *were* a family," I say. Then I run up the stairs to my room.

I don't know when it dawns on me that everything they'll be taking from us will include the money for my school. Instead of Morgan, I'll end up at some low-end neighborhood school with forty kids in a class instead of twelve and teachers who are too burned out to care whether we learn anything. It's almost a laugh to think of the fight I went through to become president of the Morgan School. Now Wentworth, Brandy, and Georgina will have the last laugh. Their prayers will be answered and the don's daughter will get what she deserves. In September, I'll be gone. The job at the bakery will stop being a joke. We'll need the money now.

It may be that Clive wants to distract me from everything or he just doesn't know what else to do, but at lunch he starts talking about the school fund-raiser called Celebrate and about volunteering to help and me helping him to get my mind off my life, which is useless. So I say yes because it's easier than saying no.

And then I'm getting crazy about how I'm feeling about my dad and for the first time how final it feels and how alone I am now, and I think about my grandma's funeral and how he looked after he came home, like someone cut out his heart.

I feel that way too now. I get what he went through and there's nothing you can do about the hurt. Maybe it's my imagination, but it seems like everyone at school is looking at me and then turning away when I catch them.

It doesn't help that the TV news did a report on how our family's assets were being seized with pictures of our townhouse, my dad's Mercedes, the Cadillac, even a shot of my mom taken years ago in a sable coat that she doesn't even own anymore because she donated it to charity.

Candy stops me by my locker and touches my shoulder. "I…I just feel so bad for you."

"Thanks, Candy."

She stands there staring at me, hesitating.

"What?"

She glances around then steps closer. "I never told anyone here this, Gia, but the reason we moved to New York"—she stops and looks lost in thought and then turns back to me—"was because my dad got convicted of tax evasion and he was sent to prison." Tears fill her eyes. "It was embarrassing for everyone, so we moved here, where no would know us."

"Candy, I'm sorry." I am. She looks so victimized, so hurt. I look at her expression. It was hard for her to say that. She did it to try to help me not feel so alone. Everything I thought about her world in LA and the movies was wrong.

"I wanted you to know…because I know what it feels like, in a way. So if you ever want to talk…"

I feel a lump in my throat. "Thanks."

"I think you're stronger than I am, Gia. And surer of yourself. I think you'll be okay. I really believe that."

Me? "Feeling sorry for yourself doesn't help," I say.

Then Brandy and Christy come down the hall, and I cross my arms over my chest, stand taller, and start walking.

Ro catches up with me in the hallway.

I pull her over to the side. "Did you see the TV last night?"

"I'm so sorry, Gia."

"We'll have to move."

"Where?"

"My grandma's apartment. It's small, but it's decent. It's a few blocks from my house. Everything will be different, Ro."

"But you'll get through it, Gia. You're strong. "

"Everybody thinks that. What do they know?"

"They can take your money, but not who you are inside, Gia. Your belief in yourself, everything that your dad gave you, they can't seize that."

"When did you get so fucking sure of everything?"

She smirks. "When you survived the bakery. I saw what you were made of."

We meet Clive in the dining hall, and after we get our food, we sit down together at our usual table.

"I heard that there's a van outside from CNN," Ro says. "Someone heard that the reporter is going to wait until you come out at three o'clock to get a comment or whatever."

"Oh good, I'll tell them how terrific it feels to see your dad put away for life."

No one says anything and everyone kind of stares down at the table.

"If they're really out there, Gia," Clive says finally, "I'm going to go into the office and have the school call the police to ask them to get the van off school property because it must be harassment or something."

I'm not sure he's right, but since I'm a minor, that sounds reasonable and why not try to chase them away if we can.

I can't help thinking that yeah, in fact, the cops will be here after school because I'm meeting Michael, which is humorous in a dark way, so at the end of lunch everyone goes off to class and I stop at the bathroom.

A moment after I sit down, I'm hit by the nauseating scent that Christy shrouds herself in, which means she probably followed me in along with her joined-at-the-hip friend Georgina, who comes in next because they even pee in tandem.

It's awfully quiet, which makes me wonder because the two of them are incapable of *not* talking. I wait and then think *screw this* and go out of the stall and I'm face-to-face with them.

Christy looks at Georgina and Georgina looks at Christy and they both smile these little, smug, full-of-themselves smiles. For no reason, I hold my hand up to them like it's a gun.

"BANG, BANG, BANG!" I shout.

They look at each other and run from the bathroom.

For the first time in a week my mouth curls up into a smile.

THIRTY-SEVEN

Bio seems to last for hours instead of forty-five minutes and I'm getting a migraine. So when Klosky, the bio prof, is rambling on about proteins being made from polypeptides and that amino acids are the building blocks of polypeptides and that the RNA made from transcription is used as a template that determines the sequence of the amino acids in a polypeptide, I get that woozy, low-blood sugar, hazy brain fog and the sounds all come together in my head as white-sound soup. And anyway it's warm in the room and my sweater is too thick and everything is putting me to sleep.

But fortunately there is a merciful God and Klosky doesn't call on me. When I look up at the clock and see the class is over, I simultaneously hear and feel a vibration in my bag, which is on my knees, and it feels like the sound is coming from inside me, which freaks me out, and I jump.

It's my phone, I realize. It's a text from Michael. *I'm on NW corner. CNN at main. Avoid.*

Ro was right. I'm glad Michael warned me. I slip out the side entrance and the only ones outside are a group of parents. Michael is standing away from the corner because he has this way of hanging back, which I guess is a cop thing because they learn to watch and wait before they pounce. I should remember that. I go toward him and as usual get weak just looking in his direction. He's wearing a black turtleneck sweater over faded jeans and he looks up and stares at me with those intense, brooding eyes. I rush across to him and want him to crush me in his arms, but he glances anxiously at me.

"Let's get out of here before someone sees you."

Michael puts an arm around my shoulders and leads me down the street, and I don't know where we're going. But if he wants to try walking across the East River, I'm in.

He knows where we're going and it's not the water. We finally stop at a small Euro-type bistro on Madison Avenue. He asks for a table in the back, and since it's three thirty, most of them are empty. Michael faces the door, and I sit with my back to it. I look at him, trying to catch my breath.

"I haven't seen you…in so long," I say.

He sits with his hands tented, covering his mouth. He doesn't answer but he holds my gaze as the electricity fires up between us again. His eyes darken. He feels it too, only he pretends he doesn't and shifts his gaze to the table like it's his safe zone.

"I know," he says.

"What will it be?" the waiter asks, appearing out of nowhere, breaking the mood.

"Coffee with milk," I hear myself say.

"Black," Michael says.

The waiter turns away and we're back to staring at each other again, the air weighted, the silence thick with what's ahead.

"Tell me about your Thanksgiving." I want to break the tension and get him talking normal and everyday and us stuff, not about my dad or the mob or everything ahead for us. "So you went home—to Maryland?"

"Yeah."

"And?"

He looks at me hard as if he's deciding if he even wants to go there, and I'm suddenly getting this sinking feeling that I do not want to be getting, but whatever, I could be wrong. I could be, because sometimes I am, and screw my internal radar.

"My mom's an alcoholic, so the whole Thanksgiving thing is too much for her."

Something personal. It takes me by surprise.

"So you cooked?"

"Yeah," he says with a half smile.

"Are you good?"

"Pretty good, yeah."

"What's your specialty?"

"Chestnut stuffing." Then he inhales sharply and shakes his head, squeezing his eyes shut for a moment. "Why are we talking about this, Gia?" His mouth is set in a hard line.

I draw a deep breath, trying to hide that I need more air. "I don't know, Michael. What should we be talking about?"

"Listen," he says. "I've been thinking…about everything…"

Everything? Here it comes. I can hear the words before he says them and what I want to do is jam my fingers in my ears so I can't hear anything at all, but I don't. Instead I look right back at him like I don't follow.

"So, Thanksgiving, tell me, I want to know about your family." I stare him down to delay *everything* and force him to shut up about *everything* and maybe make him want to forget what he is going to say or at the last minute change his mind altogether or…I, I don't…

"It's fucked up," he says. "I have a brother who's a recovering junkie." He pauses to give that time to sink in.

"I'm sorry."

"I'm sorry too," he says, his jaw tightening.

"So he was there?"

"He's always there. He lives with her. He's not working so he can't afford a place of his own." He looks away. "He lives in the bedroom he grew up in, like when he was six years old." He shakes his head in disgust.

"And your dad, when did he die?"

"He's been…out of the picture for a long time."

"Is your brother…clean now?"

"For now."

"So you're, what, his big brother and you try to take care of him and your mom?"

"Right."

I stare down at the table and think about my family. He has three people and we have three hundred with aunts and uncles and cousins and people that aren't really family but sort of are by now and people and even neighbors around day and night and people calling all the time and…

"You know why I became a cop, Gia?"

"Why?"

"Because I hated the crazy, sick people that my brother got involved with, the ones who ruined his life, and I wanted to bust their asses and lock them up."

"The pushers?"

"The pushers and the people behind them," he says, his face hardening. "You know who they are?"

Before I can say no he glares at me.

"The mob." He waits for that to sink in. "They bring in the shit and distribute it."

It takes me a few seconds to feel the impact, and I wince. I put my cup down so hard that the coffee splatters everywhere.

"So that's what this is about. You're blaming me? It's my fault?"

"I'm not blaming you, Gia. All I'm saying is I can't separate you from them and your dad and the whole picture."

"You don't know me. You don't know my dad, Michael. You just hate us, like everybody else."

"No, I hate the business," Michael says. "The restaurants, the carting, the waste disposal, the gambling, the tax evasion, the payoffs—the payoffs to cops, cops that they squeeze and then they own. Do you understand that? Do you have any idea what goes on?"

"That's not my life."

"That's not what I asked you."

"I don't fucking know, Michael, okay? My dad doesn't sit down with me and go over his business."

He looks back at me like he's deciding whether to believe me. "Maybe you actually don't know," he says, "but I can't *not* see it. I'm not blind and I can't not see how the mob squeezes people and fucks up their lives. To me it's personal."

"Oh, I get it. You see it all and you're not blind—blind like me?"

He stares back at me and just shakes his head.

The write-off, the stereotype. It's who I am to almost everybody and they can't let go of it or see past it. Only why does it continue to surprise me? How could I imagine that he'd be different? He's a cop. He thinks like a cop. It's in his blood. Ro was right.

I didn't choose to be born into my family. I never endorsed what they do, even though most of the time—he's right—maybe I am blind, because I have no idea what the hell they really do, because my dad doesn't exactly come to me for advice, at least not unless he's buying my mom a birthday present.

Now all this pushes my buttons and makes me crazy and depressed and alienated because no matter what the truth is, I'm blamed and guilty by association, and the fury rises up in me. How could I be stupid enough to imagine that this cop would be different and see past that? How could I possibly imagine that he'd want to know me or feel anything for me other than rage?

"If you're going to be a good cop, Michael, maybe you better sharpen your skills a little so you don't lump together the guilty with the innocent—"

"Gia, I'm—"

"And automatically accuse someone who might not be guilty because of your own prejudices and fucking stereotyped way of seeing the world."

He stares at the table and shakes his head then looks up at me. "I've tried. And there's more to it—"

"I don't want to hear more, Michael, because you know what I think? I think you haven't tried at all. You never tried to see me for myself. You never took me out when I just about threw myself at you. You never made any effort to find out who I am. What did you do, kiss me back? Call me in the middle of the night and breathe in the phone? Is that what you call trying?"

"I was—"

"All you do is nurse your grievances and play clean cop and purist and Mister Self-Righteous—"

"Jesus, stop—"

"No, I won't stop," I say, getting angrier by the second. "The world's not black and white. And for whatever it's worth, I'm sorry your brother is a junkie or was a junkie because that sucks. But don't blame me, I didn't do it to him, although maybe it's easier for you to think that so you can trash the don's daughter from your high and mighty place and keep your distance and not give or risk losing something, and you can devote your life to chasing bad guys to make up for the shit your brother got into." I get to my feet and Michael jumps up at the same time.

"Gia," he says, reaching out and grabbing my wrist. "You don't—"

"Don't, Michael." I pull my hand away so hard that my hip slams the table, sending the dishes clanking to the floor and smashing. I run toward the door and he runs after me, grabbing my arm.

"Listen to me, God dammit," he hisses.

"What are you going to do, Michael, arrest me for disorderly conduct?" I say, shaking free of his grip. I reach into my bag and take out a joint and throw it on the floor in front of him. "Here, here's something better, okay? You want to take me in. You'd like that, right? That's your fun. Go ahead, c'mon…"

"Gia," he says through his teeth. "Don't do this—" he says, grabbing my upper arm.

"Let go of me," I say, struggling to pull free. "I hate you." My eyes fill with tears and I shake my head and all I want to do is punch him and punch him, but I pull free and then run out of the restaurant toward the subway where I don't expect to find CNN or New York 1 looking for me anytime soon.

186

THIRTY-EIGHT

I get off the subway in Midtown and walk robotically with no destination. I need to be outside and in motion and the blaring, urgent street sounds are the perfect sound track for my rage.

I replay everything with Michael again and again, feeling helplessness and fury at the same time. The way we met. Where we sat down. I thought he wanted to see me but the only thing on his mind was blaming me for his problems and ending it. But studying that script again and again gets me nowhere, so I keep going, trying to walk until exhaustion edges out rage.

Then I think about my dad and stop. I turn and walk back uptown to the Empire State Building.

I've only been to the office once before, but my feet take me there as if the address is programmed inside me.

I have to see him face-to-face.

In all the years I've known Super Mario the day I remember best is that one day. It was before Christmas when I was very small. Even now though, I remember every moment of that day.

His company was having its office party. My mom dressed me up in a new red velvet dress with a matching coat that she made herself and a hat with white rabbit pom-poms on the ties. I had on red tights that kept riding down and black patent leather ballet flats that were too big so they kept slipping off in the back.

My dad took me up there and showed me the view. I drank eggnog and had cookies shaped like Christmas trees covered with green sugar sprinkles. I felt so grown up that day because my dad let me climb a ladder and help the secretary hang candy canes on the tree. After the tree was decorated, Super Mario handed me a big box wrapped in red paper with gold stars and tied with a gold ribbon. It took me forever to untie the shiny ribbon and tear away all the glittery paper. Finally I opened the top of the big, white box and pulled out an enormous furry white teddy bear with a thick, jeweled bow around its neck.

I remember looking up at Super Mario and seeing his face light up because he was as excited about giving me the bear as I was getting it.

"This is the best present I ever got," I shouted. I still love that bear. He sits in the middle of my bed now leaning against the pillows, almost fourteen years later.

Every other time I saw Super Mario was either at our house when he came to dinner or on the news with microphones from every radio and TV station in his face as he made a statement about how the charges against my father were fabricated, insisting, "my client maintains his innocence and will be vindicated."

Only now Super Mario isn't on the TV or at our house. He's in his office at his desk when I call.

"Gia," he says, surprised it's me. "Yes, come, please. You know I'm always happy to see you."

The office is beautiful like everything Super Mario surrounds himself with, including his blond wife, Ella, and his red-haired comare, who Anthony says is half Super Mario's age.

The waiting area has beige linen couches with brocaded pillows with gold tassels. The walls are lined with dark polished wood bookcases with glass doors and antique brass locks. He bought the bookcases in Venice from an old villa they were renovating, and he had them sent by boat to New York, where a carpenter worked on them for months so that they could fit into the walls of his office like they had been made to go there. They are filled with old books bound in dark red leather with gold writing on the outside.

The woman at the reception desk is blond and young. She has perfect features and large blue eyes. Her full lips are covered with a light layer of pink lip gloss. They must pay her a lot, because I know her jacket is Chanel because of the little gold buttons with the letter *C*. She can't be more than thirty.

"I'm here to see Super Mario," I blurt out like a total idiot.

She hesitates for just a moment and then smiles. "Mario...Della Russo?"

"Yes, sorry," I say with an embarrassed laugh. I can't remember the last time I called him anything but Super Mario.

She's about to pick up the phone, but she hesitates as if she's studying my face. "Are you Gia?" she asks. "Gio's daughter?"

Very slowly a sick feeling spreads through me. *Gio?* No one calls my father that. No one. Only the few people closest to him: my mom, some of his oldest friends. I swallow and then I look at her face. "How did you know?"

Caught. I see it in a flash.

But this sexy broad is smooth. She recovers. "He talks about you whenever he's up here."

Only my father isn't *up here*. Rarely. Super Mario comes to us. That's how it's always been. When they need to talk they go to the apartment near the social club, the one where the old lady lives who's deaf and nearly blind. She lives there rent free.

"Oh...I see." I turn away from her and sit down, grabbing a magazine from the nearest table and opening it over my lap. I stare at it, unable to focus on what's on the page.

My dad's no different from the rest of them. I can't lie to myself anymore. I think about him and this woman together. I imagine them in bed. His face and body over hers. In a hotel. Or her apartment. She looks like she could live on Park Avenue. Maybe my dad even pays her rent or buys her designer clothes. I feel nauseous. Is there anything worse than imagining your dad or mom with someone else?

I can't bear to think of how it would hurt my mom. Unless she knows. Unless somehow she's made peace with that after all these years because it's part of the package and by now my mom is a pro when it comes to denial. Then I have another thought. This woman probably isn't the first. There have been others before her.

Seconds go by. Maybe minutes or more. I glance up and see Super Mario looking down at me, studying me. I jump. "You scared me."

"I'm sorry, Gia."

He glances at the magazine in my lap, which I now realize is open to an ad for weed killer. He doesn't say anything.

"Come," he says softly, reaching for my hand.

I follow him down a carpeted hallway to his corner office with a panoramic view of downtown Manhattan and the glistening Hudson River that's the same steely blue as some of the buildings surrounding it. I stare at an ocean liner with a brick red smokestack and wonder where it's been or where it's headed and think about how it would feel to pack up and sail far away, but not just on a vacation, to start another life someplace where no one would know me or anything about my family. A place where I could just be me without the baggage.

"I remember the last time you were here," he says, smiling. He holds out his hand so that it's about three feet from the floor. "You were this big, eh?"

"I remember it too...and the teddy bear you gave me with the beautiful jeweled collar. I still have him."

"Beppo," we say together and then laugh.

Mario and I look at each other and our eyes change at the very same moment. He motions for me to sit in the chair opposite his desk, but instead of sitting behind the desk, he comes around and sits in the one next to mine. We're so close our knees nearly touch.

"Gia," he says softly, reaching over and putting his hand on top of mine for a moment. His fingers are long, his hand large and warm. Everything about him has always been comforting to me. Being in his presence is like entering a safe harbor.

This is the only time I can ever remember when he seems lost for words, and a sense of dread creeps up my spine. He exhales a heavy, resigned breath.

"There must be something you can do for him, Mario, something."

He leans forward, resting his elbows on his legs, and drops his head between his hands for a few seconds, staring at the floor before looking up at me.

"Gia...you know I would give my life for him if it would help." He shakes his head helplessly.

"But you always get him out, Mario, no matter what."

"But now..." he whispers.

"What?"

He shakes his head. "They have so much, Gia, so much more against him."

"So?"

"Gia..." he says almost pleadingly.

"What?"

"Gia, it's Frankie."

"Can't you say he's lying?"

He shakes his head. "It's different now," he says, so low I can barely hear him.

"Try Mario, please? There has to be something."

"Whatever there is to do, Gia, I will do it. You know that." He reaches out and squeezes my hand. "You have my word."

I look back at him and see something I've never seen in his eyes before. Defeat. I'm about to leave and then I stop.

"Mario..."

He looks up at me.

"Did he ever try to get out of the life?"

He narrows his eyes and shakes his head. "It's not something he could escape."

"And Anthony?"

He holds his hands out helplessly. "Maybe there's still time. But you," he says. "You'll be different."

I nod my head. Somehow he knows.

I stand and toss my backpack over my shoulder and then walk toward the door, but I turn back to him. "One last thing."

"Anything, Gia."

I think of the receptionist. I can't help it. "The girl who sits..." But then I catch myself. I see him glance at the door. He won't tell me. He'll never admit it. What was I thinking? "Nothing. It's nothing. Forget it."

THIRTY-NINE

The fund-raiser. Is there anything in the world I feel like doing less now than celebrating? But tomorrow is the night and pretending is something I'm good at. At the very least, I try to focus on some of the good things in my life because you're supposed to count your blessings and be thankful, the church says.

So there's my mom and my brother and Ro and Clive and Candy and Clive's parents because of the article, then there's the *Vogue* story coming out, although that could go either way, depending on how everyone sees it, and then yes, I am in a decent school, at least until the end of the semester, so I feel a little better and work on putting something on my face resembling a smile.

Beyond the bogus smile there's the issue of clothes, so out comes the backless dress again even though I know what I'm opening myself up to because there are more than a few people in my school who have no taste whatsoever and they wouldn't recognize a couture dress if Armani came in with it on his own back, so all they'll immediately say is OMG, Gia is such a total slut, yada, yada, yada.

But anyway I call Clive and since this is a black-tie gala, he's in the middle of getting dressed.

"This feels totally strange," he says.

I start to wonder about his neck although I'd never just come out and ask, but I'm thinking that he can't possibly wear that ratty navy cashmere scarf with a black tux, can he? I'm super curious to see how he'll handle that, and I ask him if he wants me to come over and help him get ready and put in his studs or do his bow tie or whatever.

"No, it's fine. I'll meet you there."

As I'm about to hang up I hear, "Wait, Gia. I wanted to tell you yesterday. I found out something about Michael—"

"Don't tell me, I don't care anymore."

"But it's—"

"Clive. Promise me something."

"What?"

"That you'll never mention his name again to me."

"You don't want to even—?"

"It's over. He's history."

"But I—"

"Clive, please?"

"You're sure?"

"Positive."

As I get ready, my mind briefly flicks back to Michael and the restaurant and the blame and, yes, it is so over because we're at opposite ends of the world and screw his secrets or whatever because he blames me for everything. And now I'm convinced what I should celebrate is ending things with him. I put him out of my mind and blow out my hair and then run downstairs and get in the car because Vinnie is driving me to the restaurant, which is this really classy place.

When Morgan does things, they go over the top. One of the groups being celebrated is the Botanical Gardens and their people are bringing in to-die-for orchids in rich purple and the faintest shades of celadon and yellow, and even some in black. A major league florist was invited to decorate the restaurant so he's hanging plant vines everywhere and the place is turning into more of a tropical environment rather than just a pricey Asian restaurant called Asian Fusion Odyssey.

The work of the Humane Society is also being celebrated, and their people are there with brochures and freebies like refrigerator magnets with pug faces and what have you, but then I see them bringing in cages with dogs for adoption, and I wonder who approved that. But whatever, because I love dogs, and I hope that the rest of the school does too and doesn't go ape shit and say things like, "I mean, I personally love dogs but what if someone is allergic? Or what if one of them bites someone and we get sued?"

I'm walking around looking at everything and then I stop dead in place. "Clive Laurent, oh my God!" I scream at the top of my lungs because he looks so totally adorable.

"Gia, what is it?" he says, rushing up to me. "You're scaring me to death."

He's even had his hair cut so it's layered perfectly, and he's wearing this black tuxedo with a black shirt under it, and instead of the ratty blue scarf, a beautiful, long, red silk scarf is knotted around his neck and it looks so opulent and extraordinary that I kiss him on the lips, and he laughs.

Clive and I walk around eyeballing everything, and there's just one area where there's no display.

"I wonder what they're going to put in that space," I say.

"Who knows," he says, taking my arm and leading me in the other direction.

Then Ro arrives. I really don't get to see her dressed up that often except at weddings. She's wearing an extraordinary navy blue dress with an oversized bow across the bodice and I'm guessing that it's Prada off the truck or something that could pass for Prada. Her long dark hair has been blown out and looks fabulous. She says that Dante is coming too, which I guess is cool because he's such a douche that I usually have a good time with him.

Celebrate is feeling like prom with everyone in black tie. Candy, who is a clotheshorse like me, is wearing a dress she bought from a second-hand store in LA where the stars dump their gowns after the Oscars.

"I have no idea who wore this," she says. "All they told me was that it was someone who was nominated."

It's a pale yellow gauzy gown by Valentino that's super simple, and with her long blond hair, Candy looks like she could be at the *Vanity Fair* after-party.

Ro and I and Clive and Candy make the rounds when two guys carry in a giant rectangular box that someone said is a cake, but you can't see it because it's inside. They finally get a table with a tablecloth and put the box on top of it.

"Just leave it inside for now," Clive says.

"So you do know," I say and look at him funny.

He doesn't answer or maybe didn't hear me, and we walk off.

To me, the highlight of the event is the dogs from the Humane Society. There are six cages with seven dogs. Just looking at the dogs with those sad, sad I've-given-up kind of downcast eyes makes me want to cry because I mean that loveless life and the loneliness...

The first cage has two puppies, probably the easiest to adopt out. The other five are a young beagle, a very alert and wary German shepherd with pointy ears, a senior golden retriever, a skinny black lab, and a graying pit bull named Herbie with a very resigned expression on his face as if he's a poster dog for discrimination against pits and he has thrown in the towel on anything ever changing for him.

Everyone with a beating heart who walks by stops and plays with the dogs.

"I'll adopt this one for sure," says a boy I don't know from school. "My mom loves beagles, so I'm sure it will be okay with her."

He thinks they're going to fling open the cage and let him walk off with the dog.

"Here's an application to take home," a woman from the Humane Society says. "After you fill it out, come back to the shelter with your parents." Then yada, yada, yada, after paying the fee and getting recommendations from people who'll vouch for the family as responsible dog owners, they'll consider letting them take the dog. Then I'm thinking that the lengthy process with all the paperwork is similar to what you have to do to apply to Morgan—without the dog payoff in the end.

The night goes on and we sample all the food like baby back ribs from a barbecue place that started in Austin, Texas, and Asian fusion noodles with bok choy and pea pods with peanut sauce and an over-the-top macaroni and cheese comfort food from Per Se and jumbo shrimp from the Palm and I don't know what else, and then we return to the cake box.

"Yes," Clive says finally. "Open it now." He turns to me. "Gia, I want you to share the first piece with me."

I look at him like, *what?* He doesn't say anything so I stand there with Ro and Candy and Clive while this guy who must have been the baker carefully slices open the box with a long knife. I look at the cake curiously. It looks like a certificate of some kind, only up in the corner is a face. *My* face. And at the top, in chocolate lettering, is the word *scholarship*.

"Clive?"

"My parents have created a scholarship in your name," he says. "This coming year, it goes to you. After that, it goes to girls with strong academics who need financial help and can't afford a school like Morgan."

"I can't accept…"

"Gia," Clive whispers to me, his fingers tightening on my arm, "you can, and you have to, because the scholarship is as much for me as for you. I can't imagine finishing school here without you. *You* are what *I* want to celebrate at our school."

For once in my life, I'm speechless.

After about a thousand pictures of me with almost everyone in the school, my scholarship is literally eaten up.

"We haven't told the school yet," Clive says. "I wanted you to know first."

"You didn't have to do this," I insist. "You don't have to feel sorry for me."

"I don't feel sorry for *you*, Gia" he says. "I felt sorry for *me* at the thought of you leaving. And anyway, you said you'd be there for me," he says. "You gave me your word."

"I did…"

"So?" He holds out his hands.

I wipe away the tears and in a little while the event starts to wind down, but then I see Christy and Georgina, which kills the mood. I feel like spraying them with whipped cream to hide their smug smiles, but they walk away, and five seconds later there's a scream.

Christy's near the pit bull's cage and she's shaking her head yelling, "He bit me! He bit me! He's so aggressive, and I think he has rabies because his mouth is full of foamy saliva."

But then a guy from the Humane Society rushes over and says very deliberately, "No, he does not have rabies, and he has had all his shots. Where did he bite you, young lady?"

"Here," she says, holding out her hand, and he looks and narrows his eyes and keeps looking, and she shrieks, "Are you blind?"

Even though it's barely a scratch, someone says we should call an ambulance and have her taken to the emergency room just in case, which is total manure because she's just trying to ruin things. Not only that, but who is she taking it out on—poor, homeless Herbie who has nothing left to lose? So I hate her even more for that and maybe she should be tested for rabies.

The lights come on after that, destroying whatever is left of the mood, and everyone streams out, and the pace of clean-up quickens, and the dogs get picked up and their cages are loaded onto a van outside, which is totally sad.

"Do you think we should go over to Lenox Hill Hospital just to see how she is?" Clive asks.

"No fucking way," I say because I'd rather go to the shelter and apologize to Herbie. If there's anyone I'm concerned about it's him and what may happen to him now after the bogus bite incident because you know how things can escalate.

FORTY

Something about the downcast expression in Herbie's face starts eating into me. The sadness, the resignation. And, omigod, he's been living in the shelter for months. I can't help thinking of how Clive felt—like there was no one in the world out there for him.

"You can't change the whole world," the man from the Humane Society said. "But you can change the whole world for one dog."

"Anthony," I say, barging into his room. He sits at his computer and ignores me. "There's this dog…"

He still ignores me.

"And not just a dog, but a very sad and pathetic dog."

He still ignores me.

"Anthony, remember how much dad loves dogs? How his face would light up when he looked at one?"

He takes his fingers off the keyboard and turns to face me. "So?"

Anthony picks me up at school the next day and looks at me warily. "Are you sure you know what you're doing?"

"Anthony…"

"What?"

"He has no one in the world and he's sweet and all good and we're going to give him a real life and a happy home outside of that miserable shelter and he's going to help all of us start to…I don't know…open our hearts and feel love again?"

"I don't know…"

"I *do* know Anthony. And Daddy would be proud of us, you know that. He loves dogs. He loves to save dogs. You remember that, don't you?"

Anthony looks away.

"Don't you?"

"Yeah," he says, biting his lip.

"A *pit bull*?" my mom says, stepping back to the couch and grabbing onto the arm. "A *pit bull*?"

"Mom, he's not a pit bull, he's Herbie. And he's ten years old, Mom, which makes him a senior, and he's friendly. Don't stereotype him."

She sits there and watches Herbie, and Herbie watches her back.

"Is he Italian?" my mom asks.

"*What?*"

My mom starts to laugh, then so do I, and so does Anthony, and we're laughing so hysterically that we can't stop, and Herbie's just watching all of us like, *what?* And then I try to remember the last time we all laughed like that and I draw a total blank.

I fill the dog food bowl I bought Herbie with a cup of his senior diet chicken kibble and put it in front of him. He practically inhales the food.

"See, Ma?"

"He's Italian," my mom says. Then she goes over and pats Herbie on the head. "You're a good boy," she says to him. "A good boy."

Herbie looks up at her and licks her hand. A moment later her eyes fill with tears.

FORTY-ONE

With everything going on with the school fraud bullshit and my dad not here and Frankie turning and Michael breaking my heart, my skin starts to get red and itchy and all across my stomach and up my arms I break out with a gross, blistery rash.

"It could be stress," says the derm, studying my skin through a magnifying glass.

I've now met the one person in the world who doesn't know that my dad has been put away for life. She writes me prescriptions for hydrocortisone cream and antihistamine pills and then looks up at me.

"What do you do to relax?"

Relax?

I don't have an answer to that so we talk about exercise, and she tells me that after her mom died she started running and now she's addicted. She's lost over ten pounds and has a tighter body. She says it totally helped her deal with all the shit of being a doctor with the insurance reimbursement mess, never mind that being the mother of a six-year-old makes her nuts.

I guess because I'm listening so hard she tells me that she doesn't sleep with her husband anymore and that they're heading for divorce because he met someone online, and I'm thinking about telling her that she needs a shrink more than I do, but running does sound kind of cool, and after I get into shape I could learn to box, which would be totally out-there.

I pay the twenty dollar co-pay and leave with the prescriptions and at the front desk scoop up about twenty freebie samples of Eucerin cream and Neutrogena SPF 50 and slip them into my purse. Then I realize that the nurse was watching and she shoots me a dirty look.

FORTY-TWO

"I'm going to start running," I tell Ro.

"Gia, people like us are always running."

"I'm tired of it, aren't you?" I say, broadening the subject.

"That's the way it is, Gia."

I don't really accept that, but Ro does. She isn't haunted like I am and doesn't walk around with a black sheep mentality. I only realized that one Christmas when I sent her a card that showed a tree filled with birds that were all looking in one direction.

Except for one of them.

And because my brain is so buzzed I actually didn't even notice that except on some level I guess I did because why else would I have chosen it? She looked at the card and crinkled up her nose, pointing to the odd-ball bird.

"That is so you, Gia."

I try running with Herbie, but he prefers walking or, actually, sitting in his bed in the kitchen where he can watch my mom and get food treats, so I go by myself. But first I go online and look at all these stretchy outfits with great leggings and tops and jackets. Then I close the screen. What am I thinking? I can't buy clothes anymore. I can't buy anything anymore. I put on a pair of running shoes from the back of my closet and walk around my room. It feels funny to have my feet flat on the ground. I go outside and walk/run for about three blocks and realize that I am totally out of shape. I'm seventeen, not seventy, so hello, exactly what is going on with my cardiac situation?

The next day after school I go running again and the next day after that, even though I don't tell anyone about it, because, let's face it, no one exactly sees me as Miss Jockette, and anyway, when you want to get into something like running, suddenly everyone you know has other stuff to do.

So I take the bus up to the track around Central Park, and who do I see but Jordan the Jock, and I really don't know why he's so nice to me these days unless he's relieved that he lost. He's running too and he slows down.

"Hey, Gia. I didn't know that you run."

Does that make me more appealing to him? I don't know what to say because, I mean, do I run?

"I'm starting to get into it," I come up with and then kind of look away. He gets the message that no, I do not want to have him for my new running partner, so he sprints ahead and I'm left behind huffing and puffing, which is pathetic, and wondering whether this is worth it, you know?

But I never give up, so I keep the running thing going for heart health and relaxation or whatever and even try to convince Clive for the eightieth time to come with me, but he very politely says, "hmm, no, I don't think so, Gia," because I think Clive doesn't like to sweat and doesn't care about runner's high and endorphins—whatever they are—and getting into the zone.

Every day I go a little farther and within two weeks I'm going about three miles a day, usually around Central Park. The rash is better even though I think it has nothing to do with the exercise and everything to do with the hydrocortisone cream because if you're more relaxed, you should feel that way, right?

One day I'm running in the park and I decide that instead of going home, I'll go to Clive's and have dinner with him. So I call him up and he says, "cool, we can go out for Japanese," and when I get there, I sit down and drink an entire bottle of water and then try to wash up and make myself look human again, and Clive is changing into another shirt, and I kind of stop dead in place and stare at him.

"Do you ever just think, fuck it, I'm not going to wear a scarf anymore?"

His face turns dark and as serious as it was when he first told me what happened, and my stomach tightens.

"No," he says. And a moment later, "If it were you, Gia, would you just let everyone see the scar?"

That's the kind of question I never asked myself because why would I? I don't know what to say at first and I think about it for a few seconds. "Yes, I would because I don't think you have any reason to hide it and you shouldn't have to because it's part of who you are now."

"Hmm, maybe. I don't know, Gia. I don't know if I can."

I look at him some more and get totally emotional, which I hate. "You know something, Clive?"

"What?"

"I love that scar," I whisper, my voice cracking.

He narrows his eyes and kind of slumps a little as he looks at me like he doesn't understand.

"The scar means that it didn't work. You healed. You're here now, alive, with me, Clive, and that is so, I don't know, life affirming? It's such a symbol of then and now."

Then Clive gets teary-eyed too. "You're right, Gia," he says, nodding. "I never thought about it that way."

Then we curl up together, and I guess Clive is in the mood to open up because he starts talking about his parents, who he never talks about.

"Ten years after I was born, my mom became pregnant," he says. "I guess it was unexpected and it made her happy...so happy." He pauses and looks off in the distance and then turns back to me.

"But a few weeks after birth...my baby sister died of a heart ailment. They had all these doctors come in to the hospital...from all over the world. And still...nobody, nobody could do anything." He stares out the window and shakes his head. "My mom was nearly destroyed by that because she always, always wanted a girl. She was so depressed she was almost institutionalized." He scratches the back of his head.

"And after that she withdrew from me and changed so much. I just couldn't reach her anymore. I felt...I felt like my parents were blaming me for living after the baby died...Then they sold that apartment and bought this one, but that didn't help, and so they started traveling all the time after that...trying to run away, I guess...and leaving me here with a governess while they were starting more magazines everywhere... and I felt like I was being punished."

"Oh my God, I can imagine," I say. That makes me feel horrible and so sorry for Clive even more because you'd think they'd hold on to him even tighter, but people don't always act the way they're supposed to. Then I think about my dad and mom, and even though our lives are not like anyone else's, I know they'd both kill for me, and that means everything and keeps me grounded. I look over at Clive and think back to being in Paris with him and remember that in passing he said something about starting therapy with his parents when they got home, so maybe people can change...

"You know what you said...in Paris...about room service and fancy hotels and everything not making you happy?"

He nods.

"You were right. That's all bullshit. It's all staging. None of that matters."

"Hmm, staging...I would never have thought of it that way," he says, the corners of his mouth turning up.

FORTY-THREE

I go home and pretend I don't see the cartons. There are more of them each day as my mom and Anthony start to pack up the house. I've been putting off packing mine and they lie flat against the wall of my room.

While I can't deal with packing up my life and giving up my room and especially my princess bed, I go to my closet and pull out six pairs of fabulous heels. I carry them into Anthony's room and put them on his desk.

"Time to eBay these."

"I thought you loved—"

"They're shoes, Anthony. Just shoes."

In the middle of finally going through all my stuff the phone rings.

If it isn't enough that Dante has a 911, he is now the owner of a Harley, and I mean how cool is that?

"Wanna go for a test drive?" he asks.

And duh, do you think I'd say anything but yes? Even though my mom is shaking her head and going, "Gia, I don't like motorcycles. You could fall off. You could kill yourself," I'm like, "Ma, Dante loves me, he's going to crawl. He'll be careful. Do you think he wants to kill me?"

I put on jeans and a leather jacket to kind of look the part. And even though I hate helmets, I run over to Ro's and borrow one and put it on even though it flattens my hair. In the meantime Dante is sitting in front of the house waiting impatiently and, like a complete asshole, he keeps revving up the engine over and over, which is totally stupid, but kind of funny. And then Mr. Giancana from across the street comes out and yells, "Keep the noise down, keep the noise down, you stupid kids!" And Dante mutters something under his breath, and then we take off and go up the FDR.

He's getting off on weaving all around the traffic instead of being stuck in it, which is always what happens, even with the 911, which can go from zero to sixty in four-and-a-half seconds, which Dante always reminds us, like it matters in Manhattan, and then he turns around to me and keeps saying, "How cool is this, huh, Gia?" And I'm like, "Yeah, unreal," and hanging on to him and telling him to go faster. Then a cop car goes by so Dante slows down and when it passes he goes faster. A car nearly cuts us off, and Dante curses him out and then cuts him off and gives him the finger, and after about an hour of intense speeding, I say, "I have to go back and do homework."

"C'mon, Gia," he says, "don't be such a killjoy."

He's talking about going upstate, which would take four hours, and asking why we have to get back so soon, and we're having this stupid conversation while he's going like seventy-five. I'm starting to get cold and cranky and I hear a siren and think, oh shit, we're going to get pulled over. And crap, this is not what I need. But no, the cop isn't chasing us, because, thank God, there's someone who's going even faster than we are. And I look at the police car and start to think, could it be Michael? Omigod, what if it is Michael, would he bust us? And how intensely weird would that be?

Only no, it's not Michael, because the cop is some fat, beefy guy with reddish skin, and I am starting to think that I've lost it because New York City has, what, about thirty-five thousand cops, so why is that thought even entering my mind now?

For a fleeting second I think about what Clive found out about Michael. I'm tempted to ask him just to know once and for all what the mystery is all about then decide no, that's stupid and just forget it.

I close my eyes and concentrate on the wind blowing my hair and I pretend I'm sitting on the wing of an airplane as it flies through the open sky carrying me to a different life.

FORTY-FOUR

Dante heads downtown. We stop at a red light and in the next lane there's a bus and I look up and see a huge ad for *Vogue* and I realize that this is the new issue, and no, I'm not on the cover and was never supposed to be, but I am inside, at least I think I am.

"Pull over, pull over," I yell. I make him stop at a newsstand and I buy five copies.

I look and look and then there they are, my pictures. For a few seconds I just stare because at first I don't recognize my own face and I need to examine what's on the page in front of me. It feels like one of those tests at the eye doctor's office where they click, click, click, and things either get fuzzier or sharper and you raise your finger when everything is finally 20/20.

First is a full-page picture, the first of a series of portraits of us in a kind of portfolio with the headline: *Underage and Over the Top*. That had to be John Plesaurus's idea, I realize, because he's such a deviant. But whatever, the pictures are killers, and I show them to Dante, who looks and looks and says, "Holy crap, Gia, you look gorgeous."

"We have to go home," I say, so he takes me back, and I call Ro and Clive and Candy and show my mom, and everyone is like, "Gia,

I'm running out right now to buy it." And then I look online, and there it is too. At that moment there are only two people in the world I want to call up and tell.

Only I can't. Which just sucks.

On the way to school the next day, all I keep thinking about is *Vogue* and the pictures and what people are going to say, but when I get inside there is this strange mood in the air and I can't decide if it's me or if something is going on. I wave to Clive and he comes over and whispers in my ear and I realize that no, it's not me, there really is a creepy vibe.

No one is supposed to know but at Morgan nothing stays secret for long, and someone heard someone who overheard someone, and the next thing we find out is that the school paper has a story about it even though the administration didn't want that. But since this is the USA and we do have free speech, they decided they couldn't "curtail the school paper's freedom to tell the truth." So it says that Christy, Georgina, and Brandy have been "asked to leave"— otherwise known as being suspended—for an indefinite amount of time for "misconduct."

Bottom line: They stole the ballots. And removed enough votes.

To make. Me. Lose.

Only why did they confess? I talk to Clive and Ro and Candy who spoke to other people who spoke to other people who saw stuff on Facebook, and the story is that Mr. Wright interviewed each of them separately and must have turned the heat up and brought in their parents and—bingo—Christy started crying and admitted everything.

After school Clive and Ro and I talk about celebrating but then think how lowbrow is that, so we hang out without exactly drinking Dom and reflect on the depths of their depravity or what have you while in our own quiet way we rejoice that they'll be gone, at least until the beginning of the new school year. And from this day forward, Morgan will be a better place—or as Clive says, "a more noble institution."

Ha ha ha.

FORTY-FIVE

I make the mistake of telling Dante that I want to get into boxing, so the next thing I know he's calling me up to come over because he found me gloves and a punching bag, which is already hanging from his basement ceiling like a side of beef in a meat locker.

I immediately start hitting that sucker again and again and it feels so good that I keep on going.

"If you want to kill your hands, Gia, keep going."

He makes me take off the gloves and he wraps my hands with tape like the pros do, which is probably ridiculous at this point, and then he shows me the moves. "Face the bag with one foot in front and one behind," he says, "and jab with the first two knuckles." He jabs, jabs, jabs, punching straight out, and then so do I and then cross hook with my left hand, and it's like, jab, stun 'em, and cross, hurt 'em, and I get a rhythm going and I'm starting to sweat.

"Okay, Gia, let's take a break and I'll show you the uppercuts," Dante says.

But I'm jabbing, jabbing, jabbing hard and thinking of Wentworth and Christy and Brandy and jabbing, jabbing, jabbing, and cross hooking, and—whoa—this boxing stuff is very, very good for totally getting rid of the stress, and I keep going and going and going and…

"GIA, ARE YOU DEAF? STOP!" Dante yells.

I look at him. And stop. And if that bag was a person, we'd need a priest.

The next day we train again and I'm dancing around the bag keeping my elbows in close to protect myself and learning to uppercut to the rib cage and then do the head-on kicks to the stomach and the side kicks and the roundhouse kicks and finally the kicks from the back of the body that you save for when you want to seriously do damage like break ribs, and then two hours or so have gone by.

"You wanna go out for dinner?" Dante asks.

I catch my breath and realize I'm more exhausted than I've ever been and never mind food, the only thing I need is sleep because tomorrow I have to be up at the crack of dawn.

To visit my dad.

In prison.

FORTY-SIX

It's three a.m. and I'm so wired I can't sleep. Before breakfast we're flying to Denver and then driving over a hundred miles south to Florence, Colorado, a place no one has heard of unless they're in law enforcement or the family of someone who's locked away in the supermax prison there and I'm twisting and shifting in bed and I'm cold and hot and in between and I get up and pee and get back into bed and try to sleep all over again.

But then my phone rings and my heart gets crazed. I glance at the caller ID, which I don't have to because I know who it is, and think about how he just picked the wrong time to do this because—screw you, Michael, I'm just in the worst possible frame of mind and I don't know what to say or not to say to you anymore and I can't even go there now because I'm shaking like I'm living on a fault line and the earth is opening beneath my feet.

Are you glad they put my dad away? Are you breathing easier now? Or are you calling to say you're sorry for me? I don't need your pity so go away and just leave me alone.

It rings and rings and then he must hear my voice in his head because it stops.

Anthony and my mom are both dressed in blue. Anthony is in his best suit, a navy silk Brioni and a starched white shirt with a blue-striped Armani tie. My mom is wearing a royal blue woolen Valentino dress with a single gold cross around her neck. The rest of her crosses and all of her jewelry, including her diamond engagement ring, are gone now, part of the payback to the government.

I'm in a funereal black pantsuit with dark heels and sunglasses and a small gold cross on my neck. I'm searching in my drawer for a tie to hold my hair back when my hand lands on a red painted stone with a black and white spotted design, my Aboriginal gratitude rock.

It fits securely in the palm of my hand. I hold onto it and then drop it into my bag, which is already stuffed with tissues and Xanax because visiting your dad in the country's most secure prison is not a walk in the park.

I think back to after school when I said good-bye to Clive and Ro and Candy. They all looked like they were about to burst into tears. I pretended not to notice.

"We'll all go out to dinner next week…somewhere interesting," I said.

"Definitely," Clive said. "I'll look for a new place, maybe Thai?"

"That would be cool," Ro said.

Everyone nodded in agreement.

Silence.

Uncomfortable stares everywhere but at me. We were all doing a miserable job of trying to look cheerful.

I gathered my books together quickly. "I better go."

Just as I was rushing toward the door, Ro ran over.

"Gia, wait," she said, wiping her eyes. "Tell your dad, tell him that…

we love him and pray for him every day. And Gia, I'm just so sorry for you."

Where was my hard-ass friend when I needed her?

"As if praying helps…"

"Gia…" She came toward me with her arms out, but I couldn't let her hug me because…

"I'm sorry, Ro, I'm being such a bitch."

"No you're not, Gia. I wish I could trade places with you—"

She actually meant it.

"I'll tell him, Ro." Then I ran.

My hands are functioning without a brain, stowing things in an overnight bag. You'll get through it, I keep telling myself. Like I have a choice.

We get off the plane almost six hours later and follow Anthony to the Hertz desk then leave the terminal and walk to the parking lot, slipping and sliding on the icy patches covering the ground. The sky is steely gray. My breath hovers in front of me like a frosty ghost.

We drive to a cheap motel and eat burgers and fries from a fast food joint and watch TV shows with forced laughter and take aspirin and try to sleep, pretending that the heater isn't clanking loud and that the bed isn't lumpy. In the morning Anthony drives us to the prison.

I read about it online to get prepared, to know something, anything, about where my father would be spending the rest of his life.

Thirty-seven acres. Four-hundred-and-ninety beds. Cell furniture made out of poured concrete. Showers run on a timer so they can't flood. Toilets that turn off if they are stopped up. Sinks without stoppers that could be used as weapons. Fourteen hundred remote-controlled steel doors. Twelve-foot-high razor wire fences. Laser beams, motion detectors, cameras, and guard dogs monitor the prison 24/7 in addition to staff. One of the few journalists ever to tour it said the inside was filled with "an eerie silence," a description that sounds like it was lifted from the latest bestseller about life in a dystopian universe.

Only this is real.

Nonfiction.

ADX, the only supermax in the federal prison system, was built in 1994.

No one has ever escaped.

We enter and I see a large black-and-white photo of Alcatraz in San Francisco Bay. ADX is sometimes called the Alcatraz of the Rockies. They're proud of that, I think. There are also photographs of people responsible for the prison. The only one I recognize is President Obama.

After they take our pictures and search us, they take all our stuff. I turn over my handbag and so does my mom. It makes me rethink everything I keep with me every day and how it could be used by someone trying to escape: a nail file, a tiny Swiss Army knife that holds a pair of scissors, tweezers, and a pen. Useful tools. Even the small, smooth gratitude rock. I doubt that the Aborigines ever thought about how it could be used by an angry inmate against a prison guard.

Anthony empties his pockets, handing them his phone, his wallet, his keys, and his pocketknife, a larger one than mine. We walk in stages as they unlock doors in front of us and then lock them behind us. We're under lockdown now too. We're inmates. We can't bring gifts, not even food.

"Would some lasagna be so terrible?" my mom keeps repeating. "Just something from home to make him feel better. One meal. Only one meal."

Only no one here is interested in making the inmates here feel better or at home. They're interested in only one thing: keeping them locked away.

We go forward, only our stripped-down selves. After I don't know how many hours of waiting, waiting, waiting, waiting, and waiting, and doing nothing except dreading and living in hell and making promises to God in exchange for mercy for my dad, we go down a long, underground hallway where there are one word signs. *Loyalty. Honesty. Integrity.*

Isn't that like too much too late? And what's the purpose now, to make everyone feel guilty for what can't be changed? We enter a concrete room like a bunker with video cameras all around, recording every eyeblink, every hiccup. We wait more and more and all I can do is bite at my cuticles until blood seeps out and I have to suck it away until it stops. Then I play with the cross around my neck, running it back and forth along the chain and think of songs in my head and try to recite poetry that I memorized in the fifth grade and then make more deals with God and ask him to step up to the plate right now and prove himself to me because if ever there was a time…

Then.

Suddenly.

Out of a dungeon room. In the back somewhere. A form takes shape.

My dad.

And he's…oh my God, so, so different now.

No silk designer suit or fine cashmere bathrobe. No confident stride. A short-sleeve prison uniform. His legs shackled together so he can take only small baby steps. His hands cuffed, attached to a chain connected to a black box attached to his waist. Hair clipped so short it shows his scalp. His face drawn, his perpetual tan gone yellow. He's thin, so thin, hollowed eyes as if life has been gouged out of him.

My daddy…

How can I stand this?

But he can still smile. They haven't stolen that yet. And it changes him back, a little.

"Daddy!" I call out, my voice coming out high-pitched and shrill after not speaking for nearly a day and a half. Only how stupid to call him because he can't hear me behind the thick glass partition. He can't hear anything inside this tomb. There's a phone. That's why there's a phone. We have to use it to talk to him.

My mom goes first.

"How do you feel?" she asks in a pitying voice, holding the phone in her left hand, her right in a fist in her lap.

He shrugs and she listens while I try to lip-read his answer.

"How do they treat you?" she says and then, "what do you eat here?" Then more questions about "the room" because she won't say *cell*, and answers I can't hear or lip-read, but I watch his face. That's enough. My dad is tough. Sure of himself. He's been beaten up by fists and real life and been in and out of prisons before.

Only he's never had to face anything like this.

No enemy is as tough as solitary.

My mom gives the phone to Anthony. He talks about business and everything is straightforward. Emotionless. Only it isn't. All that is kept behind Anthony's eyes because he's good at that. He's been trained by the master. Finally it's my turn.

"I'll give you Gia," Anthony says. He crosses his arms over his chest, like he's giving my dad a hug.

But my dad holds up a finger.

"What?" Anthony says.

"Be clean," he says.

Anthony looks unsure. He raises an eyebrow. "Dad, I…"

"Listen to me," my dad says, staring intently at my brother. "Listen to me. It's over."

Anthony hands me the phone, and I fall silent, stupid, forgetting everything I wanted to say and the whole script that I practiced again and again. I'm dumb. My mouth is dry. All I can feel are the hot tears about to flood my eyes, tears I've tried to fight off and vowed to hide inside me.

"It's okay," my dad starts, studying me. "It's okay, my Gia," he says, because saying it isn't okay would hurt me too much.

"What do you do…every day?" I ask, remembering a question.

"I read, I pray…" He smiles. "And all the memories, I have all the memories and go over them. Like our home movies, remember?"

I swallow and nod.

"You tell me…about everything," he says. "How is school?"

I tell him about Clive and Ro and the election and what Christy and Brandy and Georgina did. "They tried to cheat—to steal the ballots, Daddy," I say haltingly. "But we didn't let them get away with it. I spoke to the principal and asked for a recount and they found the missing ballots and counted again and I won." Only now it sounds like some kind of hollow victory to me. "I won," I repeat. "I'm president."

"President!" he says, his eyes lighting up. He nods. It makes him so proud. I talk more and more to give him information to fill up his now empty life.

What I don't tell him is about the scholarship because it would tear him up. He'd know why Clive's parents did it. He'd know that without their help I'd be out of Morgan and he doesn't need anything else to haunt him while he's lying on his back in his cell for twenty-three hours a day, a cell that's always lit and monitored 24/7. Only a single hour to exercise in a space that resembles an empty swimming pool so none of the inmates know their location for possible escape. He doesn't say that, but I know it. I read it. Still I ask him about his "room."

"There's a window and I can see a sliver of blue sky," he says. "That helps."

A sliver? A tiny fraction of the outside world. That's what they've left him. I feel like I need to double over because of the hurt. This place will drive him insane. But I snap to. Herbie. I'll tell him about Herbie.

"We adopted a dog, Daddy."

My dad's eyes widen. "What kind, a puppy?"

"He's a senior, Daddy, a pit bull. A ten-year-old pit bull named Herbie."

He nods his head, understanding.

"Old," he says, shaking his head, "without a home."

"He had a sad life in a shelter and now he lives with us." I hold up a picture of Herbie, the only thing they let me keep.

My dad's face softens. He smiles.

"And he likes mom's cooking. She's always feeding him."

"He looks like a good boy," he says. "You did right—they give back so much."

"I wish you could meet him," I say, my voice cracking.

"I wish I could too, Gia," he whispers, his eyes clouding over.

Seconds of silence and we just sit there and stare at each other with all the memories of our lives together flowing between us because this has to last. Finally we go on, talking normal, everyday things. Words, words, and more words back and forth like a volley over an invisible net to keep the lifeline alive. The neighborhood, the church, the priest, my friends, my schoolwork, movies he'll never see, music he'll never hear. Whatever we can grab to keep our mouths moving—and it all feels like lies and hypocrisy and empty talk without meaning or joy or laughter because we're afraid to divulge too much because it will show him that we're living. While he isn't.

I don't want him to think about what he's missing or how everything's empty now without him at home. But he knows. My dad knows everything. Still I don't want to make his life here even worse, if that's possible.

Minutes go by and then hours. I'm so, so bone tired. He is too. But no one wants to turn away because this visit has to last him. Five visits a month, that's all he gets. Only we're more than halfway across the country so we aren't flying back to Florence, Colorado, next week or the week after. We can't afford to. So we talk and keep talking like guns are pointed at our heads. And none of it matters except that we connect.

I pick up my hand and press it against the glass wall. He puts his in the very same spot, as close as we're going to get for the rest of our lives.

"Who loves you more than anyone else in the whole world?" he whispers.

"You do, Daddy," I say, pinching my leg so hard that I break the skin.

Neither of us says anything and I shake my head as the tears flow.

"Please," he says, "please don't cry." He glances up at the clock.

"Gia," he says finally. "Remember our secret?"

I nod.

"Remember Beppo?"

I squint. *What?*

He lifts a finger as if to silence me then turns it into a fist that he presses against his mouth, pretending to cough. He glances up. The room, they're listening, the gesture says. "Take good care of him," he says, looking at me pointedly.

A message. But what?

"Time is up," the guard says.

My dad gets to his feet. He makes a kiss with his lips, then slowly turns away.

"I love you Daddy!" I shout. "I love you!" Only he doesn't turn back, so I shout it again, louder. "I love you Daddy! I love you!" because I forgot to say it, I forgot to say it! All that time together and I'm so stupid, so stupid, I forgot to tell him.

"Gia!" Anthony says.

"I forgot to tell him, Anthony!" I scream. "I forgot to tell him!"

"He knows it, Gia," he says softly, stoically, his own eyes filling with tears as he takes my arm and pulls me away. "He knows it."

But I pull away and run back to the glass and pound on it. "Daddy, come back!" I shout. "Daddy, Daddy, please!"

"Lord help us," my mother cries. "Lord help us."

"He's gone, Gia," Anthony says. "He can't hear you anymore."

Then he drops his face in his hands and starts sobbing too.

The wind is blowing hard and it's starting to snow as we walk to the parking lot. The ground is icy and uneven and it's hard to walk without slipping. My face feels as numb as my insides. Anthony takes my mom's arm so that she doesn't slip on the ice. I nearly fall once and then again.

"Can't they salt the parking lot? Is that so fucking hard?"

Anthony turns around and stops, reaching out an arm to me. I take his arm and we walk slowly, stepping carefully, crossing the frozen tundra.

My mom sits in the front seat next to Anthony and I stretch out across the backseat.

"Turn up the heat," she says, putting up the collar of her coat.

"It's as high as it can go, Ma," Anthony says.

"That's all it can go?"

"Ma, it takes time. It'll get warmer. It takes time."

"This is how it is here for your father all the time," she says. "It doesn't get warmer for him." She looks at Anthony but he stares ahead and doesn't answer. She shakes her head and closes her hand around the cross on her neck.

"Not even a plate of food from home," she says, shaking her head and staring out the window.

I close my eyes, lulled by the motion of the car, just like when I was a baby. Only now my dad isn't driving.

No one talks on the way back to Denver. We're out of words and energy.

So much of the day is a blur, but what I do remember is the cold, the bitter, unrelenting cold, and the sun that never came out and how it felt to leave the prison, like I was leaving a cemetery, and looking up at the wide-open steel gray sky and thinking about how I am outside and free while my dad is locked inside like a wild animal for the rest of his life.

I also remember strapping myself into my seat near the window on the plane and wondering after we took off whether my dad could hear the plane overhead or for just a fleeting moment even see it pass his sliver of sky and know it's us and understand how we feel about leaving him alone in the middle of nowhere.

When I finally open my eyes we're back in New York City and I wonder whether it was all some kind of wicked nightmare. I imagine that when I get home and walk into the kitchen or the living room, my head will clear and my dad will be sitting there waiting for us like before in his tan cashmere bathrobe. He'd look up at me and smile and open his arms to me.

"Gia, don't worry," he'll say and tell me that I'm safe and that everything will be fine because that's how it's always been for as long as I can remember.

Only he isn't there when we get home.

All we have of him now are the pictures on the glass shelves in the living room: My parents' wedding photo in the big, gold frame. A picture of both of us on Christmas day, near our tree. A picture of the whole family at the beach, all of us happy together, dripping ice cream cones in front of our faces. And one of just my dad when he was about twenty-five. He's wearing a suit and tie and he's looking very proud of himself. It's the day he joined the life.

We all walk into the house and stand there for a minute before taking off our coats. I hug my mom and even Anthony, and my mom looks up and whispers a prayer.

From now on, it's only the three of us.

And Herbie.

FORTY-SEVEN

I'm sitting on Clive's bed and he's on his computer writing a paper when he brings up Michael.

"Don't mention him, please." I hold up my hands and he shrugs and I change the subject. "I'm thinking of taking boxing classes to keep going with this fighting thing."

"Cool."

"Well, it's cheaper than shopping." *Or staying home and feeling sorry for myself because my dad's locked away and Michael is so over.*

Clive is wearing a black T–shirt and jeans—with no scarf.

"If you could face a supermax prison," he said, "I can face the people at Morgan or any place else."

But the strangest thing is when he took off the scarf, no one noticed. Or if they did, they didn't say anything, which says not only that most of the people in the world are wrapped up in themselves and oblivious, but also that what's inside your head is not always reality.

I wake in the middle of the night. Only this time it's not the phone. It's the conversation. The one with my dad.

"Beppo, Beppo," he's saying. I sit up in bed and pull my furry bear toward me. He's about four feet tall and fat and furry. I touch his face, running my fingers over the silky white fur. Then I examine his jewel-covered collar. Make-believe emeralds, diamonds, and rubies. When I was little, I was convinced they were real and having the collar made me rich.

"See what I have?" I used to say to my dad. "Real diamonds and rubies."

That made him laugh. "Yes, I know, Gia," he'd say. "You're a rich little girl."

I run my fingers over the stones, feeling their hard, faceted surfaces. They're attached to a thick ribbon, so I slide my finger beneath it and check the length of the band. Is there a message? A secret zipper?

Nothing.

I turn on the lamp on my night table and then lift him up. Two legs, two arms, and a round, fat tummy. I run my finger over the fur.

What were you trying to tell me? What is it about Beppo?

We'd been talking about my secret plan for the future when my dad mentioned Beppo, so it has something to do with that, only what? My dad is used to talking in his own made-up shorthand. He's been bugged by the feds for so long that he's learned to say what he has to without them figuring it out. Only that's not how he ever talked to me before.

Then suddenly it hits me. I lift the bear and shake him. I examine the seams. The left side is smooth and neatly sewn, that's not it. Then the right. It's smooth and perfect too. I turn him on his stomach.

Now I see.

The back seam has been opened and re-sewn. Tiny, perfect stitches, but these were carefully done by hand. I run into the bathroom and grab the cuticle scissors, nearly tripping over the edge of the scale, then run back to my bed and carefully snip open the stitches, one by one until the opening is one inch wide. Two. Three. Then four. I peer inside.

And there it is.

Like a mule that has swallowed drugs to smuggle across the border, Beppo has been stuffed with cash.

When was that done? How? Who did it?

It had to be my mom. She was a designer and a seamstress. Her sewing is flawless. But was she in on this? She probably stuffed the money inside a long time ago. She helped my dad all the time and never asked questions.

My dad is away in prison for the rest of his life, everything he put away for us gone except for what's inside Beppo. Now I know. My dad had no doubts about how things would end up for him, and he wanted to make sure that no matter what, I'd have money for my secret plan for the future: to go to law school.

I count the crisp hundred dollar bills. I make piles, five thousand dollars in each. I'm so wired that I make mistakes and lose count so I start over. It's four a.m. when I finally finish.

A quarter of a million dollars.

My ticket to a different life. A life where I will stand up for people, or maybe helpless animals, who can't stand up for themselves.

FORTY-EIGHT

"Start a boxing club," Clive says.

I look at him like, *what? Are you kidding?* "Do you think I want to hang out with the uppity bitches in our school?"

"I thought it would be fun, but you have a point there."

So I'm a one-person boxing club, running every other day and boxing two times a week which my mom can't understand and neither can Anthony who should be working out with me, but that's another story.

After Clive and I go out for teriyaki salmon and vegetable tempura and miso soup inside shiny black lacquer bento boxes so that the whole thing feels like a black tie dinner, I go back to his house where I practically live now and change into sweats.

"Gia, be careful," Clive says. "Remember what Anthony keeps saying."

"I'm careful, I'm careful."

"Do you want Thomas to ride along with you?"

"I'm fine, Clive, don't worry."

I don't know if it's the full moon or my music or something inside my head or someplace else, but I run to Riverside Park and keep running along the Hudson River as the sun sets and the sky gets darker and the lamplights cast a hazy yellow glow on the water. I start to get crazy thinking about things like when the American Indians were here before us and how they believed not in a separate God, but a godliness in the whole world, in the mountains and the rivers and the sky and in the plants and the animals, a kind of spiritual web that connected everyone and everything.

All that makes me feel like I'm part of a bigger plan. Maybe it's not exactly what the priest in our church says, but I can't actually pinpoint the last time I was there anyway because, even though my mom prays on a daily basis, I don't go anymore. I'm not sure why that is, but I think it has something to do with feeling that religion has let me down and hasn't given me any right answers. Either that or I'm asking the wrong questions.

I run and keep running and start to think about everything in my life, and then—flash—there's Michael's face and I remember exactly how he looks with his movie-star green eyes and thick dark lashes. And how he looked at me and how he kissed and tasted and how hot it felt to kiss him back and feel his lips on mine and be held in his arms, and I try to forget that because it's over and hopeless and stupid, and I start running faster and then see a car slow down on the side of the drive and I watch it out of the corner of my eye even though it's probably nothing, and I try to out run the memories and shake off the emotional whiplash, and pretend, pretend, pretend I'm getting over feeling what I'm feeling, but my brain is stronger than my heart. And it's just not buying it.

A figure gets out of the car and walks in a crouched-down way and crosses the highway, darting past cars going sixty that are honking at him like, *what the fuck?* He heads toward the running path, which is totally insane and suicidal, and I run faster and faster, and he crosses one lane and waits and then he's almost near me when I hear an ear-splitting crash and whine and *wham* of one car careening into another and then another and then—oh my god—the guy running toward me gets hit and his body goes shooting up into the air like a rocket. I scream and scream and can't stop screaming and so does everyone else on the running track and I stand still, frozen, as the body drops to the ground and a car horn gets stuck and won't stop beeping and it's like a nuclear alarm to the world of something insane and out of control taking place, and inside my head somewhere I hear my dad's voice screaming, "Run, Gia! Run away! Run for your life!"

I turn and go the other way, my heart pounding like it's been squeezed up into my mouth, and I don't stop running, sweat covering me like a layer of oily rain. I keep going and going until I'm back at the other end of Manhattan, where I slow down and finally start to walk again.

One foot. In front. Of. The other. My body trying to feel normal again, even though I doubt it ever will be because of the image of the crash and the body propelled toward the sky is now tattooed on my brain.

FORTY-NINE

The next day's paper reports that a pedestrian was killed while attempting to cross the West Side Highway. There were conflicting reports from eyewitnesses as to whether he stepped out of a car or he came from the path along the river. There was no identification on the body, the paper said. No one could come up with any motives. There's only a small picture, something that looks like it was taken by Weejee, the crime photographer from like the '30s and '40s who took lurid pictures of dead bodies at crime scenes.

But the picture is enough for Anthony to recognize it.

"Fucking Sal," he says while he's drinking coffee at breakfast. "Got what he deserved."

I don't dare say anything because he'll be furious at me for running alone along the river, but my heart registers panic.

"Sal One-Eye? The one that Dad hated?"

Anthony nods without looking up.

They called him One-Eye because he lost an eye during a fight and wore an eye patch for the rest of his life. It always made me cringe to hear about him. Was Sal after me? Even with my father locked away in prison, were they still going after him by going after me?

I vow that I'll never go running alone after dark. Clive's right. I should start a club, at least a running club, because there's safety in numbers.

All day at school I'm thinking about the day before and what could have happened and how stupid I was and if anyone knew, not that I'd tell, and somehow I get through the day, and even with my dad away and Michael out of my life forever and all the shit that enters your head at night, after running thirteen miles around the track at the health club because it's brightly lit and safe but not much fun, I manage to sleep.

Only after I hit the pillow all the craziness gets woven together in a patchwork of fantasies and the dream begins. I've decided to bring Michael home with me to meet my mom and Anthony. Ro thinks I'm insane.

"He's different," I say.

"He's a cop," Ro says.

I invite him anyway.

"You sure?" he says.

I'm not sure of anything. "My mom will love you."

I invite him for Saturday dinner and the day before my mom is standing in the kitchen making manicotti when she turns to me. "Is the boy Italian?"

The boy? "He's not Italian."

She exhales and draws another breath. "Is he Catholic?" she asks, holding out her hands.

"He's Catholic, Ma."

She touches the crosses on her chest, like her prayers have been answered, at least some of them.

We're interrupted by a knock at the door. Michael's standing there holding a bouquet of flowers. He holds them out to me, but I can tell this is weird for him. He doesn't know how to act, but he smiles at my mom and his cop eyes scan the house.

I panic that he'll turn and run, insisting that it's wrong and stupid and crazy, or worse, that he'll go up to Anthony's room and find grass or coke and change back from boyfriend to law enforcement officer again and bust my brother.

But that's not what happens.

We open the wine and Michael pours some for my mom and then for me. We toast.

And then Anthony walks in. He looks at Michael and does a double take. He walks toward the kitchen and motions for me to follow.

"That's the same cop who—"

"Yes, Anthony."

"You bring him home with you? You know what Dad would say?"

"Do you see Dad here, Anthony?

We eat together in the dining room and Anthony mutters a "how you doin'" in a guarded way then fills his plate, ignoring Michael who sits and waits.

Our eyes meet across the table, and then Michael casually asks Anthony about his car. Anthony looks up and they start talking car stuff and the air changes and Anthony goes on about his beloved Jag with this kindred spirit, and I'm sitting there like, *okay, can you guys just shut up about cars and carburetors and the throttle body needing to be replaced,* whatever the hell that is.

But never mind that because then they move on to head gasket failure, which seriously sounds like car impotence, and then my phone rings and I answer it because it's Clive so I go to the living room to talk, and when I get back it's not like I was missed because Michael and

Anthony are still talking car failure. And I'm wondering about this cop, the one who never talks.

After I help my mom clean up and Anthony and Michael finally shut up, I grab Michael's hand and pull him upstairs and show him *Vogue* and he looks at the pictures and shakes his head and says, "did your dad see these?"

"No."

He laughs. "That's good."

We make out and he tastes like merlot and I lock the door and finally Michael catches his breath and says, "Baby, I better go."

Then I wake up and that make-believe world vanishes. I'm alone.

Again.

FIFTY

I convince my mom not to worry because I'm going to Clive's and that Thomas will be waiting for us at school and yada, yada, yada, even though now with my dad away my mom and Anthony keep saying, "be careful, be careful," and if they ever had a clue that the crash on the West Side Highway…

"It's game change time," Anthony says, "and Dad has enemies."

Clive has to stay after school and retake the history test he missed when he overslept. "Wait for me in the library," he says.

Only it's beautiful out and it's daylight and other kids are around and so are parents and I could use some distraction, so I decide to walk uptown and look in the stores. I text him.

Text me when you're done. Going out for air.

I walk west toward Madison, checking the street both ways because my radar is in high gear, but no one is around and nothing sets off my internal panic meter. I stop at the ice cream truck because the mac and cheese for lunch was gross and I threw most of it out so I'm fainting from starvation. I wait in line and finally get a chocolate éclair bar because they're out of the strawberry shortcake, my number-one fave. I head down the street, peeling off the paper, then start thinking about Michael and the chocolate ice cream sandwiches and how he looked and what that was like and how it went nowhere and crash-landed, and I look everywhere but he has not magically appeared.

Just thinking about him is depressing and a waste of time so I try to push those thoughts away and focus on what kind of cashmere cardigans I should look for and what colors I need and want and settle on dark green and camel to match what I have. But I'm distracted by an asshole in an SUV who guns the engine and goes flying down the street and—hello—didn't he see the sign that says *slow* because there's a school on this block, and, like, where is the cop on the corner when you need him, and then the asshole slams the brakes hard and stops with a screech.

And I get chills.

I turn around to figure out what's going on, and, shit, my ice cream falls from my hand and splatters all over the street, and I open my mouth but then look up when a door slams on the SUV and somebody gets out of the front seat, and I stop because he looks vaguely familiar, only I can't place him.

Then he crosses the street to my side and walks toward me.

And. My. Insides. Tighten.

He comes up close and then closer so he's walking next to me, keeping pace. Step by step. This freaks me out. A small smile on his pock-marked face.

"Hi, Gia," he says, like my name is a dirty word.

Adrenaline shoots through me. I try to hide the fear that rears up. I pivot abruptly and speed walk back to school. To safety. It's not far. I'm almost there, less than one block.

Be calm, a voice inside me says. Don't show him you're scared.

I'm trying. To look calm. And not afraid. Trying to hold back from breaking into a run.

An eighth of a block more. I can make it.

He reaches out suddenly and grabs me roughly on the upper arm, dragging me toward the street.

"Let's go for a ride, Gia. Sal couldn't get you. But I can."

"No!" I yell, yanking my arm free. He grabs it again and I freak and scream, "Let go of me!"

Where the hell is everybody? I look around frantically. The street is deserted now. My body jerks alive with panic. I fixate on being strong. I have to get away. It's life or death.

Boxing. Fighting. All of Dante's lessons flash in my brain. All the practice. The drills. It's like he's next to me and has prepared me for this.

Jab, Gia! I slam his jaw as hard as I can with my left.

Surprise them, Gia. I jab again.

It stuns him. He freezes. His grip loosens. But before I can reach out and punch him again and again and again the way I'm supposed to, he recovers.

This isn't Dante's basement anymore, where it's just me and the bag. He has the advantage now. He's bigger and stronger. He comes back at me and yanks my arm so hard I lose balance. I'm thrown to the street and fall back. My shoulder hits the pavement hard, then I slam my head, and it stuns me and I forget, I forget to be tough. I forget to pretend, and the strength leaches out of me. I want to cry. I need help. I hurt everywhere.

I lie there overcome. Then he's crouching over me and grabbing my arms to pull me to my feet.

My head. It throbs. Blood rushing in my ears makes me deaf.

Everything starts to go around and around. I stare up at the bright blue sky. My dad. His sliver of sky. All he sees. All he has. He's lost almost everything he has to lose.

And that. Can't. Happen. To me.

"Let's go," he hisses. "Get up, you bitch." He yanks my arm again, nearly pulling it from the socket. I come to life and reach under the leg of his pants and dig my nails into his skin and then pull hard at his ankle to make him fall, to break his grip.

It works.

He stumbles and falls to his knees, but he manages to get up and he's over me again, breathing hard, angrier now, furious that I hurt him, furious that I made him fall. He tries to grab me again. He yanks my hair. Only now I can't fight as hard. I hurt all over. My whole body has turned to deadweight.

I see my dad yelling no. Telling me to fight. To be strong. To win. I'm going to faint. Everything's getting fuzzier. Stay awake, stay awake, my brain is yelling. Get up. My brain? Or my dad?

Somewhere outside myself, an arm reaches over me. I'm trapped on the ground. I push against it, but it doesn't move.

Then there are voices. People are around me. Kids from school or people from the street?

"It's Gia," a voice says.

"Jesus," says another.

Then a voice from above me yells. "Get back! Get back! Police! Stop!"

I'm trying to focus only on a figure leaning over me. Who is it?

"Are you okay?"

"Okay," I whisper.

I don't know what's happening anymore.

Then there's a hard click. The safety. A gun.

My eyes open wide.

Then again. "Are you all right? Talk to me."

Then I know. I am.

"Did you get him?"

"He got away."

He leans away, not hovering over me anymore. He pulls out a pen and scribbles down numbers. The plate. I lie there as he calls it in. "Can you get up?" he asks, turning back to me.

Only when I focus, I see that it isn't him. It's another cop, somebody I've never seen before.

"I called an ambulance," he says. "They'll take you to the hospital."

"No, I'm okay."

"It looks like you hit your head pretty hard."

Am I conscious or not? I can't tell. And then I hear the siren and feel them lift me up and carry me onto the gurney.

Then everything goes black.

When I open my eyes I'm in a curtained-off room. "I'm okay, I'm fine," I say.

A doctor nods as a nurse is taking my blood pressure and then cleaning what must be a cut on my head because the gauze looks bloody.

"You can go as soon as your mom comes," she says. "The MRI was normal."

And then the curtain parts and I see…Michael.

"Gia," he says, walking toward me.

"We'll be finished in a minute," the nurse says.

"It's okay," I say.

Michael steps toward me and touches my shoulder.

"What are you doing here?" I ask.

"I heard it come over the radio," he says. "I got here as fast as I could. How are you?"

"Not ready for my close-up."

He shakes his head. "You look good to me."

Michael sits with me while we wait for my mom. He reaches out and takes my hand, and out of nowhere, my tears start and don't stop. Fear, relief, shock? He reaches into his pocket and hands me a tissue. I expect to hear *why are you crying?* Or *don't cry, you're safe*. But he doesn't say either of those things. He leans toward me and takes me in his arms, pressing me against his chest.

"I know, baby, I know," he says over and over, and those words go beyond what just happened to me and they comfort both of us because of everything we've gone through and all the months of not being together and finally losing my dad.

"I'm sorry, Gia…for everything."

I never thought I'd hear that. I never thought I'd feel what I am feeling now and all I know for sure is that no matter what, I don't want Michael to let go of me because I am so scared and so mixed up about my dad and all the things he did and I want to forget the past, all of it. I bury my face in his neck.

"I wish I could take you home," he says.

That's not what I want to hear. I thought things were different finally, but they're not. I'm just blind and stupid because he obviously still blames me, and I'm just so weary of all the back and forth and the bullshit and his fear of getting close to me because of who I am even though he knows I can't change that and I don't even want to.

"Don't keep saying that, Michael. I don't want you to take me home."

He shakes his head. "My home, Gia."

And I'm like, *what did he say?* I look at him again and I know it wasn't my imagination.

He said it. *My home.*

Does this mean he accepts me for who I am? Or at least he wants to try?

Never before have I moved from despair to ecstasy in a split second. How can a two letter pronoun do all that?

My.

A single word that can change everything.

"Let's start over, Michael."

"Fresh start," he says with his half smile.

FIFTY-ONE

My mom comes to the hospital with Anthony, and since they found out what happened, my brother is in a rage and they're huddling around me, super protective.

"Saturday night?" Michael whispers.

We've crossed the line back to relationship from the planet Splitsville.

"Saturday night," I say before he slips away and my eyes close because I feel like Dante's punching bag.

The newspapers pick up the story of course, and instead of my dad's face on the front of the *Daily News*, it's mine, because what's bigger news than a kidnapping attempt on the don's daughter who happens to go to one of Manhattan's snootiest private schools?

I get into bed that night and turn on the eleven o'clock news and after it's over the phone rings.

"Did you see the news?" Michael asks.

"Ha, I'm famous."

"Christ," he says.

"Thanks for coming."

"Yeah, well…"

"If I wasn't feeling so crappy now..."

"Yeah, if only...Saturday?" he says.

"Saturday."

Then the Percocet kicks in and I yawn.

"Go to sleep, Gia," he says softly.

"I love you, Michael," I blurt out. *Did I really say that?*

"Gia..." he says, exhaling hard.

Say something back, Michael. Please.

"Good night, baby," he says finally. Then the line goes dead.

I'm in school the next day, now with a friend of Anthony's, Angelo, as my new driver and bodyguard even though I don't know how Anthony's paying him. And when Clive gets all the details about why I didn't return his fifty calls or texts or emails he looks shaken and upset and keeps saying, "oh my God, Gia, oh my God, if I had known..."

"But I'm fine, Clive—"

"I know, but—"

"Really, I'm fine."

"But I was inside, right inside, taking the damn test, if I had known..."

He finally calms down after I tell him a hundred more times that I'm fine and how another cop saved my life and that "everything's different now."

"So now do you want to know what I found out?"

"About?"

"About him, about Michael Cross," Clive says impatiently. "The report. I've got the whole thing now...assuming I'm not dragged off to prison for hacking into—"

"Yes, yes, tell me."

FIFTY-TWO

It's been so long since I asked him to find out about Michael that I forgot he said there was more and that he managed to get past a security firewall and yada, yada, yada.

"What did you find out?"

"Well, it's not really about him," Clive says.

"What do you mean?"

"Well, it is and it isn't."

"Clive…"

"It's about his dad."

"He was a cop too."

"Yes, but it gets complicated," Clive says. "Come over after school and I'll show you everything."

Patience is not one of my strengths. Waiting and wondering and worrying churn up my insides. Not only that but also I'm now getting that quickening in my heart, the kind of amped-up feeling that says my body knows something ahead of my brain.

Only it's twelve o'clock, and I have three more hours until I go to Clive's.

"Gia," Mrs. Collins says.

I look up at her, startled. I was spacing.

She asks the question again. Something about the significance of Ophelia to Hamlet? I haven't thought about that.

I stare back at her like an idiot. "Sorry," I answer apologetically.

She studies me briefly and shakes her head. "Please pay attention," she says in a gentle, pitying sort of way. "You're in outer space."

At three o'clock, my new bodyguard, who has a body like a defensive lineman, drives me and Clive to Clive's apartment.

"I'll be fine from here on," I say. Then add, "Thanks, Ann," because I call him that, which makes him nuts.

He exhales. "How you gettin' home?"

"Clive's driver."

He looks at me uncertainly.

"It's fine, Ann, I'll text you if anything changes."

Clive and I get into the elevator, and as soon as we get to his floor and the door closes behind us, I turn to Clive. "Show me."

He holds up his hands and goes to his room. He comes back with a manila folder. He opens it and looks at me questioningly. "You sure you want to hear it?"

"His dad is dead now, so it doesn't matter much anyway. But whatever. What did you find?"

"First of all, his dad isn't dead," Clive says.

"What?"

"He's living in Tennessee…in a small town there."

"Maybe his parents are divorced and his dad left," I say. "That's not a big deal and Michael could be mad at him or think of him as dead…"

I think back to the time I asked him about his father. He talks so little that I've just about memorized his every word. We'd been talking about Thanksgiving. He was on the Henry Hudson, waiting for speeders.

"What about your dad?"

Silence.

"No dad," he'd said finally.

"Did he…die?"

"Yeah…he's dead."

"Well," Clive says. "Here's the interesting part, Gia. His father was a cop—"

"I know that, you said—"

"And he was promoted to detective, but two years later there was an internal affairs investigation. I can't get the actual report, I tried, so it was hushed up I guess because these people can usually get almost anything…but I got a summary from them—"

"Them?"

"My dad's people, his sources," he says, leaving it at that.

My heart is starting to pound in my chest. "What…what did he do?"

"He took payoffs, Gia…"

"From?"

"People in…your dad's organization."

"What? Clive are you sure?"

"It's a summary of a report by internal affairs, Gia. They're the ones who investigate these things."

My dad and his associates sometimes got tipped off about things they weren't supposed to know. I would hear bits of things, never whole conversations. They had connections everywhere, I knew, but I never imagined it would get close to me, not like this.

And then I remember the fight with Michael.

"The cops that they squeeze and then they own," he said. "To me it's personal."

No wonder he hates people like my dad. He blames him, he

blames us, but not only for how it ruined his brother, but what it did to his dad too. He couldn't even forgive his own father.

The wall between us is even thicker than I imagined.

FIFTY-THREE

I consider telling my mom I have a date then decide no, why go there. Homework with Clive is my default lie, so I use it again even though I'm on shaky ground.

"Be back by eleven."

"Ma, if it gets late and we're working, I'll call you."

"Gia…"

"Don't worry." I'm out the door before she can answer.

The phone rings when I'm in the cab. "Are you really…?"

"Yes, Ro. I'm four blocks from the restaurant."

"Am I supposed to say have a great time?"

"You could, if you're my friend."

"I am your friend, Gia, that's why…" She sighs. "I mean a cop—and not just *any* cop."

"For once in your life can you just forget that?"

"Can you?"

"I gotta go," I say, pressing End.

I meet Michael in an Asian restaurant on the Upper West Side. He's already at the table when I get there. Prepared. In position. I spot him before he sees me. He's lost in thought. This can't be easy for him, a date with the don's daughter. I only hope I'm not being trailed by a photographer from one of the tabs.

He turns suddenly and spots me. He stands, stepping away from the table. I slow down, catching my breath. Seeing him has the usual effect on me, as if some powerful aphrodisiac has filled my insides, heating my blood. I can't believe how beautiful he is. The deep-set green eyes. The dark hair just long enough to brush against the collar of the black pullover sweater that outlines his shoulders. Jeans that cling to his narrow hips. I kiss him on the cheek.

"How do you feel?" he asks.

"Alive?"

He gives me his guarded smile as his eyes do the nanosecond cleavage sweep that takes in my white silk blouse, unbuttoned enough to show the top of the nude lace demi bra underneath. He takes my hand.

"Come, sit down."

I sit next to him on the banquette. I'm nervous. I can't help it. All I could think of for the past few days was how this night would go.

"Hungry?"

"I didn't eat all day."

"Why not?"

You, Michael. I just shrug.

He knows, but he doesn't know what to say so he changes the subject.

"The food is good here." He lifts his chin, motioning toward the menu in front of me. There must be a hundred appetizers, main dishes, and sides. I stare down at the menu. I might as well be looking at the Oxford English Dictionary of food options. Words, words, and more words, and I don't know what I want, all I know is I want to be next to Michael and nothing else matters.

"What do you like?" he says.

Why does everything he says sound like something else?

"Whatever. You decide."

We have corn and crab soup to start and then noodles with peanut sauce and beef with orange sauce and a whole fish with ginger.

I don't think of fish as Michael food, but what do I know about how he eats or lives or does anything, other than chasing speeders.

"You've been here before?"

"Yeah," he says with a smile.

To poison things, I wonder whether this is his go-to spot for dates and I fixate on how many other girls he's taken here. *Shut up, Gia.*

"What?" Michael says.

"What, what?" *Caught.*

"You looked worried," he says. "Something in your face changed."

"Are you a face reader?"

"Comes with the job. Tell me, what is it?"

"I was wondering if you bring all your dates here." My heart is kicking now. Why the hell did I ask him that? I don't want to hear what's he's going to say.

Raised eyebrow. "All my dates?"

"Mmm."

"No."

"Do you…have a girlfriend?"

"No."

"Not ever?"

"Not now."

I feel myself relax. "What happened?"

"It was a while ago," he shrugs, dismissing it gently. Not that I expected him to spill.

"What about you?" he says playfully. "A main man?"

"No."

"Never?"

Does making out with Dante count? What about Marco Valente when I was in the eighth grade? Almost every weekend, we made out in the back of his dad's car. I let him touch me, but with my clothes on.

"No one...special...except Herbie."

He frowns. "Herbie?"

"Yeah, he's the sweetest."

His jaw tightens. "So why aren't you out with...Herbie?"

"He's older, he likes to go to bed early."

"What?" He looks at me curiously as I reach into my bag and hold up the picture of Herbie.

"You had me goin'," he says as the food arrives.

I guess I'm hungrier than I thought because I manage to finish everything. Michael watches me, amused.

"Do you always clean the plate?"

"I eat like a horse."

"I wouldn't have guessed that."

"Why?"

"Because you're thin."

"Too thin?"

He shakes his head. "Not too thin," he says, his eyes holding mine. "Perfect."

Did he really say that? I look up at him and swallow, embarrassed. I know I'm blushing.

Perfect.

It's not a word that anyone has ever used to describe me. Attractive, hot maybe, pretty, but never perfect. It's not a word I would ever use to describe myself either because I always feel that everyone else has the edge on me and that I never measure up, no matter how hard I try. The stereotype is part of it, but deep down I believe that I'm not as good or good-looking as everyone else.

I want to say it out loud. *Perfect*. Michael Cross thinks I'm perfect. He reaches into my lap and squeezes my hand, sending bursts of electric current shooting through me.

We leave the restaurant and walk uptown along Broadway. The street is alive with people, students from Columbia University, parents pushing baby strollers, people my age holding hands with their dates. We look through the windows of restaurants and thrift shops.

"How are you doing…without your dad?"

I stop, not only because it's a question I've been afraid to ask myself, but because it tells me that he's thinking of me as a girl who lost her dad, not a girl whose crime boss dad is locked away because he deserves to be, which is what a cop would be thinking.

"The house is so empty now. He was always such a presence. Such a power." I shake my head. "Now there's no one to turn to for the…"

I'm speechless, suddenly thinking about my dad and what he meant to all of us. He was always the final word, the strongest opinion. It gave us such security to have him decide things because he was always so sure, so right. I don't even have to finish the sentence.

Michael nods, he understands.

I'm going to tell him what I know about his dad, I decide right then, because it's like the elephant in the room, and if there's one thing about me that everyone knows, it's that I can't keep things inside for long.

"There's something I found out."

He looks at me questioningly. "About?"

"You."

"What?" he asks quietly with an intensity that scares me.

"Your dad, Michael."

"What do you know?" he says, showing his impassive law enforcement face again, the one that doesn't give anything away.

"That he was a cop…"

He looks at me and waits.

"And what happened…the investigation. The bribes."

"How do you know?"

"I wanted to find out about you so I could see you again. I know someone who can get information, so I asked him."

Michael looks off as though he's lost in his memories. He shakes his head. I want to reach out to him to get him back, but he's drifted off away from me. Was I stupid to tell him? Did I just ruin everything? Maybe he hates me now for snooping.

"I…I'm sorry."

"Me too," he says, his face expressionless.

"Maybe I shouldn't have told you…I don't know. But I understand now…about how you feel. You might not believe me, but I'd hate it too. And I'm sorry."

"It was his fault. It has nothing to do with you."

"How can you say that? It was my family."

He stops and turns to me. "He fucked up his own life," he says. "He was corrupt. And stupid. I can't blame you for that. It has nothing to do with you."

"You don't speak to him anymore?"

"No."

We walk without talking. I watch a muscle pulsing in his jaw. He looks haunted and hurt and I'm suddenly filled with this overwhelming sorrow.

"I didn't think you could separate me from…" I shrug.

"I didn't think I could either," he says, his voice softening. "But I want to try."

We stop in the middle of the street and Michael takes me into his arms.

FIFTY-FOUR

His building is an old walk-up with so much paint chipped away on the hallway walls that it reminds me of a moonscape. As we climb the steep stairs, I smell fried chicken. Somewhere on a lower floor there's a baby crying and the sound of people arguing. When we get to his apartment on the fifth floor, I'm breathing hard. I can't imagine how I'd feel if I didn't run.

"It's a hike," he says, looking back at me, amused.

"I'm in decent shape. I run five miles a day."

"You surprise me," he says. "We can run together."

"And I box."

He smirks. "I don't. I'll remember that."

It's a one bedroom apartment with bare white walls. In the living room there's a beige tweed couch and a matching club chair with an ottoman, the kind of furniture that comes from Craigslist. There's a small, neat kitchen with tarnished copper-bottom pots hanging on a pegboard above the small stove. I haven't seen the bedroom yet because it's off to the side down a small hallway. If he owns any posters or art, they're hidden away. What I do see is a wall of CDs, which is not what I expected, only how did I know what to expect?

Michael opens the refrigerator. He reaches inside and holds up a beer.

"Do I need to show you ID?"

"No, but if you say yes I'm going to bust you."

"What?"

"I'm kidding."

He opens a beer and hands it to me and opens another one for himself. He leads me to the couch.

I sit in the corner and take a swig of the beer. "I never thought I'd be here."

"I never thought you'd be here either," he says.

"You remember the first time you saw me, in the car?"

He nods.

"What were you thinking?"

He smirks. "When I saw who you were? I thought I was fucked."

I raise an eyebrow. "That's not what I meant."

"I know what you meant."

"Well?"

He stares at me intently and I feel as though I'm going to ignite.

"I thought," he says, his voice deep and husky, as he slides closer and starts to kiss the side of my face, "that you were the hottest girl I had ever seen."

Before I can answer his lips are over mine and his tongue is inside my mouth and he tastes all beery and good and I'm kissing him back and he pulls me onto his lap and it feels like we're about to swallow each other up, and everything I ever thought about the instantaneous attraction between me and Michael Cross comes to this combustion point, and he's breathing hard and so am I and his fingers are slowly unbuttoning my shirt and helping me out of it.

"Look at you," he says, eyeing me appreciatively as he slides one finger under the strap of my bra and slowly slips it down so he can kiss my bare shoulder. I try hard to catch my ragged breath as the tension inside me builds and I reach up and slide my fingers through his hair and then grab it tightly, all the time trying to ignore that nagging voice in my head: *Say something, do something now, because this is it*, and I know what's coming and everything is moving too fast.

"You on the pill?" he whispers, "otherwise no worries, I have—"

I pull back. "I…"

"What?" he says. "What is it?"

Is this going to ruin everything? "I…I'm not. On the pill. I haven't needed to…"

He tilts his head to the side. "What do you—"

I inhale and climb off his lap. "I've never…I'm a virgin, Michael."

His eyes widen, the surprise so clear on his face. Gone is the straight-faced cop whose face gives away nothing about what he's thinking. I've definitely shocked him.

"Whoa," he says, leaning back and catching his breath, then exhaling sharply. "I didn't think…you seemed so…"

For a painful few seconds, neither of us says anything. "Are you mad?" I say, barely able to get the words out.

He narrows his eyes. "Why would I be?"

"Because you didn't expect it, I…I don't know."

"Gia…" he says, reaching for me. "I'm surprised, baby, that's all. It's fine. We don't have to—"

"That's not why I stopped, Michael…I just wanted you to know… first."

He catches his breath. "I don't want you to feel pressured…"

I hate this, all the talk, the explaining. It now feels like the temperature has dropped from a hundred and ten to like forty in the shade.

"We don't have to if you don't want to," I say because now I'm feeling stupid and hurt and getting mad and I don't know what else to say, and he's probably totally turned off because he's convinced I'm some kind of tease, which guys hate. I stare out the window.

"Gia," he says, reaching for my chin and turning my face back to his. He kisses me lightly on the lips. "You don't know how much I want to."

"Then okay…"

He stands up and reaches for my hand, leading me into the bedroom.

Ever since I met Michael, I've fantasized about what it would be like to be with him. How it would feel to have him kiss me. How it would feel to have him undress me and see me in front of him, undressed. I've fantasized about what he would look like. How he would feel inside me. And how it would feel to finally lose the V-card so I could be like everyone else and move on with my life and think that sex is cool and all right and not a huge deal.

Even Ro's done it—Ro who never seemed to go crazy over any guy. Once when we had a sleepover she finally told me. I knew even before though because after she met up with Chris Ruggio, a gorgeous friend of Dante's who sold grass but also did some modeling, she couldn't stop talking about him. One day she ran into him on the street and he took her out for coffee and she hung out with him for the afternoon, even though she never told me where they went.

She acted quieter after that day. Not herself. Like she had to process it on her own before she could talk about it.

I read stuff online that girls wrote about what it felt like the first time. You're there but you're not, some of them said. It felt like they were in another place watching themselves play the part of the virgin. I understand that now, the self-consciousness. The super-awareness.

Michael pulls his sweater over his head and tosses it on the floor. He leaves his jeans on and then gets into the bed next to me, leaning up on one elbow, his head resting in his hand.

I finally see the lean, hard body. He's the one who's perfect. He's ripped and strong and totally hot. I wait for him to undress me, but he doesn't. He reaches out and touches my face, using just the tip of his finger to trace the outline of my jaw before running his thumb back and forth lightly across my bottom lip.

"I can't believe how beautiful you are." He kisses me softly, playing with my hair, running his fingers through it as if it's made of delicate strands of silk.

I smile back at him, shy and embarrassed, and wait, but he stops touching me and rests back on the bed, closing his eyes.

"What is it?"

"This is tough," he says, squeezing his eyes shut.

"What is?"

"To go slow with you, not to jump you," he says, removing the hand over his eyes and turning toward me, the slightest smile on his face. He pushes a strand of hair away from my face on one side and then the other before he slides his hand behind my head and tightens his hand around my hair. His touch is hypnotic.

I edge closer until our lips meet and we start kissing again. It's almost painful when you're trying not to go crazy, but you are. It's like denying that you have to inhale when your body needs oxygen. We are skin to skin, still partly dressed, only it doesn't feel that way and I'm in a place I've never been before, feeling more toward Michael than I've ever felt toward anyone.

But my brain can't be quiet and I'm wondering if this is different from what he felt with other girls before because I want it to be singular and special for him too, more intense than with anyone else so that he'll remember it, no matter what.

We kiss until we can't just kiss anymore and he slides out of his jeans and I'm wearing only my thong and Michael has touched me past the point of combustion and now it's time. He slides the thong down over my hips and reaches for the foil packet.

This is it, this is it, are you sure? my conscience asks, catapulting me back from that other world. But before I can think, Michael is over me then inside me, moving slowly at first.

"You okay?" he says softly.

I nod because I can't speak and his mouth is over mine while his body moves insistently in a slow, hypnotic rhythm until I feel something that I've never felt before, at least not in that way, and he calls my name with an urgency that sends me over the top, and then he stills and drapes himself over me and we lie there breathing hard, two bodies that have become one.

Tears run down my cheeks as he lifts his head and softly kisses my eyes.

FIFTY-FIVE

The one place you don't want to go after making love for the first time is to your own bed in your parents' house. But it's almost eleven and my mom is expecting me.

"Don't leave," Michael whispers, pressing his forehead against mine. "Can't you say you're staying at a friend's?"

"I already lied about where I was going."

He frowns and gets up without another word, grabbing his jeans as he heads to the bathroom. I watch him with an empty feeling. Is he mad? When he comes back, he's dressed and so am I.

"I'll take you home," he says, nuzzling my neck.

The traffic is light as we drive down to lower Manhattan. I feel a strange combination of hyper alertness and exhaustion. I glance over at his profile and study his face. He's back to his intense, expressionless cop face, not giving anything away. I lean over and rest my head on his shoulder. He turns and flashes me his smirky smile.

"You can let me out here," I say when we're a few blocks from my street.

"I hate this," Michael says.

"What?"

"You getting out here and walking alone."

"I'm fine."

"I'll follow you in the car."

"Omigod, I'm totally…"

His jaw tenses. "Gia, you're not walking home alone."

"Okay, follow me." It reminds me of my discussions with my dad. I start to open the car door, but he reaches out and grabs my upper arm.

"Let's not do this again."

It's over? "Wha…what do you mean?"

"We have to figure something out."

I look at him, not understanding.

"Next time, I want you to stay with me. All night."

"I will," I say, relieved.

I start to turn and—

"Gia!"

"What?"

"It was incredible."

There's a game I got as a gift when I was in third grade when we played Secret Santa in school. My gift was Tell Me! It's a box of fifty fun questions designed to get families talking. As I'm cleaning my room I see it stuck in the back of my pajama drawer. I open the box and look at some of the questions:

Has there been someone special you could turn to when you were sad or upset?

What have you had your heart set on but didn't get?

What is the most fun you've ever had?

As I read through the questions, the idea comes to me and I immediately tuck it into my bag.

Michael and I meet again the following Saturday and have dinner in a small Italian restaurant near his house. After veal piccata, spinach, and spaghetti (with sauce nearly as good as my mom's), he turns to me.

"What do you feel like doing now?"

"Going home…I brought a game."

He cocks his head to the side, his slow, sexy, gorgeous Michael smile spreading over his face. "What kind of game?"

"A fun one that I doubt you've ever played before."

"I'm game," he says with his snarky cop smile.

We end up back at his apartment and I take out the box.

"Tell me?" Michael says. He eyes the box suspiciously.

Will the game work with him? Because he was right, I barely know him.

I look through the cards. "It's easy. I get to ask you one question and then you get to ask me one.

"That's all?"

"That's all."

"How do you win?"

"It's a talking game. You don't win."

"I guess you're going to win then."

"Why is that?"

"You're a better talker."

"Maybe you are, Michael. Let's find out." I pull out a card. "First question," I say. "*When did you have to muster up all of your courage in order to do something?*"

He looks at me, his eyes growing more intense.

"Last week," he says, "when I took you out." He kisses me on the lips and grabs the cards. He looks through them and finally looks up at me. "*What has been the most unlikely friendship you've had?*"

"You, Officer Hottie." I pull the cards back and search through them. *"What is the worst thing you've done in a fit of anger?"*

"I don't know if I want to answer that," he says, all the humor suddenly gone from his face.

"Answer," I say, holding his gaze.

He looks at me intently. "You sure you want to play this game?"

I nod.

"I beat up a pusher. A guy who sold to my brother."

"Did you…?" I hold my breath.

He shakes his head. "He survived." He grabs the cards away. *"What's the biggest trouble you've ever gotten yourself into?"*

"I went out to a bar one night…Uptown."

The corners of his mouth turn up. "And?"

"When I got home, I walked in through the basement. My dad didn't know it was me and he suddenly grabbed me by the shoulder and dragged me in. I was lucky he had a flashlight or he would have slammed me with the baseball bat in his hand and killed me."

"Shit," Michael whispers. "Why didn't you tell me? Does he know about me?"

"That's not one of the questions."

"Gia, tell me," he insists.

"No."

"Are you going to tell him?"

"I don't know."

"I want you to."

"I…I don't know. He won't understand."

"You have to tell him."

"Why?"

"I don't like secrets." He drops the cards on the table and closes the distance between us.

I grab the cards and slide away. "*What adult did you have the most fun with growing up? Why?*"

He looks at me and doesn't answer.

"Your dad?" I whisper.

"Yeah."

"Tell me."

"We would go out and play baseball," he says, looking down. "He loved baseball and so did I, so he took me to games all the time." He shakes his head.

"What?"

"I didn't know," he said, staring off, lost in thought.

"Know what?"

"That he got the tickets, the box seats, as part of his pay package," he says icily.

"From…"

"Yes," he says. "From them. But that was a long time ago. A long time ago."

"Do you miss him?"

"That's not one of the questions," he says, his jaw tightening.

"Do you, Michael?"

"Sometimes."

"Why don't you get in touch?"

"It's over."

"You should try."

"Maybe some day, I don't know."

He grabs the cards away from me. "This is getting too heavy, Gia." He searches through them. "*What everyday person has inspired you? How?*"

"My dad," I whisper.

Michael narrows his eyes. "How?"

"He's strong. He's not afraid to show his love for us. He's done bad things, I know it…I can't pretend anymore, but he couldn't have been a better father."

He nods.

I take the cards back from him. *"What is the most physical pain you've ever had to endure?"*

He stares at me.

"Answer, Michael."

"Looking at your pictures. The ones from *Vogue*. And trying to pretend that I didn't want to see you."

I swallow. "Do you still blame me?"

He shakes his head back and forth and exhales. "No."

FIFTY-SIX

When I get home from school on Monday, I sit down at the computer. I don't try to write my English essay or do my math homework or go over the chapters for the art history quiz.

I try to write a letter to my dad.

I've written him before. I write at least once a week, especially when I have fun things to tell him about Herbie, because Herbie's always doing things that make us laugh, like lifting up his ears and tilting his head toward the TV if he hears a barking dog or something strange on Animal Planet. Or stealing dirty socks out of the laundry and hiding them in his bed.

But this letter is different. Michael wants me to tell him that I'm seeing him. I start the letter ten different times, each one of them different.

Remember the time Ro and I were stupid enough to take Dante's car and cut school and drink beer and then a cop pulled us over, well…

Of course he remembers it because Super Mario probably charged him twenty grand for all the hours he put in bailing us out.

Dear Daddy, you always ask me stuff about my friends, so here's something that I know you never expected to hear: The cop who picked us up on the Henry Hudson ended up being my boyfriend…

Dear Daddy, this is crazy, I know, but there's something I have to tell you. I'm now dating a cop. And not only a cop, but small world, the son of someone who used to take payoffs...

I try to write it in different ways, goofing on myself, then getting serious, but no matter what I say, it all sounds wrong.

Then I realize why.

This is not something my dad has to know. He's not home anymore. He's locked up now, halfway across the country for committing horrible crimes. And as hurt and conflicted as I will always be about the man who was the most loving father I could imagine, I also see him now for who he is. I'm less than a year away from going to college now and whether he approves doesn't matter any more.

My dad isn't the feared mob boss now. Someone else has taken over. The police don't come to our house anymore. Our family isn't on the TV or in the newspapers now, at least not on the front page. The running is over. There's a calm to our lives that I have never felt before.

For the first time in seventeen years, I can date whomever I want. I don't need his approval. I'm not living in his shadow anymore.

Our lives are totally different since he left. We live in a small apartment now. Anthony and I sleep in single beds in a room we share with a screen between us. The fancy cars are gone and so is the jewelry. We don't eat out anymore unless someone else pays. I take the subway to school.

My brother is different too. He works for a company selling Italian suits. He has an honest job, I think, at least for now. He seems calmer these days, more resigned to things. We lost so much, but along the way I gained something no one can take away from me: a separate identity.

I'm not the don's daughter or Mafia Girl anymore. I'm Gia now. Just Gia.

And that feels good.